Hollaran's World War
TIM MAHONEY

"Set in the uncompromising grit of Newark, *Hollaran's World War* is as swift and effective as a tracer, as illuminating as a midnight flare—a remarkable feat in view of the author's canny reluctance to capitalize on the horrors that have warped Hollaran and woofed his buddy. . . . There is anger . . . but an anger tempered by humor and especially insight. Enough insight, in fact, to span both sides of the bozo line."
— *Los Angeles Times*

"Mahoney's first novel becomes addictive . . . and in its slightly manic manner and breakneck pace does succeed in documenting some significant repercussions of the Vietnamese experience." — *Publishers Weekly*

"Sad, funny, touching . . . a harrowing journey. . . . It's cleverly done and good reading." — *The Washington Post*

"Both timely and timeless . . . Tim Mahoney effectively explores basic yet sophisticated responses to complex problems in this sometimes angry, often comic story of one veteran who learns to get even with 'the system' without taking revenge." — *Grand Rapids Press*

"There are no hunks, no heroes, no blood—first or otherwise. And nothing is left of Vietnam but the scars and the metaphors. It may not be prime time, but try *Hollaran's World War* as a dose of reality, and leave the rest to Sgt. Fury." — *The Detroit News*

Hollaran's World War

Tim Mahoney

A LAUREL BOOK

Published by
Dell Publishing Co., Inc.
1 Dag Hammarskjold Plaza
New York, New York 10017

Interior designed by Virginia M. Soulé

Laurel ® TM 674623, Dell Publishing Co., Inc.

ISBN: 0-440-33631-7

Reprinted by arrangement with Delacorte Press

Printed in the United States of America

December 1986

10 9 8 7 6 5 4 3 2 1

WFH

For Spear, for Swider, and most of all for Riley

Acknowledgments

For gracious help given during the writing of this novel, the author thanks Bill, Clark and Bharati, the Iowa Writers Workshop, and the James A. Michener Foundation.

CONTENTS

While it's Tommy this, an' Tommy that, an' "Tommy fall be'ind,"
But it's "please to walk in front, sir," when there's trouble in the
wind.

Rudyard Kipling, Tommy

Hollaran's
World War

1

Why I Hate Helicopters

I've heard some pretty fancy explanations for why I hate helicopters. My first shrink, the private shrink, says my feelings, even the lousy ones, are valuable. I must face up to my fears and hatreds, she says. Experience them, think them over. She says I might have to suffer a little before I get better.

My second shrink, the VA shrink, he has a different idea. I should ignore my negative feelings, he says. My obsession with helicopters, he says, is just a cover-up. For the fact that I can't seem to fit back in. For the fact that I'm failing in just about every area of my life. I've got to let go of my fears and hatreds, he says. And get down to the business of making my life a success.

The VA shrink is a pretty insistent guy. "Tell me," he says, late into one of our Friday morning sessions, "since you insist on talking about these . . . mere machines . . . when did this phobia first manifest itself?"

I squirm in my chair. Because of the question and because it's sweaty and stuffy in here and because it's late. I don't answer him right away and he says, "Well?"

Doc, I say, I've told you all this before, haven't I? I don't really know how it started except one day I was riding in a chopper over there and I just had the urge to jump. I don't know where it came from, Doc.

"Highly irrational," he says. And breathes out heavy, a

frustrated man. He sits back in his government issue hospital chair and digs a pack of mentholated cigarettes out of his suit coat pocket. "Do you think," he says, and holds a gold Gucci lighter up to the cigarette, "that maybe fear and shame and guilt had something to do with it?" He lights the cigarette, blows smoke toward the ceiling.

Fear and shame and guilt over what, Doc? I ask.

"You tell me," he says. And just looks at me. And I just look at him until he goes out of focus, and all I can see is the window in back of him. Newark Airport out there, a mile away. And I could swear I hear just faintly the chop of the blades of a helicopter. Well, I'm thinking, it's finally come down to this, hasn't it, Doctor Pyle? You're more subtle about it, but you're just like everybody else. I've been asked this question in a dozen different ways by uncles, cabdrivers, strangers on the street, girls I've met in bars, little kids in my old neighborhood. All they ever want to know is, did you kill anybody over there? I have never answered this question with anything but a stare.

"Once again, Mister Hollaran," Doctor Pyle says, "you've managed to exasperate me. Just when we touch a sensitive area—"

Doc, I say, and cut him off. It's late, we're out of time, aren't we? I've got to get going.

"The moment we begin to talk about your urge to destroy yourself—" he says.

Doc, really, I say, and get out of my chair.

"Why don't you tell me?" he says. "What is so attractive about suicide?"

Suicide? I say, and lean in toward his desk. Who said anything about suicide?

"Well," he says, and taps his cigarette on his big, full ashtray. "To jump from a helicopter in flight . . . what else would you call it?"

Doc, I say, I just wanted out. Don't you understand, man? I didn't want to be there anymore. I'd had enough, I'd seen enough.

"See?" Pyle says, and points a finger at me. "Your fight is

not with helicopters. I've told you over and over, helicopters are only a symbol."

Symbol, hell, I say.

"You're shouting, Mister Hollaran."

I *hate* helicopters, I say. They're not symbols, they're the worst goddamn things man ever invented, and I wish you could understand that. I hate them all, the way the blades rotate, the popping sound, the winds they stir up and the smell of the exhaust. I hate the rotors, the engines, the floorboards, the instruments, the seat belts, the landing lights, everything. I hate the people who fly them, the people who make them, and the people who fix them, too. My idea of a good time, Doctor Pyle, would be to watch the midair collision of a thousand helicopters.

"Control yourself," says Pyle.

I'm late, I say.

Pyle nods. I think he notices my hands gripped tight on his desk, my arms shaking with adrenaline. Jesus, and I took two pills just an hour ago. "I want you to stay until you feel you've got yourself under control," Pyle says.

Got to go, I say, and back toward the door.

Pyle stands and comes around his desk. "Listen to me," he says, almost shouting. "Why don't you ever listen to me? You're in a dangerous condition, Mister Hollaran. Mister Hollaran!"

I push through the frosted-glass door and I'm out, running, past Pyle's secretary, who tries to wave me down for another appointment, past the coatrack and grab my army jacket without breaking stride, turn the corner into the green-tiled corridor. Running with all my might and working into my jacket at the same time and feeling for my keys, almost bump into a nurse carrying urine samples, turn around, dodge an old drooling guy in a wheelchair, turn the corner, my shoes skidding, run for daylight at the end of the hall. Past the smoky dark dayroom with its wall map of Vietnam, past the rooms blue with the glow of TV, huffing already, pain in my side, past the cafeteria window where a guy with no arms is being fed by a guy with his jaw shot away.

Head down, Hollaran, run. Push the glass door, down the
stone steps, past the flagpoles flapping with flags, America,
New Jersey, the VA. Out into the parking lot and the cold
sting of an ice storm. Running in slush, shoes taking on cold
water, buttoning my jacket, a hard wind blowing ice drops
right into my face. My car at the edge of the lot, the bottom
half of it rust, the windshield already iced over. A trick to
opening this door, lift, push, then pull, must be something in
here I can use for an ice scraper. Paw through the glove
compartment, crumpled parking tickets, a can opener, nuts
and bolts, they just kind of fell off the car. Got to be something, feel under the seats, there, cold metal, a butter knife I
once used as a screwdriver. Now start the car, twist the key,
pray, a miracle, the engine sputters, catches, starts to race on
high idle. I get out into the wind and scrape ice, my hands red
cold, trying to clear a patch just big enough to see out. Scraping the windshield, my hands already numb, I've got to buy
myself a pair of gloves this year.

Now in the car finally, breathe a smoky breath, let down
the emergency brake, the car stalls. Damn it, why does it do
this? Grind. Grind the starter, come on. A sick whirr, slowing
down, oh no. Wait, Hollaran, patience, count to sixty, let the
battery recover. Tapping on the steering wheel, fifteen, sixteen, that's enough, turn the key, whirr, click, silence, Jesus!
Pound the goddamn dashboard, come on, you bastard. Turn
the key, turn it, turn, slam my hand into the windshield. Out
of the car, kick it, shard of rust falls in the slush, kick it again,
now shoulder to the doorjamb and push, come on, Hollaran,
push. Groan, feet slipping in slush, a Mercedes goes around
with an angry beep, push, strain, up a hump and then a little
hill, hop in, slam it into second, pop the clutch, engine flick-
ers, dies. Pop it again, nurse it, life, okay now, give it revs,
revs, revs. Go, slam the door. Don't stall now, you bastard.
Out of the lot, blowing the horn, can't stop, might stall. Swing
a wide right, look quick, zoom in front of an orange garbage
truck and straight across the road, steer for the Turnpike
entrance. Through the tollgate on a roll and grab the little
computer card from the machine.

Relax, Hollaran. It's all Turnpike now, breathe deep, slow, Doctor Rhinehart's method. Two pills in you so let them work. And blend in with the traffic, pay attention to your driving. If only I could get a little heat in this car.

Slowing down, getting into the rhythm of the drive. Every minute or so, wiping the frost from the windshield with my hand. Hell, I've been this late before and nothing's happened. Relax, breathe deep, let the shoulder muscles go. What's there to worry about? What's the worst that could happen? Don't think about that, Hollaran, drive. Relax. The windshield wiper beating a slow time, only the one on my side works. It's like I'm in a tunnel of frost and can only see straight ahead.

Not that you'd want to see what's on either side of the Turnpike around here, because it's Newark, the worst piece of real estate on the planet. With its bombed-out, burnt-black buildings, with its vacant lots full of rubble and broken glass, with block after block deserted and in ruins, Newark looks like some dope-crazed B-52 pilot mistook it for Hanoi. I can't help but think of war and destruction whenever I make this drive. I've seen Vietnam and I've seen Newark, and Newark loses.

After miles and miles of ghettos, Newark changes and becomes the junkyard, scrapyard, and garbage-heap capital of the world. There are so many junkyards that some have developed specialties. If I could see, somewhere around here there'd be a yard full of auto batteries, heaped in pyramids. Then maybe a half mile later there's a chemical dump, hills and valleys of fifty-five-gallon drums. Past that there's a scrapyard full of tires, acres and acres of just tires, with the smell of burning rubber so strong it stings your throat. A little farther out in the meadows are the scrap-metal yards, with twisted, rusting auto bodies, just oceans of them. Right along there you can smell the Meadows dump, where they're filling in the swamps with garbage from Manhattan. New York has been getting away with that for years, trucking its garbage into Newark, or sinking it in the ocean to wash on the shores of Asbury Park. New Jersey! Sometimes I wonder if I'm bound to live my whole life here.

Driving along in the right lane at forty-five now, as fast as the old Volks will go. On my left a trailer truck blows past, kicks filthy ice water onto my windshield. And I notice when the wiper clears it that there's no more sleet coming down, a small patch of blue sky out there. I want to clear the fog in here so I roll my window halfway down, and in comes a blast of cold garbage-dump air. And I can see out there on my left, in between the rush of trailer trucks, the tremendous skyline of Manhattan. Empire State, Chrysler, World Trade Center. All my life I've lived on the lousy side of those skyscrapers.

If only the radio in here worked, I'd know just how late I am. My boss, he doesn't like me taking time off for "treatment," as he calls it. Every Friday when I'm at the VA, I have this paranoid vision of Johnson sitting at his desk, tapping his fingers, watching the clock. That's my boss, John Johnson, he's fifty-something, he's worked for Jersey Sheet and Tube since he was in high school. He dresses in only gray suits and gets his hair cut every Monday, and in front of the other workers he likes to kid me about being a hippie. Except he's not kidding, really. He's called me in his office a couple of times to tell me it looks bad to have one of his salesmen "out of uniform," as he puts it. Can't you fit in? he tells me. Can't you try to get along?

Nobody'd ever guess that three or four years ago I was the fair-haired boy around JS&T. The company big shots believed in me. I had myself fooled that I had a future selling steel. There were all kinds of implied promises back then, and I was convinced that after a few years of "seasoning" on the order desk, I'd be out there with my own territory, an expense account and everything. The youngest guy in company history to do that.

I guess I was pretty much caught up in it, because I worked hard and dressed nice back then, and any rebellious thoughts I kept until after hours. Harold Young, who's dead now, he was the sales manager back then, and he treated me like his own damn son. Took me out on his sales calls and introduced me to the buyers, and gave me all kinds of advice. Never ignore the little people in an office, he once told me on the way back from a Manhattan call. I made that mistake as a young salesman, he said, and as a result, we don't do a dime's business with Patterson Aero-Jet today. Because clerks have a funny way of becoming purchasing agents. And he laughed when he told me that. He was the one who nicknamed me T-Bone, I don't know why, except maybe that my first name begins with a *T*. Everybody in the office was calling me T-Bone in those days. They just yell out Hollaran now.

In a strange way, I'm glad Harold Young didn't live to see everything get so screwed up. He died while I was in Vietnam, cancer, a big lump on the back of his neck, people told me. I didn't know anything until I came to ask for my job back and found John Johnson was the boss. He told me the news and said, I *guess* I can find a spot for you *somewhere*, Hollaran. Guess? I said. You've got to rehire me, it's the law. Johnson nodded and said he'd see what he could do. He also said he didn't like the tone of my voice.

That's the way it goes, I say to myself, driving down the Turnpike, my hands practically frozen to the wheel. You come back from the big bad Nam and all of a sudden things seem different. Only they're not different, really. It's just that something happens to you over there. Well, something happened to me, at any rate.

All of a sudden there's red light everywhere and I hit the brakes. My car does a little slide but then stops all right, and ahead of me there are three lanes of stalled cars and trucks. Stuck in traffic. Just what I need.

A whole minute goes by and nothing moves. Already I'm breaking out in a nervous sweat, the cold drops running right down my side. I look ahead and see the flashing lights of a trooper's car, way up there about half a mile. It's going to be a long wait. I can only hope that Johnson will be out of the office when I get back.

A big green trailer truck on my right idles placidly, a deep rumble, while I'm racing my little putt-putt of an engine. Come on, come on. I'm cursing now, whimpering when

that doesn't work, then beeping the horn in desperation. The
traffic moves forward like a big slow centipede. Five minutes.
I know it's been at least five minutes. Out there in the slush, a
trooper in yellow-striped pants and an orange rain jacket
waves traffic to the left. I lay off the horn when I see him.
Traffic stops dead again for at least two minutes.

I'm practically in a panic by this time. I'm cursing the
state trooper, Doctor Pyle, the rain, the traffic, drivers everywhere, New Jersey, my Volkswagen, John Johnson, Jersey
Sheet and Tube, every Volkswagen ever made, my heating
system, my radio, and finally, when there's nothing else left,
myself. Still the traffic won't move. I must be a good ten
minutes late.

Finally the jam breaks loose, and the traffic starts to
creep along at about a mile an hour. I'm gunning my engine,
hitting the brakes, gunning it, hitting the brakes. I get up to
the obstruction, a trailer truck jackknifed across two lanes,
surrounded by flares and state troopers. After that the highway's wide open, and I'm pushing the Volks for all it's worth
toward Elizabeth.

I'm really sweating, soaked under the armpits, by the
time I pull up in front of JS&T. I'm out of the car and running
before the engine quits. I stop at the office front doors, a
quick look at my reflection in the glass, and then I take a deep
breath. I walk in and the clock says eleven thirty-five, I'm
twenty minutes late.

I'm barely inside the door before Jerri, who's been
JS&T's receptionist since about the Civil War, hands me one
of her pink memos. She's busy now, answering a phone call,
speaking into this tiny microphone that looks like it grew in a
semicircle out of her ear. I know what the note says, but I
open it anyway. *Hollaran See Mr. J. Immed.*

I walk to the elevator and push the button that says UP,
it'll take forever to get here. And I've never figured that out,
because there's nothing between the top and bottom floors
but a big shaft. That's because this wasn't built as an office
building, really, but as a railroad-yard control tower, sixty
feet tall and built like the letter *I*. The railroad's long since

gone, asphalt poured over the tracks, forklifts running where locomotives used to churn their wheels.

There's a ringing sound and a big green-lit arrow pointing up, I step into the elevator car, the door closes, I'm wiping my sweaty palms down the legs of my corduroys. When the elevator door opens, I'm up with the accountants and managers and the people who are trying to put in a computer system, and then my knuckles are rapping on the gold name JOHN JOHNSON imprinted on a smoked-glass door.

"Come in," says a muffled voice, and I can feel the pull on my stomach muscles, but when I push the door open the office is empty. Then I realize where Johnson is, in his private bathroom. I sit down to wait for him, in a fuzzy chair that reminds me of being in a Lincoln Continental. Johnson has a nice view, big smoked-glass windows. When you sit in this chair and face Johnson, you see all of Manhattan behind him.

There's the flush of a toilet and then a splash of water in the sink, and finally the polished-wood door opens and Johnson says, "Tom!" like he's surprised. I start to stand, but he waves at me and says, "No, no, sit down, Tom." But warning lights are flashing for me, and I could swear I hear the noise of helicopters somewhere. Since when does Johnson call me Tom?

He sits across the desk from me and adjusts his half glasses until they're down on the end of his nose. "How are things going down there, Tom?" he says. "Are you caught up on your orders?"

Kind of, I say.

"Have you got that big Esso job written up yet?"

No, I say, not yet. In fact, I'm working on that order right now. It's a real big one, I say. I didn't think we'd get it. I had to do some pretty sharp pencil work to bring that one in, I say.

I finish talking and there's a silence. Johnson leans back in his big chair, puts his hands in back of his head, and then turns away from me and looks out the windows. I figure maybe there's a tugboat or a big barge down there on the Arthur Kill, so I lean forward for a look. But there's nothing on the river at all, except for the usual oil slick. For all I can figure, Johnson is just staring down at the steelyard and the warehouse sheds. Then suddenly, without even looking at me, he says, "While that order's lying on your desk, guys down there are sitting on their butts, waiting for something to do. How can we run a business like that?" He finally looks at me. I squirm in the chair. I say, Hell, I take a lot of orders. I can't write them up all at once, can I, Mister J? Johnson likes it when you call him Mister J.

"The point is," Johnson says, and starts using his hands to dust his sleeves, "that you used to be a top producer around here. Now I look in the order book and see only three or four under your name. And every time I look around for you, it seems you're out getting some kind of treatment."

But Mister J, I say, I make up the time.

"Hollaran," he says, "orders come in between nine and five. That's when we need you here. Every time a phone goes unanswered in here, bingo, a couple of hundred bucks goes down the drain." He stops talking and stands, paces, his hands in his pockets. "Look," he says, "maybe it's none of my business, but can't you knock off this treatment stuff? Or do it at night?"

They don't keep office hours at night, I say.

"Who doesn't keep office hours at night?"

I don't want to use the word *psychiatrist*, it just makes me feel too weak. So I answer Johnson with the word *therapists*. The therapists, I say. They don't keep night hours.

"Hollaran, I don't mind telling you, I don't believe in all this therapy that's going around these days. These people are nothing but modern-day witch doctors. And the fees they get away with. I can't imagine why anyone would . . . would need their services."

I'm sure he's ready to fire me, my only hope now is an appeal, sincere. I say, Look, Mister J, ever since I came home from the army I've felt kind of shaky.

"Shaky?"

I don't want to tell him hostile and angry, I don't want to tell him about the nightmares, the phobias, the hallucina-

tions of helicopters. Shaky, I say. Unsure, Mister J. Confused.
It's like I've got to start all over and I don't know anything
anymore. Can't tell up from down, left from right, I don't
know why. But Mister J, ever since I came back—

He interrupts me, just by saying, "Hollaran." Then he
puts his two hands down on the desk, leans over, and looks
me square in the eyes. "I'm a veteran too," he says. "There
are lots of veterans who work here. And they all seem to have
fit in pretty nicely."

They're all World War II veterans, I say.

"Yes," he says, "and that was a real war, a world war.
Vietnam was just a little firecracker. And yet there's been
more whining about that little firecracker than about anything I can remember."

I say, strictly to myself, So that's where you're at, Johnson.

"Frankly," Johnson says, and starts pacing again, "your
attitude, your dress, and your behavior just haven't been up
to par. It comes across in everything you do. I've gotten
complaints from the buyers. They don't want to talk to you
anymore, Hollaran. They say you're hostile, curt, and rude. A
salesman can't be those things, Hollaran. So, starting Monday
morning, I want you to report to the warehouse for work."

The warehouse?

"And if you manage to get your personal life in shape,
we'll see about bringing you back up into the office."

The warehouse? I'm saying to myself. What the hell can I
do in the warehouse? I don't know anything about sheets and
tubes, they don't even heat some of the buildings down
there, I don't *know* anybody in the warehouse. I can picture
myself out there, freezing all day, cutting up greasy bar stock
or something, dressed in JS&T blue.

"And that's really all I have to say to you, Tom," I hear
Johnson say. But what I hear louder is the sound of helicopters, an earsplitting noise, like one is hovering right over me.
I find myself fumbling with the doorknob, I say something to
him, a stupid, shocked, mumbled thanks, and then I'm out

the door and into the hall. I have to put my hand up on the wall for a moment, I feel like I'm going to fall over. I push the button and the elevator door opens, the bell rings, the big arrow flashes red and points down.

2

Why I Like Glenn Miller

It's well after dark when I get home, throw open my apartment door, and flick on the light. Damn it, roaches, running for cover across the sink and cabinets. I drop my packages on the kitchen table and run for the sink, hot water will kill them every time. On with the faucet, hand under it, water freezing, come on, get hot. There must have been six, eight, ten roaches, but now all I can see is one pair of waving antennae under the rubber dish-drainer. At least I'll get this one. Then I'll pour scalding water behind the sink and maybe get some of his buddies, too. Come on, please, water get hot. I really know my antiroach warfare by now. I even went and got a roach book out of the library, on the theory of know your enemy. I've tried every trick in the book, too, sprays, traps, mothballs, boric acid trails, nothing works. Hey, this water isn't even getting warm. Take the easy way, violence. I reach over and pick up the dish drainer, smash it down. The roach scurries over the side of the counter, disappears.

I kick the sink cabinet hard, and go over and sit on the edge of my bed. Another weekend in this place. One big cold room with a so-called kitchen lining the far wall. And my furniture, this lousy single bed, a card table and two folding chairs. Unless you count the stacks of cardboard boxes I haven't unloaded yet. And I've been here, what, eight or nine months?

I go over to the table, dig my supper out of a brown

paper bag. A little Tastykake blueberry pie, a bright-colored
box of fried chicken, a six-pack of bottled beer. I open the
chicken box and there's a breast and leg in there, cold and
looking pretty greasy. I close the box. Twist the cap off a beer,
this won't be the first time I've had a six-pack for supper.
Who would believe that at one time I was considered a pretty
fair cook? And a professional, too. Well, sort of. Anyway,
that's what's in all those cardboard boxes. Pots and pans,
knives and colanders, spoons and gadgets and bowls. I have
to laugh when I look at it all. Because at one time I had this
big idea, I was going to go to chef school in New York. And
then travel the world, all the better places, cooking in hotels.
And then come home someday and open my own little restaurant. The dreams of a young boy. It seems like a hell of a
long time ago, really.

Another swig of beer and maybe it's time for a pill. I
open the white drugstore bag, there's a bottle of Maalox and
a plastic vial of tranquilizers, Doctor Pyle's prescription. I'm
going to need a couple of these to get to sleep, even with the
six-pack. Or else I'll be up fuming the whole night. Because of
John Johnson, the bastard. He beat me, he won, I'm sure he
figures the next step is for me to quit. Well, never. I wouldn't
give him the satisfaction. Besides, I need the paycheck. So
I'm not quitting, Johnson. I can take it in the warehouse.

Sure, Hollaran. And have another beer while you're at it.
Up with the full bottle, tilt it at my lips. Open the vial and pop
a blue pill, wash it down with beer. And watch out, Hollaran,
this could be dangerous. But I've done it before. And what's
my alternative? To stay up all night and stew about Johnson?
I can't believe I walked out of his office this afternoon actually thanking him. Why did I do that?

And it was worse this afternoon than it's been in a long
time. My hostility, I'm talking about. Because when I was
shopping, I had to keep my hands in my pockets. So I
wouldn't reach out and just slap people, strangers. I've had
that kind of lousy impulse ever since I've been home, and it's
guys like John Johnson who trigger it. Middle-aged, well-
dressed, prosperous, smug, I could reach out and just bare-

hand them right across the face. I damn near slapped some older guy in the bookstore tonight, all he did was take a couple of quick steps to get in line ahead of me. I looked at him, saw the spot where I knew I was going to slap him from behind, I was hearing the noise of helicopters and everything, so I ran out of line and just hid. Made myself stay in the corner where they sell the self-help books. And by the time the guy left I had decided to put back the joke book I wanted to buy. Instead I bought this book *Psycho-Cybernetics*, I've heard a lot about it. It's supposed to help people feel better somehow. I'm going to read it tonight, unless I get too bombed.

The reason I'm so hostile to those people, the three-piece bankers and businessmen, is that I blame them for sending me over there. I also blame my family, the government, the Church, the whole way I was raised. Doctor Rhinehart's helped me understand all that. But she says there's something else I need to understand if I want to get better. It's the most important thing of all, she says. What? I've asked her over and over. Oh, no, she says, you'll have to find that out for yourself. You'd never believe me if I told you. But before you can find the answer, you must first acknowledge your feelings, Mister . . . she can never remember my name.

Sometimes I think I must be *really* nuts, having two shrinks. I didn't do that deliberately. When I took on Doctor Rhinehart I meant to stop with Doctor Pyle, but somehow it never worked out that way. The two shrinks, they don't even know about each other. And the kinds of advice they give, you'd think they were from different planets.

Experience your anxiety, says Doctor Rhinehart, and your anger and hostility too. Let the feelings flow through you.

But they're bad, I say.

Who told you that? she says.

They make me feel bad, I say.

Oh, is that all? she says. Perhaps that is appropriate,

then. Perhaps you are right to feel angry and hostile. After all, you've been in a terrible war.

But that was a year ago, I say.

Only a year? she says. Probably you are just now getting ready to confront its consequences.

Just now? I say.

Yes, she says, and you will know you are healing when you start to see that not everything about Vietnam was bad.

Sometimes I think the woman's crazy. I guess that's why I stick with Doctor Pyle. Besides, he believes in tranquilizers, and Doctor Rhinehart won't prescribe them. She says they're exactly what I *don't* need. But Pyle says I *do* need them, and whether I feel anxious or not, I should take one every four hours.

But they're not working, I tell him.

Are you taking them regularly? he says.

Well, no, I say, sometimes I skip a few, and then take two or three when I start to feel real bad.

That could be dangerous, he says. Why don't you take them as prescribed?

I don't know, I say.

Are you afraid they might work? he says. Afraid that if you take them you'll forget about Vietnam and start facing your real problem? Which is to get over your feelings of failure and make yourself a prosperous life. Isn't it time, now that a whole year has passed, to stop fighting the Vietnam war? Are you listening, Mister Hollaran?

Yes, I'm listening, Doctor Pyle, you wiseass. And I need another beer. Don't you think I've tried to declare an end to this stupid war? Why do you think I've drunk a thousand beers? And popped a hundred of your little blue pills? And hidden myself away in this apartment? Because I'd like some goddamn peace, Doctor Pyle. I'd like it but I'm too angry, at you and everybody else in this world.

If I had the guts, if I wasn't so ashamed, if I could find the right words, I'd like to tell you, Pyle, just what kind of year it's been for me. A walking, breathing, wide-awake nightmare, and I can't seem to get rid of it. Can't seem to really come back from the Delta. Can't stop sweating. Can't shake the helicopters, and all their noise, lights, hot rotor winds, they're driving me crazy, Doctor. And I still can't tell who the enemy is, could be anybody. Never know. Got to be on guard every minute. Yes, I'm lonely, Doc. Why is this war still going on inside me? Tell me, you're the psychiatrist. Why do I feel so bitter and hateful and hopeless? I'm waiting for the answer, Doc. I've been like this every minute, every day, all year.

Of course I'm sick, and the proof of it is I'm standing here by myself, talking like my two shrinks are in the room. This is what happens, Hollaran, when you spend too much time alone. And whatever happened to all my friends? I went to high school just a couple of blocks from here, but I don't seem to know anybody anymore. I hear things like, Scott's in grad school in Colorado, and Wally married Lorraine and they have two kids, and Sully's working over on Wall Street and just got a big promotion, and Buzz and Janet just bought a house in Roselle Park. Sure, they were the smart ones, those guys. They stayed in college or quick got married and had antidraft babies or joined the Air National Guard and spent six months drinking beer in Florida. Of the whole graduating class of St. Veronica's, only three of us that I know of ended up in Vietnam. I'm the only one who made it back home.

You can't count Eddie Sadowski in there, because he never did graduate. I believe it was April of the tenth grade that he finally turned sixteen and dropped out. Eddie's about the only friend I have left, really, and I'd call him right now only he doesn't have a phone. Won't get one, either. Doesn't want any contact with the world. He always tended that way, but since he came back from Vietnam it's gotten worse. He was a helicopter crew chief over there, and was shot down once, but that's about all he's ever told me. We're not real gabby on the subject of Vietnam, and Eddie's a guy I've known my whole life.

Eddie got smart after he came home, went to school on the GI bill, learned to fix oil burners, and now he makes piles of money, works whole days of overtime. Plus he's on a VA pension, because he limps around, all gimpy in one leg from the chopper crash. What's happening to all his money I don't know, but he sure isn't spending it on housing. He bought this old house on a VA mortgage, and lives in it all alone, with practically no furniture. The house is down in the port section, near JS&T, and its neighbors are junkyards and oil tanks, and warehouses and factories, half of them abandoned. This doesn't bother Eddie at all, in fact he craves the solitude, and anyway, whenever he's home he's always working, down in the basement, some big noisy secret project. Twice now I've asked him what he's doing down there, and he's just ignored the question.

I guess I could drive over to Eddie's, but I'm finishing my second beer on an empty stomach, and I don't know. Maybe I should eat something. I go to the table, dig a chicken leg out of the box, hold it up to my nose and sniff. Cheap shortening. Take a bite anyway, awful, a burst of cold oil in my mouth, and the meat has the texture of an inner tube. Force myself to swallow. Pick up the whole box of chicken, two quick steps to the garbage, it's overflowing, lay the leg and the box on top, push it all down with my foot, pack it in, ought to take this out to the alley someday. Now to the refrigerator, open the door, empty, toss in the blueberry pie, in the morning I'll be desperate for something to eat.

No use putting the beers in there, they'll be gone before they even get warm. I'm sick of this, really, a year of this, and nothing's any better at all. In fact now it's worse, all the things I've got to stew about all weekend, and right now it gets dark so early, a dreary time of year, and Christmas coming up, and nothing in it for me anywhere. I sit down on the bed.

Feeling sorry for yourself, Hollaran, so knock it off. Nobody told you to take on the whole world at once. No, but I can't see my way past this weekend, really. Can't see myself Monday in a blue warehouse uniform. Weekend's shot, really, because all I'll do is think about it. Turn it over and over in my mind. Why not admit that you lost, Hollaran, and Johnson won? Never. The bastard. I'll get him back if I have to dedicate my life to it. But how, Hollaran, how?

I don't know. Get up off this bed. Four beers left, line them up on the table. Open the vial of pills. Your hands are shaking, Hollaran. Four pills. A little blue dot next to each beer, and that'll take care of me. Until tomorrow morning when I wake up sweating. Don't think about that. Pill on the tongue. Mouthful of beer. Swallow.

Sandra. Why not try? Nothing to lose now and I'll be passed out in an hour anyway. Go over to the windowsill, pick up the phone, dial her number. *My* old number. Let's see, must be about seven-thirty, could be a chance. First ring, and a sweat breaking out under my arms. Big drink of beer, third ring, fourth ring, my stomach balled up tight. Still ringing, raise the window shade. Nothing out there but a brick-wall garage, one weak yellowish light on it. Sleet coming down heavy, on a slant, hard wind out there. A depressing view and I pull the shade down. Still ringing, lost count now, must be thirteen, fourteen. Of course she's not going to answer. No way would she spend *her* weekends alone.

Leave the phone off the hook ringing, put it down on the windowsill. Let it ring all night, make her answer. A trick I've tried before, only to wake up at dawn to the wail of the phone company's trouble signal.

Click of the phone still ringing, and where is that woman anyway? Out with some young stud, out dancing if I know her. Do you know her, Hollaran, at all? I thought I did, once. And it makes me bitter when I think of all those paydays at Vinh Long Army Airfield. Me in a line of suckers standing in front of the base post office. Waiting for an hour, two hours to buy a U.S. postal money order, send it back to the States. How many guys in that line like me?

God damn it, just the thought of it, answer the goddamn phone, will you, Sandra? How many guys in that line came home to be locked out? It was a year ago, a year and a couple of weeks ago that I got out of the goddamn taxi with my uniform on, and hauled out my duffel bag, feeling good enough to give the driver a ten-dollar tip. And it was cold, and cloudy like snow when I climbed the stairs to the apartment building, shivering inside my coat because the day before I'd been in Saigon at ninety-two degrees. And dropped my duffel bag at the door of number six and knocked, no answer. And knocking away, still out in the cold. And the neighbors starting to look out the window and then I was pounding. Yelling out your name, Sandra. Knocking for ten goddamn minutes before I realized there wasn't going to be any answer. And the windows in the courtyard all full of the faces and noses of strangers.

Thanks, Sandra, thanks a lot. For never having the decency to offer an explanation. For making up excuses about why we can't meet and why we can't talk. For saying over and over, in your lousy impatient way, That's the way it is, Tom, and that's the way it's going to be. And right now I'm in great need of a pill and a beer.

Go to the table, pill in the palm of my hand now, head back, hand to my mouth, hard little click against my teeth, swallow. And go to the bed. Maybe try to lie down.

Lay the beer on the cold wood floor, put the pillow under my head. Maybe enough in me now to try for sleep. Try, Hollaran. It'd be a gruesome hangover, six and six. Or maybe worse than a hangover. I don't want to think about that. Or anything else. Want to sleep for a long, long time. Close my eyes. Breathe deep, wait for it all to work. Big breath and hold it. Let it out slowly. Start to relax. Don't think. Blank mind. Flash, the brown face of a little girl, caught in a beam of light. My eyes fly open, I'm sitting up straight, no. No, I will not allow it. A tingly feeling at the top of my skull, the beginning of panic. I roll off the bed, to the floor, sitting, hold my head, the tension in it. Let it pass, Hollaran. No, I've got to fight it. Leave it all back there in the Delta. And there's one thing that helps me every time.

Reach under the bed and drag out the old phonograph, it's a simple child's thing, orange and white, used to be my sister's. Eddie salvaged it, put it together for me, hooked it up to a simple amplifier he built from a kit when he was in high school. I just use these headphones, no need for the speakers. Click the toggle switch and static loud in my ears. Open the double-record set, the only album I have. *Glenn Miller, A*

Memorial, 1944–1969. Side one, my favorite. "Moonlight Serenade," "Sunrise Serenade," "Stairway to the Stars," "In the Mood," "Johnson Rag." I love them all. The first note of "Moonlight Serenade" and I'll have goose bumps through the whole song.

Music's not even playing and already I'm feeling better, just watching the record spin on the turntable. I've spent hours and hours like this on the really bad nights, listening and drinking until I don't have the slightest quarrel with the world. And it's only the Glenn Miller boys who make me feel that way. Who make me wonder what I ever saw in protest songs, acid music, or rock and roll. It's Sandra who's got all those albums now, and she's welcome to them.

Lift up the tone arm, put it down to music. First bar of "Moonlight Serenade" and my eyes close peacefully. No bad memories, just music filling my mind. And humming along with it. The first riff of the piano practically brings tears to my eyes.

Drifting off. Through "Sunrise Serenade." Into "Little Brown Jug," and then my head snaps, body jumps, just at the edge of sleep there, and now I'm in a cold sweat. Off with the headphones. A glimpse of a dream there, my own funeral. Just the image of my own face, surrounded by white fluff in a coffin. Jump up, go to the table, beer and a pill in my hands. And you've taken too many of those, Hollaran. Just stop and think about it. A failure's funeral. Oh, Tom Hollaran? What did he die of? Booze and pills? Didn't he just get back from Vietnam? What is wrong with those guys anyway?

No, Hollaran, no. Fuck it, I'll go of anxiety instead. Scoop up the pills. Take the vial, too. Over to the sink, on with the water. Open the vial and dump it upside down, listen to the pills click down the drain. Flush them with water. Breathe out hard. A sense of triumph. I think.

A little anxious, though. Yes, hands sweating a little. Tight muscles in my head. No, please, no anxiety attack, not now, I'm out of pills. Sit on the floor and slap on the ear-

phones. Play another side. "Don't Sit Under the Apple Tree."
With anyone else but me. Great the way Marion Hutton sings
it. Cheerful, girlish, hopeful. She wants her soldier to come
home. Ready, Marion? Sing your heart out.

3

Bozos and Bimbos

What I do every Sunday morning is go over to Eddie Sadow-ski's and rap on his garage window. I never knock on the front door, because Eddie's *always* down in the garage. So I go and knock about ten times on his black-painted garage windows, and finally Eddie yells out, "All right," and I go up the stairs to the kitchen door and wait.

It takes a couple of minutes for Sadowski to get to the door, and when he finally does open it he says, "What do you want?" He says this every time he opens the door, no matter who it is. Let's go, I say to Sadowski, get your ass in gear.

"I'm goddamn working this morning," Eddie says. He's blocking the doorway. I tell him, well, quit your goddamn working and let's get out of here.

Sadowski shakes his head and lets the door swing open a little. "No wonder I can't get no work done," he says. "Let me get my jacket."

I let myself into the kitchen, which, like the rest of the house, is mostly bare. The big piece of kitchen furniture is an old wooden workbench with a couple of barstools shoved under it. On top of the workbench there's a sugar bowl, a picnic spoon, and one of those eat-from-the-carton boxes of Rice Krispies, with milk curdled inside. There's nothing on the walls of this kitchen, nothing on the stove, nothing on the counter tops. There aren't even any dirty dishes in the sink. Eddie does not own a single pot, pan, dish, glass, or bowl, and

he doesn't have any silverware, either. He eats mostly from
cans and boxes, although sometimes he goes as far as to heat
up a TV dinner.

Sadowski comes back into the kitchen, limping on that
bad leg of his. He's got his army jacket on now, and he digs
into a pocket and comes up with this ring of keys that must
weigh five pounds. There must be a hundred keys on that
ring, but Sadowski picks out the right one, goes to lock the
basement door. He turns the key in the lock and pulls hard on
the door to check it.

Outside it's actually nice, a cool, sunny December morning, maybe the last decent day before winter really jells.
Eddie starts to roll up the canvas cover that's draped over his
jeep, and I turn my back on him. It drives me crazy, how he
babies that jeep. After he gets the cover rolled up he'll bend
down and check the air pressure in each tire. Then he'll open
the hood to check the oil and water, inspect all the hoses, and
wiggle the sparkplug wires. After that he'll take a big piece of
cheesecloth and wipe the paint job clean of any dirt, grease,
or finger marks. Then, and only then, will he start it. The jeep
will warm up for five minutes minimum, Eddie timing it with
his old aviation watch. With the engine idling, Eddie will
spray the windows, wipe them lovingly with a special cloth,
and then do his walk-around inspection. He learned to be this
thorough, he says, when he was crew chief on a chopper.

While Eddie's doing all this I'm wondering, for about the
fortieth time, why he doesn't keep his jeep in the garage
anymore. I mean, that's why he picked out this house, because of the garage. I guess you could call it a garage or a
basement or both, since it's kind of a combination. It's at least
half the house, all unpainted cinder block, with a gray clapboard afterthought of an apartment built on top. Anyway,
there's room in the basement-garage for at least two jeeps,
and Eddie was attracted to this place like a magnet. Paid the
full asking price and could hardly wait to give his jeep a nice
home. But the next thing I knew, he was keeping his jeep
outside, and had painted the basement windows black and
had put two iron bar locks across the garage door.

I can hear the jeep running smooth and it's been a couple of minutes, so I turn around, walk behind the jeep, and get into the passenger seat. Eddie's sitting behind the steering wheel staring at the gauges, studying them, one after the other. It's a fantastic set of gauges he installed himself, and some of the things they measure have me pretty puzzled. Like engine vacuum. Why would you want to know about that? I've asked Eddie. And he's just smiled and tapped his head with his forefinger. I've asked him, too, about the barometer, the compass, and the altimeter. Especially the altimeter. I've asked him many times about that and he's said, It works when you drive uphill. Come on, Ed, I've said, don't bullshit me I'm not that dumb. What's it for? And he's just smiled and tapped his head with his forefinger.

"Just one minute," Eddie tells me after looking at his watch. "Okay?" I nod at him. He knows his jeep rituals annoy me, and he tries to control himself a little better when I'm around. But he can't help himself, really. Building this jeep was his whole life for a year, and now it's the only nice thing he has.

It really is a beautiful jeep. It's a real army one that Eddie bought surplus for seven hundred dollars and then tore down to the nuts and bolts. Then day by day, week by week, he put it back together, his way. Every part was either oiled or painted, except the seats, which went out to a custom upholsterer and came back in brown leather. Eddie did everything else himself, fabricated the top, installed the windows and the gear to raise and lower them, blueprinted the engine. The engine work alone took him three months, and I remember what the garage looked like then, with pistons and valves and springs and shafts everywhere. He worked on this jeep day and night, and supported himself on GI-bill money and unemployment. He did a class job on this thing, and now it's got a deep, rich camouflage paint job, thick green carpeting, a big loud stereo, and chrome roll bars. The dashboard is especially nice, with all those green-lit gauges set into polished wood.

Eddie puts the clutch in and then waits three full sec-

onds before he eases the gearshift into first. You'll never
grind a gear, Eddie always says, if you count to three before
shifting. Well, the gears in this jeep don't even *clink*. We roll
noiselessly down Eddie's driveway, and come to a complete
stop at the road. Even though it's a deserted industrial street
and Sunday morning, Eddie takes time to look twice before
pulling out. We take a left and we're off, the jeep running like
it's lubricated with honey. Past a small auto scrapyard with a
barking Doberman inside, past a vacant rubble-filled lot
where long ago there was a factory that made locomotive
engine parts, then around the bend to where the Arthur
Kill's on our right. A river so black with oil and sludge and
crud that it hardly flows anymore, and hasn't been known to
freeze in a century.

We're headed across town toward Lucky Leo's, our first
stop every Sunday morning. It's maybe a f e-minute ride
and I occupy myself by thinking about Eddie and this jeep.
When he first started building this thing, Eddie had big plans.
He was going to start a little home industry, customizing
jeeps and selling them for a lot of money. He quit the auto-
parts place that hired him fresh out of the VA hospital, and
swore he'd never work for a company again. Somehow he got
on unemployment, and then there was the skeleton of a jeep
in his garage, and then he went down to Trenton and registered himself as a business. Sadowski Custom Enterprises, A
Sole Proprietorship, that's the legal name of his business, and
it's printed on this certificate he brought back from Trenton.
I remember how proud he was the day he nailed that certificate up in his garage.

But then something happened, and I'm still not sure
what. I remember that Eddie went away for a weekend, a
practically unheard-of occurrence, and it was when he came
back that he painted his windows black. He never did sell his
first jeep, and never built his second one. He took a crash
course in oil burner repair at night school, and pretty soon he
was working for a company again. Working almost double
time, actually. Hardly sleeping, spending every spare moment down in the garage. I know he picked the oil burner

business because there's so much overtime in it, but he seems to be tighter with his money than ever. And all I get when I ask him about any of this are grunts, mumbles, shrugs, and vague little half smiles.

When we get near Lucky Leo's, there's no place to park, as usual, a Protestant church down the street and services just letting out. We won't even look for parking here on Westfield Avenue, because Eddie will never leave the jeep on a main street. He lives in constant dread of a scratch, a nick, a bump, or his worst nightmare, a sideswipe.

Eddie turns down the side streets and we prowl for just the right spot. He will not park too near a driveway or a corner. Finally after twice around we find a good spot with a big new Chrysler idling there. We wait behind the car, but it just sits. "What's with this bozo, anyway?" Eddie says after a minute, and then pulls up parallel with the Chrysler and tells me to roll down my window. I do that, I see this guy in the car, hands on the steering wheel, talking to his wife. "Hey, pal," Eddie yells out, but the guy doesn't notice us. "Hey, bozo," Eddie says, and then puts two fingers in his mouth and lets out an ear-busting whistle. That doesn't work either, and finally Eddie just lays on the horn until the guy turns and rolls down his window halfway. He's an older guy with a veiny red face, a lot of alcohol come to the surface. "A bozo all right," Eddie says to me, and then yells at the guy, "Hey, pal, you leaving?"

"You need this space?" the guy asks. He looks a little bit afraid, and I can tell he's not going to give us an argument. I'm thinking we must look scruffy and maybe mean, two guys in old army jackets on a Sunday morning. The guy rolls up his window and starts backing out of the space. "What'd I tell you?" Eddie says to me. "A regular bozo."

The word *bozo* has a special meaning for Eddie Sadowski, although I'm not sure I can define it just right. A bozo, according to Eddie, is an American man who produces nothing, fixes nothing, has no particular skill or aptitude, yet is powerful and prosperous. John Johnson is a good example of a bozo, because he's made a living selling steel, yet it's hard to imagine his manicured fingers reaching down to *touch* a greasy tube. Salesmen and managers are nothing but bozos, according to Eddie, and so are bankers, foremen, clerks, stockbrokers, insurance agents, public relations men, corporate officers, consultants, and all government workers except mailmen.

To avoid being a bozo, a guy should do something directly useful, or get his hands dirty somehow, or risk something on the job besides a paper cut. Cops and construction workers, bartenders and repairmen, cabinetmakers, musicians, pilots, barbers, housepainters, cooks, cannery workers, bank robbers, those guys are okay by Eddie as long as they do something real for their living.

Actually, I would count as a bozo under Eddie's system, except that I once humped a rifle and pack around the Mekong Delta. That makes me all right forever, according to Eddie. I could even become a life insurance salesman, the kind of bozo Eddie hates most, and still I'd be okay. Because the true bozos, Eddie says, all found a way to avoid Vietnam.

Sometimes I point out that I was *drafted* and *forced* through infantry school and *shipped* to Vietnam, all against my will. And that I would have been perfectly happy to have stayed home and watched the war on TV, thank you. But Eddie says it doesn't make any difference, because a real bozo will always find a way out.

We get out of the jeep and Eddie brings out this little greasy notebook and writes down the license numbers of all the nearby cars. He'll track down the owners if there's even a chip on his jeep. He pockets the notebook and then we start walking the two blocks to Lucky Leo's, Eddie limping, hitting the pavement hard with that good left foot. All around us there are bozos, coming from church with their little families, all clutching their little prayer books. Heading downtown to the bakeries, then home to bacon and eggs and the funny pages, and an afternoon of TV football. Bozos. Suckers. Eddie's walking ahead of me, he just puts his head down and limps away, and the bozos, like always, step aside.

Lucky Leo's is a defunct eight-lane bowling alley stuck

off in a corner of Elizabeth where practically nobody lives
anymore. The building itself is a brick L-shaped thing, dark
with soot on the outside, just like when it was called the Alley
Cat Lanes. It's the inside that Leo made different. It's the
inside that has people standing in line outside the door on
weekend nights.

In the mornings, though, especially Sunday mornings,
Lucky Leo's is always empty. Eddie pushes in ahead of me
and we grope, almost blind, coming out of the sunlight and
into this black cave. Eddie bumps into a barstool, steadies it,
and sits down. I feel my way into the space next to him.

"Be right with you boys," Leo's voice booms out. He
knows it's us. From the sound of his voice, he's working somewhere in the back room, where the lanes used to be. That's
Leo, always working. He did a nice job on this place, deco-
rated it like an old-time casino, a gambler's motif. Along a
side wall there's a bank of antique slot machines, cast-iron
ones with brass pull-arms, the handles shaped like animal
paws, the coin slots welded shut. Where other bars would
have ordinary tables and chairs, Leo's got old blackjack tables
and casino stools. A craps table holds a sandwich bar, or will,
if Leo follows through on his plan to start serving lunch.
Poster-size playing cards are nailed up here and there along
the walls, especially jokers, Leo loves jokers. Foam dice the
size of washing machines sit in each corner, and the center-
piece, behind the bar, is a huge roulette wheel, immobilized
at the insistence of the state liquor commission.

I don't have to see Leo to know he's coming, the floorboards in this old place creak under his feet. Leo weighs in at
three hundred plus, and when he walks behind the bar you'd
swear a rhino was coming. He comes into the horseshoe
shape of the bar, he's smiling, wiping sweat from his face with
a blue bandanna. He gets in front of us, drops two coasters on
the bar, and, without saying a word, bends a little to make the
drinks. Every time he bends, even a little, he groans. He puts
a shot glass full of Jack Daniel's and a draft beer on the bar
and says, "Tom." Then he makes a vodka tonic with no lime
and puts it on the bar and says, "Eddie." I've put a ten-dollar

bill out, but Leo won't touch it yet. "Luck to you boys," Leo says. He'll buy the first drink every Sunday morning.

We drink to Leo, as if he needs any more luck than he's already had, and then we start our ritual toasts. Unless we get too drunk and forget, Eddie and I will toast before every sip of every drink. I pick up my beer and hold it out toward Eddie. To the Pope, I say.

"And to all his funny hats," Eddie says. We drink. Today it's my turn to buy, so Eddie takes a regular sip. If he were buying, it'd be the tiniest sip in the world.

"I was looking for you yesterday," Eddie says.

Well, I was out, I say. And try not to look at him.

"Came by a couple of times," Eddie says.

Wasn't in, was I? I say.

"Nope," Eddie says. "You're usually home on a Saturday."

Silence. And the gray-green stare of Polack eyes.

I was out looking for Sandra, I say.

"Oh," Eddie says.

I wanted to get it straight once and for all, I say. So I camped out in front of our old apartment. All day. And she never came home.

Eddie's nodding. "I came around and looked for you last night, too," he says.

Well, I was still there, I say.

"At eight o'clock?" he says.

I must have just missed you, I say.

Suspicious look in those Polack eyes. Eddie reaches for his glass and raises it toward me. "To the Honorable Richard M. Nixon," he says.

To the commander in chief, I say. I raise my beer with my left hand, and salute with my right. Eddie salutes too. We drink.

I wait out a few seconds of silence, hoping the subject will maybe die out, but I can just *look* at Eddie and tell he's not going to give up.

"You got it bad," he says, and shakes his head.

I know, I say. It's one of those love-hate paradoxes.

"What?" Eddie says. "Speak English. What did you just say, professor?"

He calls me professor because I've had three semesters of college. I've tried to tell Eddie that college is no big deal, but he won't believe it. What goes on in colleges, he's convinced, is that brainy people learn how to trick and swindle guys like himself.

Look, I say, don't ask me for a definition right now. Love-hate paradox. All I know is I'm caught in one.

"How do you know?"

That sets me thinking for a few seconds, and then I say, Because it's over but for some reason I can't say good-bye.

Eddie whistles. "You're in a rut," he says.

That's right, a rut, I say.

"Then why didn't you say that in the first place?" he says. "What's all this paragon stuff? That's bozo talk."

Okay, I say, I'm in a rut. Let's drink to ruts. I hold up my shot glass.

"To four-wheel-drive jeeps," Eddie says. "That's how to get out of ruts." We drink and it's time for Leo again and Eddie swishes ice cubes and taps his glass on the bar.

"What you need is a new bimbo," Eddie says. He'll never say woman or chick or girl or broad, it's always bimbo. "Let me think," he says, "I must know somebody who's looking."

Just what I need, I say. I barely survived this bimbo, Ed.

"Quiet while I'm thinking," he says.

We're not saying anything when Leo comes up in front of us, breathing like a horse. The guy can't walk ten feet without gasping for air. His nostrils are flaring as he bends down to refill our drinks. His full, thick head of gray-black hair, combed straight back, smells of Vitalis as he bends in front of me.

"Leo," Eddie says, and moves his thumb to indicate me. "This guy needs a bimbo."

"This early," Leo says, "I don't know."

Eddie shakes his head. "Not that kind of bimbo," he says to Leo. "A nice one, you know. Somebody with class. College preferred." He says that without any trace of sarcasm.

"You know where to find a girl like that?" Leo says. "In church."

Eddie and I both laugh. Leo puts our drinks on the bar, starts drying his hands with a towel, and says, "I mean it." I can see he's a little put off by our laughing. "I don't know what's with you guys. When all the women are in church, you guys are in here. When all the women are in here, I never see you guys." He draws a little half glass of club soda for himself and sips it. "You should have seen this place Friday night," he says. "Wall-to-wall with good-looking women. I must have made ten thousand Harvey Wallbangers."

He shakes his head, takes my ten-dollar bill to the register, and on the way back he's grumbling. "Harvey Wallbangers," he says. "I thought college kids were supposed to drink beer." He lays my change on the bar and shakes his head like there's some big tragedy going on. "Kids today," he says, "they got more money than they know what to do with. That's the problem."

I have a hard time working up much sympathy for Leo, especially when he complains about success. He's a guy from the old neighborhood, he must have been around thirty when Eddie and I were in gram_ _ _r school, and back then we kids called him Two-ton Leo. He lived by himself in a little basement apartment and never seemed to go to work. The adults in the neighborhood, especially my father, had him figured for a petty mobster. All us kids were warned to stop teasing him, stay away from him, don't take anything from him. That was hard because, as every kid on the block knew, if you went down to Leo's and talked nice to him, he'd get out a 3 Musketeers or a Milky Way for you.

But then when I was around fourteen, Leo disappeared. The whole neighborhood jumped with rumors for weeks, people saying Leo had been given a cement overcoat by the Mafia and dumped into the Arthur Kill. Or he had moved to Miami to become a bookie. Or the FBI had nailed him with bags of heroin and put him in Sing Sing. We kids even invented a rumor that he had run away with the fat lady from the circus. For the next couple of years Leo was reported everywhere. California, Singapore, Trenton, Alaska, Sicily, Argentina, Brooklyn, and the Panama Canal. Supposedly he was a crooked contractor, a phony priest, a pimp, a con man, a Communist, a Mafia don, a union goon, a CIA agent, a smuggler. I don't know about any of it, except that a few years ago Leo came back to Elizabeth with plenty of money, did a first-class job renovating this place, started playing music from the thirties and forties, and had lines of college kids forming outside the door.

By the time Leo finishes grumbling and starts walking toward the back room, I've just about drained my shot glass. So I pick up my beer to make up for lost toasts and say to Eddie, To college girls. One for me and one for you.

"College bimbos," Eddie says. We drink together. Eddie swallows and says. "But they're all yours, pal. I'm through with college bimbos, let me tell you."

Laura? I ask.

Eddie nods and gives me what's supposed to be a meaningful look, his lips puckered. All I know is, Laura's a nurse he's gone out with a couple of times, she's taller than he is, and she's studying for a second degree, in social work.

"We went out yesterday," Eddie says. "That's why I was looking for you. To see if you'd want to come along."

On your date? I say.

"Yeah, well," Eddie says, and just shrugs his shoulders. A lot of times I just have to guess what Eddie means. So I think for a moment and say, Oh, you wanted me to run interference for you.

"Sorta," he says. "You know where we ended up? At an art gallery over in New York."

A museum? I say.

"Yeah," he says. "One painting after another. We must have been there three hours, doing nothing but looking at paintings. My feet were aching like a son of a bitch. They don't have nowhere to sit down in those museums."

I have to laugh at him. I say, Well, you should have just been patient, taken her to some bar afterwards, you know, made your moves there.

"Nope," Eddie says. "I could see we weren't going to get anywhere, you know how it is. We're standing there looking at this one painting, and she's going on and on about how concrete it is. I tell her, concrete? I don't see no concrete."

I say, Ed, she didn't mean cement-like concrete.

"I know that, professor," he says. "I was just giving her a little gas, that's all. I don't know why they teach bimbos to talk like that in college."

Don't let it throw you, I say. They're saying the same things we are, they're just using longer words.

"Yeah, well, it's them longer words that throw me for a loop. I'm staying away from college bimbos from now on, believe me."

Come on, I say, your toast. Glasses up. What'll it be?

"To college," Eddie says.

To college? I say.

"I always been for it," he says. "I figure every guy who's in college is one more guy who ain't in oil burner school. And the less guys in oil burner school, the more overtime for me."

Okay, I say. To college.

"To overtime," he says. "Drink up."

We go through that round and call Leo for another, and I'm getting a little woozy already, drinking on an empty stomach. When Eddie and I get enough to drink, our toasts start to get kind of antisocial. In fact, ever since we've been back we've been rooting for a big trauma, like maybe six feet of snow in Manhattan, or a power failure during the Super Bowl, or a Teaneck-to–Cape May traffic jam on the Parkway. Today I offer a toast to the Arab oil embargo, then Eddie toasts to the hope of an explosion that will end gas heat once and for all. "To oil burners," Eddie says.

I thought you hated them, I say.

"I do," Eddie says. "Look at this." He shows me his hands, which I know about, which are just about permanently black on the palms, with big ridges of grease all around the fingernails. Eddie could scrub those hands all day, he could soak them in turpentine, and still the black would be there. "There's nothing as filthy as an oil burner," Eddie says. "But every time one breaks down, it's money to me."

Oh, I say, you want to drink to the *breakdown* of oil burners.

"Yeah," he says, as if it should have been obvious all along. We drink, and I figure now's the time to tell him about John Johnson putting me down in the warehouse. Eddie looks like he can hardly believe what he's hearing.

"They can't do that to you," he says when I finish my story.

I'm in the warehouse tomorrow morning at seven, I say.

"But you're a college man," he says, with no sarcasm at all. "You're going to quit and get another office job, right?"

Think about it, I say. What kind of reference do you think I'd get from John Johnson? The big steel bozos around here are all buddies, you know that, don't you?

"It figures," Eddie says. "Drink up, I'll buy." That practically sends me back off the stool, Eddie buying when it's not his turn. "Your Honor!" Eddie calls out to Leo, and holds up his glass. "Your Honor, justice, please."

"Look," Eddie says after the drinks are delivered and Leo's out of range. "I got something going and you might be interested in knowing about it. Especially now. But you got to promise to keep it quiet."

Okay, I say.

"Your word of honor, Tom," he says.

My lips are sealed, I say.

"I'm going to get the bozos," he says, very quietly. He's looking right in my eyes, he's serious. I say what do you mean, *get?*

"I got it all planned out," Eddie says.

Revenge? I say. I'd be all for it if I could figure out how. Without getting in more trouble.

"Join me," Eddie says. "We'll put John Johnson at the top of the list."

I wish you'd tell me what the hell you're talking about, I say.

"In time," Eddie says. He picks up his glass and holds it out at me, an angry, drunken expression on his face. "Fuck the bozos," he says. "You with me?"

I'll drink to that, I say.

4

CABIN FEVER

I came all the way up to the lake today, I'm still not sure why, it's a freezing, slushy Saturday, and I don't really have anything to do up here. I walked out on this little peninsula, to the remains of an amusement park, shut down for the winter. The big structure is an enormous old wooden roller coaster, the whitewash peeled off, showing the rotting gray wood and rusting bolts. I've got a can of beer in each jacket pocket, and a half-empty can in my hand. I'm sitting on a big crossbeam at the bottom of the roller coaster, shivering, drinking stuff this cold on a day like today.

I can't hide from my mind, not any longer, the basic reason I came up here. I told myself I needed to relax, calm down, get away, but the truth is, I wanted to see if Sandra was at the cabin. I came all the way up here on just that chance.

I can see the cabin from here, across a hundred yards of gray-brown lake water, across a road, up a hill, off a dirt path covered with fallen leaves. Sandra's cabin. It *was* our cabin. I married into it.

I finish my can of beer and drop it at my feet. I stand and climb, one more rung up the roller coaster studs, eight feet off the ground now, sitting on a thick crossbeam. I get another beer out of my pocket, pop the top, tip it to my mouth.

I spent a lot of summers at this lake as a kid, learned to swim and dive here. I practically lived on the beach down there, a lot of time lying on my stomach, looking at girls. A lot of time wishing there was a girl underneath me. There were hundreds of beautiful high school girls here in those days.

Once I remember there was a missing child, right down there on that beach, the one behind the penny arcades. I still remember the lifeguard, on top of his stand, whistling and waving everybody out of the water. Everybody obeyed. Then the lifeguard told us to line up at the edge of the water, and we did that right away too. Then he asked us all to hold hands and walk through the shallow part of the lake. I was holding my father's hand on one side and my mother's hand on the other, and there we were in the middle of this long human chain. Slowly we walked out into the lake, still holding hands, dredging for the body. I was scared and excited as hell, I was twelve years old and had never seen a dead person, and with every step I was terrified that I'd nudge a drowned corpse. We never did find any body, but I remember that with a warm feeling. Because there was trouble around, and we all stayed together and held hands.

I'm looking backward, always backward, it's been that way ever since I've been home. The past, that's all that interests me, it's a sign of my fear, that's what Doctor Rhinehart says. Fear of what? I ask her. Only you know, she says.

All I do know is something's wrong, really *wrong.* I wish I knew what it was exactly. I finish my beer and drop the can, it hits hard dirt down there, bounces, rolls a little. I pop open another can. Sip some and climb a little on the beams, up on the third level now, the beer having its effect, because normally fifteen feet off the ground I'd be sick with fear. Now I'm just looking out, dangling my legs, remembering. The first girl I ever kissed, it happened right on that beach. She was a Puerto Rican girl, very skinny, with big buck teeth. We were both down there in the shallow water, a hot summer day, she came up and just started talking to me, then asked my name. In a minute she had her hand around my waist. She was a brazen little girl, and we hadn't known each other for five minutes when she leaned in and kissed me, hard and dry. We banged teeth, I remember that. I was astonished that a girl would want to kiss me. And after a minute or two of shy small talk from me, she swam away, splashing water in my face, and I didn't listen to my heart, didn't swim after her. And then later that afternoon I saw her do the same thing to two other boys, she just went up to them, talked awhile, kissed them, and splashed away. That whole summer I planned all kinds of ways to meet her again. And *I* was going to kiss *her* this time. And then ask her if she'd be my girl, just mine and nobody else's. Of course, I never did see her again. I looked on every damn beach down there, too. For years I remembered that girl's name, but I've forgotten it now.

I'm walking across the beams. Pretending I'm a high-wire artist, but it's safe, the beams are a foot wide. I stop, sip beer, take a few steps, sip some more. I put one leg then another around a vertical stud, I'm across, into my balancing act once more. I finish my beer, drop the can, climb up a level, sit on a beam, put my arm around the stud, dig into the pocket of my army jacket for another can. I look above me at the roller coaster tracks, two rusty rails looping just over my head. I can see almost the whole lake now, I never remember it this dead, this empty.

Looking out like this reminds me of tower fourteen, how many times I sat in that thing, just looking out at water, river water. I remember sitting there nights, the river all lit up, it's the Mekong I'm talking about, big boat-size floats of lily pads drifting by. Most of the time I watched alone, the only one *awake* anyway, in a big bunker built on thick stilts, the inside of it smelling of mosquito oil and marijuana, two guys down on the floor, sleeping. I usually volunteered to pull everybody's guard, mostly because I didn't smoke marijuana much, it made me too paranoid. And anyway, I could never sleep on sandbag floors.

So I spent a couple of nights every week looking out over thirty feet of sandy grass, laced over with concertina wire, and set with Claymores and trip flares. There were these big floodlights, they lit everything, all across the river. But beyond that there was nothing visible, just blackness. Only because of day patrols did I know what was out there. Hot green swamp, muddy rice paddies, hamlets of seven, eight, ten

houses. It was Charley's country, full of mosquitoes, black
stagnant water, mud forts, fire ants, snakes thicker than a
man's forearm, and, I've seen it myself, the people who ate
those snakes for breakfast.

On tower guard I really had to watch in two directions. I
had to pay *some* attention to the river, even though it was
pretty unlikely that the VC would come paddling past the
floodlights. But I spent more time watching the road behind
us, because of the platoon sergeant, a near-toothless skinny
rebel named Hoover. He just loved to sneak up the ladder,
shout out the password, push through the trapdoor, and
catch marijuana smokers, beer drinkers, and draftees who
didn't follow the rule of two men awake at all times. I spent as
much time worried about Hoover as about the VC.

Tower guard was an easy, boring job, but safe, and for
me, enjoyable. Anything was preferable to pulling night am-
bushes, or listening posts, or day sweeps, or search-and-
clears, or any of the other stupid, dangerous things we had to
do. On tower guard I just loaded the M-60, turned the radio
to the night's frequency, sat back, and stared at the river. The
lily pads would flow down with the tide, and then hours later
come back up. About three in the morning the lily pads
would start to look like boatloads of VC, so I'd just stare away,
the sand, the roof, the concertina wire. Once in a while a
bored soldier would call for a time check. A breeze would
start the ammo belt clicking against the M-60. A frog would
hop over a Claymore.

Some nights there'd be a Cobra mission, out there in the
darkness, two, three, four miles away. It would start high in
the black sky with four blinking red lights. They would make
ritual circles in the sky for maybe five minutes. Then a para-
chute flare would flash, pop, start drifting down slowly, a
giant smoking white candle. Two more flares would pop,
making an arc of bright smoky sky where it used to be night.
The blinking red lights would stay high above it all, circling.

Then one of them would break out and dive, almost
straight down, letting out a narrow, neon-red river of mini-
gun fire, thousands of glowing tracer rounds pouring down

on the earth. The noise would come a few seconds into the dive, just like the sound of a chain saw.

Then the red river of bullets would stop flowing and there'd be two white flashes, and the blinking red light would turn, heading up at a steep angle. The two rockets it had fired would hit with white, lightning-like flashes, I could feel the explosions vibrate in the wood of the tower.

By then the blinking red light would have rejoined the circle, way up there, and in a minute another one would break, dive, a repeat performance. The flares would pop, the sky would glow red, the rockets would make thunder and lightning. It would go on for maybe a half an hour, and then the blinking red lights would win, or maybe just run out of ammunition. They'd rise even higher, form a straight line, and head for our base. I'd watch them get closer and closer until they weren't just blinking lights but real helicopters, loud and low, zooming over the tower, landing on the runway behind me.

I remember very clearly the one night something different happened. It must have been almost dawn, I was sitting in the tower, watching a Cobra attack, I was used to it by then, it was like nothing more than a fireworks show. The blinking red light was diving, pouring out its stream of red fire, letting go its rockets, and just as it turned back and climbed, a single green spark came up after it. One miserable tracer round from a VC rifle. Of course, the blinking red light just kept climbing, and the green spark faded uselessly into the dark sky. And the attack didn't miss a heartbeat. Dive after dive, the mini-guns rattling like chain saws, the rockets slamming into the ground and lighting pure white. I sat there and started thinking about whoever it was that fired that single shot. I imagined one barefoot VC out there, in a mud bunker, with just an AK-47, trying to survive the attack of a squad of helicopters. I had never thought that way before. The VC was my enemy, right? Then why did that green spark make something inside me move? Why did I set up this howl of delight when I saw it. I felt like waking one of the guys who were asleep on the floor, just to tell them about it. But I didn't. I sat there watching the sky long after the Cobras had come in.

Hell, I could sit here and remember forever, and I probably would if it wasn't so cold. I tip up my beer, drain it, and drop the can. Out on the far road I see the county sheriff's white cruiser, maybe I'd better climb down, the cops are probably bored enough to bust me for trespassing. I get down off the beams of the roller coaster, hop a low fence, and I'm walking along an asphalt path, a little slush left at its edges. I pass the penny arcade, boarded up with new plywood, then the Octopus, covered with canvas, then the Tunnel of Love, garage doors brought down over the entrance and exit. Up over the entrance there's this big, awful painting of an American-looking Adam and Eve, holding hands, dressed all in leaves, staring into each other's eyes. I stand and look at that painting for a moment, the words TUNNEL OF LOVE spelled out in a wooden arch over it, and I wonder what kind of society this really is. That makes children pay money to double up in the dark for their first kisses and feels. I bend down and make an ice ball out of some slush and throw it up at Adam. The ice ball hits him in the nose and shatters.

I walk out of the amusement park, cross the main road, and get behind a tree, where I let out some of the afternoon's beer. Then I take the one can left in my pocket and snap the top open. I sip beer, walking up the wide path toward Sandra's cabin. I can see that *somebody's* still coming up here, because the cabin is the only one along this path, and there are tire tracks in the leafy, icy mud that can't be very old. I'm walking uphill, there's the cabin, white clapboard and not much bigger than a good-sized family room. Nobody's fixed it up for the winter. The green wood-frame screens are still in place over the windows, and the big thick winter door for keeping out hippies and vandals, that's still leaning against a side wall.

I get up to the cabin steps and finish the last of the beer, throw the can off into the woods. I walk around the cabin once, then come back to the front and yell, Hello? No answer. I yell, Anybody home? Of course not, nobody would be inside if there's no car around. I sit on the steps. Depressed now. In a few minutes the sun will be down, it'll be Saturday night, I'll be driving back to Elizabeth, half bombed and still feeling lousy. If this was still my cabin, I'd stock it with ham and eggs and butter and coffee. I'd turn on the stereo and fall asleep listening to Glenn Miller, and in the morning I'd make a big omelet and maybe drive out for the Sunday paper. It would be nice if I could find a girl to stay with me too.

Sandra, I find myself saying, Sandra. I'm actually sitting here saying her name. I get up and walk, kick at the leaves. I circle the cabin, Sandra, I'm saying. She gave it to me good. And I let her. Why? Why couldn't I see this coming?

I find myself thinking about the day we met. At Union College, it's up in Cranford, a little two-year school. It was my first experience in a non-Catholic institution. And the first person I met there was Sandra. Because we were both fifteen minutes early for the first class of the new semester.

I walked into the classroom and she said, Hi. Are you here for Accounting 100? I said yes and smiled. A nervous smile. And sat a couple of desks away from her, nobody else in the room. Tried to keep my eyes away from her, but it didn't work. Legs crossed at the knees. Purple skirt. White blouse. Red hair. Green eyes. This is it, right? I said. And held up my brand-new accounting book.

Let me see that, she said. I stretched out of my desk and handed it to her. She leafed through it, then dipped into an enormous shoulder bag that lay at her feet, came up with an old accounting book, the same cover as mine, but cracked and dirty. She compared the two books for a moment and then handed mine back. I just have an older edition, she said. And then closed her book and put it on the floor. Laid her arms on the desk for a pillow and lowered her head. Her face turned in my direction. They should never, never start school on a sunny morning, she said. It's so depressing.

I just smiled.

You're not depressed, are you? she said.

Not really, I said. I've been kind of looking forward to this.

Accounting? she said.

No, college, I said.

She gave me a long look. Maybe to see if I was putting her on. Finally she said, I've had this class before. Twice. It's deadly, believe me. Do you know, she said, and broke off to look at the wall clock. Do you know why the cafeteria was closed?

I shook my head.

Typical of this school, she said. I got up a half hour early this morning, hoping a good breakfast would get me through the day— She cut herself off in midsentence and reached down for her bag, then stood, hoisted it to her shoulder. Maybe I'll get a cup of coffee from the machine, she said.

I could have gone with her, but I didn't think of it at the moment. Didn't think of it until she was out the door. And then I began an argument with myself about whether to follow her. Male instinct versus some basic fear, and fear won.

She didn't come back to class until maybe ten after eight. Walked in holding a cup of coffee, did not apologize for inter- rupting the instructor. A bald guy doing his best to reveal the mysteries of the double-entry system. I concentrated on tak- ing notes, and mostly forgot about Sandra. But I wasn't sur- prised to find myself talking in the hall with her after class.

I told you it was a bore, she said. But if you want to major in business . . . She shrugged. We started walking. Actually I was kind of following her, a half step behind.

I wanted to tell you, she said. There's a back-to-school party tonight, if you want to come and meet some people. Do you know Union? It's just two blocks off Morris Avenue.

I copied down the address in my accounting book as we walked. Out the double doors and into the parking lot. Where Sandra had her old faded-blue Falcon. She said she had other classes but was going to cut. It was just too nice a day, she said.

She got in the car, rolled down the window, started the engine, and I stood there feeling awkward. Finally when she was ready to back out, I asked her name. Sandra, she said.

Nobody calls me Sandy, I don't like that. Maybe I'll see you tonight, she said, and backed out slowly.

Of course I was at the party. But I made myself go late so I wouldn't seem like an eager fool. It was at an old house shared by Sandra and four other college girls. For a half hour I stood and sipped beer at the edge of three conversations. One about the Mets, one about Camus, and one about a famous clam bar in Hoboken. I was almost going to join in with that last one when I felt a touch on my elbow, and knew it was Sandra. She was a little drunk.

Tom Hollaran, right? she said. And pronounced it Howl-Ah-Ran.

It's Holler-In, I said. And how do you know my name?

I have my ways, she said. I see you're only drinking one beer at a time. Let's get serious. She went to a picnic cooler in the corner and brought me two bottles of the good stuff, imported. But before we could even start to talk, one of her roommates dragged her away to a kitchen emergency.

Sooner or later at any party I'll go off by myself, and at this party it was sooner. Out to the little backyard, crickets chirping, a warm cloudy night. I wandered the yard, beer in hand, and in the dark almost strangled myself on a hammock. Strung between two trees. I got in and sat. After I finished the beer I just laid down. Glad to be far from the party talk. And the stereo, which featured a bunch of British madmen screaming, banging, and twanging guitars.

I was close to being asleep when I heard her voice. Didn't anybody ever tell you not to drink alone? she said. And gave a little push to the hammock.

Hi, I said. Even after a few beers, something about her just plain scared me.

Are you having a good time out here? she asked.

Very, I said. I could only see the shadow of her in the dark.

Maybe you want to be left alone, she said.

Not really, I said. Tell me something, I said. How did you know my name?

Simple, she said. It was in your accounting book. Do you have room in there?

In here? I said. Sure.

She got in with just a little help from me. And her entrance, so easy, put me in a little panic. Because up to that time I'd only made love to Catholic schoolgirls. Two, to be exact. So all I'd really known was guilt and reluctance. When Sandra got in the hammock, she laid her hand and arm across my chest. Comfortable? she said. I'm getting there, I told her.

And now I find myself looking in the back window of the cabin, through the screen, through the dusty glass. Things haven't changed. There's the stereo, covered with a big clear plastic sheet. I think I actually paid for that stereo and most of the records, but they're hers now, somehow. There's the bed, folded out from a brown corduroy couch, somebody's been staying here lately, the covers all twisted, the pillows pushed together in the middle. It's like I can smell Sandra now, smell her body right through this window, damn it, I'm saying. I give the screen a whack with the side of my hand. Damn it. I'm pounding on the screen, cursing. I push the screening out of the frame, reach in, flip the hook out of the eye, take the screen off its hinges and throw it to the ground, I'm pushing on the window now, it's stuck, locked. I'm pushing up, straining, grunting, the window won't move. Down around my feet I find a rock, I back up, throw it and the glass shatters. Take off a shoe, knock out more glass, it's flying everywhere. I reach up, unlatch the window, throw it open, drop my shoe inside, heave myself up on the windowsill, I'm squirming, I fall in, broken glass everywhere, my hand is cut, bleeding. I'm breathing in gasps, I'm in the kitchen, running water, my hand under the water now, diluted blood running in streams down the stainless steel, I think I cut my foot, too, from the feel of it, I turn up the sole and I'm bleeding through the sock. Blood on the floor, running water. I wrap my hand in a dishcloth and limp to the bathroom, glass all over the living room floor, the bed, the stereo, it crunches under my shoe as I hop my way, one-footed, into the bathroom.

I sit on the toilet seat, off with the sock, the cut's down

toward my heel, rub it with my good hand, I can feel the glass
grind in there. I stand, push open the medicine cabinet door,
the shelves crammed with bottles and jars, all Sandra's stuff,
I'm pushing it around, bottles falling out, into the sink, I'm
still pushing things, in pain, looking for the tweezers, the
Band-Aids. I find the tweezers, sit on the toilet seat again,
pick up my foot, go after the glass, it's down there in the
bloody meat, I'm just drunk enough to go after it, get it, a
knife-shaped shard about a quarter-inch long, bloody, I drop
it down the sink. A Band-Aid, I'm standing on my good foot,
looking for one, pushing around the cremes and oils and
lotions and scents, everything in here but a goddamn Band-
Aid, I throw a bottle of something into the shower stall, it
doesn't break, rolls around in there, where are the goddamn
Band-Aids, Sandra? I take my foot in my hand, wrap it in
toilet paper, put my sock on over that. Now take the wash-
cloth off my hand, it's not bleeding anymore. I rub over the
cut, no glass in it, I need a beer. Hop out to the main room,
put on my shoe, crunch through the broken glass and into the
kitchen, there's a little half-refrigerator, I expect to find it
empty, instead it's jammed. Bottles of beer, Dortmunder,
good German stuff, and stuck among them, sausages,
cheeses. I pick up a beer, is Sandra drinking now? Then it hits
me, a kraut, she's going with a German, that's her new guy,
drinks Dortmunder, a buck something a bottle. I snap the
cap off one bottle, take a long drink, my foot really hurts.
Dortmunder, the son of a bitch drinks Dortmunder, what the
hell's she getting herself into? I open the refrigerator again
and look at the sausages and cheeses, they didn't come from
any supermarket, but some specialty place, a rich kraut, who
is this guy?

I limp out of the kitchen. I'm thinking about Sadowski,
we're both limpers now. I smile. I'm drunk. I'm nuts, I'm
really finally nuts, the cops are going to come, somebody
must have heard the breaking glass, I'm going to wake up
tomorrow morning, hung over and in jail, nobody to call for
bail, I'll be there for weeks, they'll find me hung. I have to
laugh, I laugh because I'm crazy, finally around the bend, I

look around, I've busted in here, really busted in, Jesus, glass
everywhere. Fuck it, I'm here now, I'm going to jail anyway,
might as well look around for evidence, who is this goddamn
kraut?

I'm in the living room, looking for something to tell me,
there's nothing of his in here, nothing by the fireplace, nothing on the end tables that's his, no pictures of him, no calling
cards, no wallet, no keys, nothing here. I pull the covers off
the bed, like I'm going to find some evidence, but nothing,
just a cream-colored sheet, I pick up some hairs from it, red,
Sandra's, red, Sandra's. Just red hair. A bald goddamn kraut?
She got rid of me for some bald goddamn kraut?

I get up off the bed and go into the kitchen, I built a lot of
this damn thing, built the oak shelving that fits over the half-
refrigerator, built this pot tree, hung up these knives and
pans and whisks and spoons, it was Sandra's old man who did
the other stuff, though, who put up the pine paneling, not
that glossy junk but good pine, the kind that turns dark with
age. He built the cabinets, too, nice ones, he was a carpenter,
I'm looking through these cabinets for evidence, but all I find
are boxes of cereal, cans of soup, Sandra could eat forever out
of boxes and cans.

I grab another Dortmunder, I'm drinking it, still breathing too hard, I'm thinking not about that kraut now, but
about Sandra's old man, a guy I never met, she hated him,
and I mean *hated* him, at least that's what she said, said it
practically every day of her life. He was a bad drinker and
beat Sandra, beat the mother, he'd be sober for months and
then start boozing, coming home late, raving, beating them,
finally he'd disappear, weeks later the cops would find him
somewhere, Texas or Alaska or Florida, collapsed in the john
of some bus station, or maybe just drunk in the gutter. He'd
come home, dry out, then start up again. Sandra told me she
spent a lot of time wishing, even praying, that he'd never
come back, that he'd die out there, but he didn't, he died
right here, one day when he was raving drunk and they were
all fighting, Sandra and him and the mother, he stormed out
the door, came back in for his bottle, then fell down dead, he

didn't make a sound but just dropped right here in the kitchen, died with Sandra still cursing him. I think about that a lot, and the lesson I learned from it all, the hard way. Never have anything to do with a girl who hates her father. Especially her dead father.

I'm going to drink all of this bastard's beer, whoever he is, he's in for a big surprise. I open the refrigerator, nothing I've overlooked, nothing to tell me who this guy is, just Dortmunder and cheese and sausages, this guy's fart must smell like the sewers of Berlin. I take a beer and go into the bathroom again, maybe something in there I overlooked. I flip through a stack of towels, all familiar, I push around under the sink, tampons and toilet paper, and there's something, a brown leather shaving bag, I open it, it belongs to that bastard, all right, the prick, he's living here, shaves with a goddamn shaving cup, Robert! His goddamn name's right on the cup! Robert the goddamn kraut. Shaves with a straight razor. I take it out, flash the steel, slash it through the air, come on, Robert, I'll take off your goddamn balls, you bald bastard, come on. I'm slashing at the air.

I'm looking at the razor now, just staring at the long shiny blade, test it against my thumbnail, just a touch of it cuts a groove. I ought to draw this thing across my wrists. Bleed to death right here and let them clean it up. Haunt this goddamn cabin forever. And punish nobody but yourself, Hollaran. Yes, and I'm tired of being like that. Fuck it, fold up the razor, put it away. Evidence, I need evidence, I'm going to find out what's going on here, though I already know, a lot of fucking, somebody fucking my wife, she's not your wife anymore, Hollaran, we're not even divorced, and what difference does that make?

I'm out of the bathroom and at the closet, open the door, the left side filled with clothes, men's clothes, I rip down a pair of trousers, look inside the band, holy Christ, size 42, this guy's a blimp, she left me for the goddamn *Hindenburg!* Size 42 polyester machine-wash no bleach, I throw the trousers to the floor, kick them, kick them again, something's under them, something white, the bastard's underwear, I squat to

look at it, no, a deposit bag, Elizabeth National Bank and
Trust Co., now what? Is Sandra sneaking money out of the
bank? I open the bag, no money, nothing inside but a slip of
yellow paper, a deposit slip, Robert Wolpenheimer, DBA
Coin-O-Rama, 1441 Elmora Avenue, Elizabeth, N.J., a goddamn Laundromat, it all makes sense now, I can follow the
connections, Sandra working the teller's cage, me gone for a
year, this guy Wolpenheimer coming in every day with bags
of coins, being friendly, then flirting, then a lunch date, then
a dinner date, then they drive back to his apartment, and
then the bastard's fucking my wife, goddamn it! I run to the
kitchen, get a big knife, back to the closet, I scream, stab,
slash at a green jacket, rip it, take that you goddamn Laundromat bastard, rip down, rip across, cut off the sleeves, I'm
twelve thousand miles away and you're fucking my wife, I'll
get you, you prick, slash across the back of a dark blue
sweater, rip down the length of a white shirt, off with the legs
of trousers, stabbing and slashing and cutting, cloth flying
everywhere, I'm growling, an animal, gasping for air, stabbing into the heart of a plaid coat, cutting a vest right down
the spine, I lose the knife, drop it down into the shreds of
cloth on the floor, I take the plaid coat in my hands, pull, tear,
growl, it rips right in two, I drop the pieces at my feet, kick,
kick it all, tattered cloth, kick it again, hard, fall down, fall on
top of the knife but it doesn't cut me, I just lie still, breathing
hard, I could cry, I actually start to cry, then I find myself
laughing, I'm laughing out of control, lying in a pile of shred-
ded clothes, my head in the closet, my feet out there on the
broken glass, tears in my eyes, hysterical laughing, I'm up on
all fours now, I back out of the closet, crawl over the broken
glass to the kitchen, hysterical laughing, I stand up, I'm at the
sink, bending over, trying to stop laughing, tears running
right down my face, I'm crazy, sick, desperate. The laughing
fades, I'm holding my sides in pain. Control coming back
with the pain, I reach for the refrigerator, open the door,
take out a beer and shake it. I open it, it spurts all over like
champagne, then settles down to a foam and I put my lips
over the top and drink. Walk back into the main room, look

around, dark in here but I can see enough, oh my God, a madman was here. I feel very, very sober now. I try to laugh but nothing comes. I brush broken glass off one corner of the bed and sit down, put the beer on the floor. Frightening to look around this room, I'm getting worried, sick to my stomach. I'll be put away, nuthouse, that'll be next. I'll have to clean up. But what about the clothes? I'll take them all with me, make it look like a burglary. Maybe I could take my stereo, too. I'm up and pacing around. I've got to make this look good, and I've got to hurry.

I get the broom and start pushing glass, stop to turn on the overhead light. Sweeping glass and cut-up clothing into one corner and I hear something, I stop to listen, something coming up the path, a car, oh my God, it's the cops, I know it's the cops, I drop the broom, I see the headlights out there, holy Christ, I'm caught, it's jail, I'm going for the back window, the headlights close and bright, the car stops, door opens and closes, I'm halfway out the window, good Christ, they're going to shoot me, and then I hear a woman's voice. "I know it's him."

Sandra's voice. I stop where I am.

"Well, then, stay here, I'll handle it," she says to someone. The kraut.

"I know you're in there," she shouts out. "I saw your car down there."

I get out of the window, run to the front door, open it. I see Sandra, tall, alone, coming from out of the headlights, walking toward me. "What are you doing in there!" she shouts.

I step out the door. I want to talk to you, I say. My voice sounds so flat, so controlled, it surprises me. I take a step toward her and she backs up. "You've got no right to be up here," she says. She keeps backing up.

I want to talk to you, I say. That's all I can manage to say, I keep walking toward her. She turns and runs. She's at the car, opens the door on the passenger side. I know the kraut's behind the wheel, but I can't see him for the headlights. I'm walking toward the car, all I can hear around me are helicopters. Let the German get out, I'm thinking, just let him get out. Sandra, still at the passenger door, says, "I'm going to get the cops on you, buddy." She gets in and slams the door and the moment she closes it, the headlights start backing away, down the path, I keep walking but the guy's driving thirty miles an hour in reverse. The headlights back all the way down to the main road, take a wide swing, start off toward the village, tires squealing a little on the asphalt.

In just a few minutes they'll be at the sheriff's office. I run back into the cabin, look around quick, have I left anything? I give a long look at the stereo, I can't run far with it, I go to the refrigerator, pack my jacket pockets with Dortmunder, I'm out the front door without closing it, give a look behind me, cabin lights blazing, I run into the woods, breathing hard, dark, no moon, trying to find a path I know, running through leaves, over dead branches, into low bushes, running, dirt under my feet, a path, downhill now, long strides, ankle twists in a rut, keep going, arms flailing, lungs aching.

Get to the car, I'm going to die breathing this hard, I open the door, get in, key in the ignition, oh no, you bastard, start, start now, the ignition gives a sick little whirr.

I'm screaming curses, screaming them between big, deep breaths, and then out there, along the lakeshore, I see it, flashing red light, then headlights, moving fast. Come on, I turn the key hard, the engine coughs once and dies, I pump the gas, turn the key, turn the key, red light moving toward me, no siren, just flashing light. Turn the key and the engine starts, dies, turn it again and get ignition, give it throttle, rev it way up there, I'm watching, waiting for the police car to come right up behind me, it's near the amusement park now, coming fast, there's a squeal, the car turning left, light going away, up the path toward Sandra's cabin. My chance now, one lousy sheriff's car in this town, I'll drive right out past the highway, stick to the back roads all the way in. I step on the gas and pound the empty seat next to me, come on. Pull out on the road, push the pedal practically through the floorboard, no headlights, the road all dark in front of me.

5

BOILER TUBES FOREVER

My idea for lunch today was to eat at the family restaurant, but it looks like I'll just go back to work hungry. That's the place, Satriano's, right across the street, it was started by my grandfather back in the thirties. It's not a really big place, or fancy, just a couple of storefronts, curtains drawn waist-high across the windows.

I've been standing on the corner here, South and Washington, it must be ten minutes. Practically frozen. Snow coming down. Well, gray sleet anyway. I've pulled the hood out of my army jacket and turned my back to the wind, and all I hear is sleet hitting canvas around my ears.

It's a funny thing, but Satriano's seemed a hell of a lot bigger when I was a kid. A lot fancier, too. It's a shock every time I see it, and realize it's just a plain little neighborhood restaurant. Because for me, the place always had some magic to it. It was in that kitchen that I discovered you could be paid, and treated almost like an adult, for doing something you liked to do. Such as making meatballs or working a big dough mixer or stirring pots and pots of sauce. I started when I was twelve. By the time I was fourteen I could cook everything on the menu, and already I had lost interest in high school.

But for some reason I can't make myself walk in there now. And my half-hour lunch is almost over. Maybe it's shame, really, keeping me out. Because to walk in wearing my greasy blue JS&T uniform, well, that would cause too many questions. I can just hear my uncle Anthony, who runs the place. Hey, Tommy, he'd say, what are you, greasing cars now? I thought you had a suit-and-tie job. Why do you want to work in that business anyway? When are you going to come back to me?

And then I'd have to tell him I can't live on what he pays. Which would embarrass us both. So forget it, maybe if I leave now I can grab a quick hamburger on the way back to the warehouse. But something's keeping me here, maybe it's just the good familiar smells of the place. Yeasty baking bread. Garlic sautéed in olive oil. Fennel from the pans of frying sausage. I wonder who's got my old job in there now.

There's an old Italian guy, a customer, comes out the restaurant door and inside there I see the hard wooden chairs, the red-checked tablecloths, everything coming back on me now. I'm walking. Can't help myself. Through the dirty slush, across the street, up the curb, past the big windows with my head ducked and hidden in the hood. Around to the alley. Smell of cold grease. Narrow passage between sooty brick walls. Duck the icicles. Around four big garbage cans on rollers. Kitchen door a screen, open in any weather. I put my back against the cold brick wall and just listen.

Dishes rattle. Hum of the walk-in refrigerator. Somebody chopping something, in bad rhythm. Anthony's voice, loud but muffled, he's in the dining room. A door opens and closes, the oven. Relentless chopping. And no mistaking that smell, garlic frying with onions somewhere.

And the heat of the kitchen coming right out the screen door. One thing I loved about this place, you're always warm. Work in a thin undershirt on even the coldest days. You're never hungry, either, you don't even have to eat a meal, just the testing and sampling will keep you satisfied. And you're always so busy, there's no time to worry, no time to be depressed, no time for anything but work, and keeping in your rhythm.

I close my eyes and all the good smells intensify. My hand reaches up and finds the handle of the screen door, hangs on. I never, never want to go near that warehouse again. I make myself that promise, open my eyes. Move away from the wall, pull on the screen door a little, it's stuck, latched. Standing right in front of the door now, I see the steam table with its buckets of sauces, its ladles, I pull on the door again, it doesn't move. Look to my left and there's somebody at the big chopping block, somebody small and skinny chopping onions with a clumsy two-handed motion. A boy, short black hair, white T-shirt, the chain of a cheap religious medal high on his neck. Pimply neck. Must be a cousin of mine, a Satriano, Gary? No, too skinny for Gary. I rattle the screen door, he's too busy chopping, doesn't hear me. Rattle it again. Knock. The kid turns around, pimply thin face, pimples as big as boils, he's thirteen tops, I don't know him.

I wave for him to come over and he walks slowly, squinting to see, the knife in his hands, chopped white onions clinging to it. "You want something?" he says.

Could you open the door? I say.

"What for?" he says.

Could you please open the door a minute? I say.

The kid steps away toward the dining room, turns his back on me. "Hey, Anthony," he yells out. "Some guy's back here looking for a handout."

I take off running. Down the alley and across Washington Street, down another alley and out on South, into my car, it starts on the first try, without looking back or around I give it gas, wheels spinning in the half-frozen slush. That little twerp. Doesn't he know what a bum looks like? Somebody ought to show the little bastard how to chop an onion. Left turn on Bayway. Gunning it, twisting, turning, through heavy traffic. A bum! Maybe I ought to get rid of this army jacket, people will be giving me quarters on the street. Left turn into JS&T's parking lot. Outer edge of it. Turn the key but the engine won't quit. Damn this car, doesn't want to start, doesn't want to stop, I stomp on the floorboard three times, that does it, silence. And out of the car. Hustling toward the gray tin building, the smallest of them, the boiler tube shed. Must be late. I'll say I forgot to clock in, write it in later, twelve-thirty. Can only get away with that so many times, though. Hustle. Through the big open garage doors, look around inside the shed, no noise, no movement, good, I made it back before he did.

Slow down and catch your breath, Hollaran. And on with the yellow oilcloth work gloves. Dark in here. And cold, no heat at all, and somehow it feels worse in here than outside. Like the corrugated tin walls and all those boiler tubes just radiate cold. A nasty metallic kind of cold. Smells of acid and steel mill grease. Stand in the middle of it all and breathe out, watch my own breath freeze. And look at all those big racks of boiler tubes. Black carbon steel pipes three inches around and twenty feet long. Thousands and thousands of them stacked in racks, all the way up to the rusty tin roof. Boiler tubes so cold that the hair on the back of your neck stands up when you touch them.

I slide along the floor, that's the safest way, it's as slick as an ice rink in here. A layer of leaked-in half-frozen rain on a greasy concrete floor, and you can go ass-over-teakettle with any step. I slide over to the big green Do All band saw, but there's no use turning it on yet. This is my first day in boiler tubes and I can't do much until Carmine gets here, and besides, he keeps all the job tickets in his pocket. So I just sit down on a stack of wooden pallets, they're the warmest thing in here. And kick idly at the big rusty pile of scrap pieces of boiler tubes.

Cold all day. The things you take for granted when you have a nice warm easy job. When you're up there in the office, you never give a thought to the guys down here. If they're dumb enough to do the dirty work, well, that's their problem. That's just the way people think, and it would have saved me a lot of trouble if I'd have learned that a few years ago.

Sound of somebody running, I look up, it's Carmine, coming in the garage door, turns the corner, his arms go out, he tries for balance, slips, hits the ground, shoulder first, gets up right away. Slides across the floor toward me. "Let's go!"

he yells, and I stand up. "The Jersey City job's got to be cut by one o'clock."

He's right up next to me now, his eyes all red veins, his breath smelling like jet fuel. He takes me by the elbow and gives me a little start toward the saw. I just glare at him. A guy my age with a stupid face and a flattened nose and big teeth. And a yellow hard hat with his name stenciled on it. "You cut, I'll measure," he says. Which is like saying you work, I'll watch.

But I don't want to fight. Because I don't count on being in boiler tubes for long. They're rotating me through all the departments, so I can be a fill-in man until a permanent job opens up somewhere. I'm hoping for stainless pipe, the guys are friendly there and they even keep a pot of coffee going.

So I go to the head of the big saw and switch it on, a loud hum. Carmine's down at the end of the cutting table, twelve feet six inches away. Exactly, because that's how long the tubes for the Jersey City job need to be. He's down there feeling his own biceps, flexing his arms, bulging up his JS&T jacket. He does that all the time, I don't think he's even aware of it. A tough guy. A boxer. "Let's go, will you?" he yells.

Sure thing, Carmine, I mumble. And it's your problem, pal, your show. Because I'm here for today but you're here for the rest of your life. So have fun bossing me around. Poisonous thoughts. Hungry and cold. I push the big black button in front of me and reach over to grab a boiler tube.

Push the tube along the rollers of the cutting table. Down until it hits the metal stop Carmine's measured out. The saw whirring, the blade on its never-ending cycle, moving through puke-green coolant at the bottom, then up through green side guards, then across the top where it'll cut, then down into the coolant again. I push a red button and steel clamps grab the boiler tube, the saw head starts down. The blade starts scratching the black surface of the tube, digs in to where the silvery metal is, green coolant squirting all over everything, metal flakes washing down into the coolant basin, the blade cuts through. A sound that sends shivers through me. I take off the seven-foot scrap piece, drop it in back of me, Carmine's measuring the job cut. Makes a self-satisfied expression with his lips and holds up the okay sign at me. "Run it," he yells out, and reels in his measuring tape.

Slide in another tube, push the red button, watch the cut, take off the scrap, drop it, bong, behind me. Carmine rolls the job piece off, and it hits the concrete with a bong. I grab another tube, push the red button again, wait for the cut, drop the scrap, bong, Carmine drops the job piece, bong. Saw whirring, grab another tube, bong, bong. You go home after eight hours of this and your ears ring like bells all night.

And I'm nothing but part of this machine, that's what's bad about it. Because I stand here and there's nothing to do with my brain but worry. Grab another tube. About everything that seems to be wrong in my life. Push the red button. And about the cops most of all. Pick up the scrap, drop it behind me. Sometimes I think about Sandra, seeing her in the lights of the kraut's big car. How much I hated her at that moment. And wanted desperately to get her back.

I'm afraid to go back to my apartment, that's the big problem right now. I just *know* the cops have been there. I'm *sure* there's a warrant for my arrest by now. Breaking and entering, vicious behavior, performing a deranged act, who knows? All I can picture is courtrooms, long corridors leading to jail cells, me in leg-irons. Sure it's stupid, but it makes me sweat anyway. Because I've done something criminal, that's for sure. And it's entirely possible that the cops would come pounding on my apartment door at three in the morning. So I'm staying at Eddie Sadowski's, at least until I figure out what to do.

What makes it all worse is that my old man's a cop, not a city one, he works for the Erie Railroad. He used to be a yard bull, rousting bums out of boxcars in Weehawken and Hoboken, although now he's a lieutenant with a desk job. Even so, he knows a lot of city cops, and I'm sure he's heard a couple of versions of the cabin story by now.

Stack of uncut tubes going down, down. Roll another one through, push the red button. And a bad smell in here, metal cutting metal, grease, the slow burning-out of the saw motor. So heavy in here you can actually taste it. No wonder Carmine spits all the time.

Push the red button. I look down at Carmine, he's whistling, does this job make him happy? No, I guess not, because he's got a real life, too. Spends most of his time hanging around gyms in Newark, at least that's what I've heard. He's had three fights for small-time money, I've heard, and lost them all. And he's probably the last white guy trying to make it in Newark as a fighter. That's practically all I know about Carmine, except that he's already gone through a couple of marriages. Push the red button.

"That's it, that's it," Carmine yells at me. I push the black button and the whirr of the saw dies out slowly. "Thirty-six," Carmine yells out, drops the last tube to the floor, steps over it, takes off his yellow gloves, comes up to me. Pats me on the back, hard. "All right," he says. "Just one o'clock now." He keeps walking past me. Isn't he going to bundle up the tubes? Strap them? Get them ready for the truck? I guess not, because he keeps walking, all the way to the end of the shed, and turns in, disappears behind the last rack of boiler tubes.

I just stand near the stinking saw for a minute, thinking. I could try to strap them myself, but then Carmine's the kind of guy that anything I'd do would be wrong. So I turn and walk toward the end of the shed, turn in where he did, a slim passageway between rusty steel racks and the corrugated tin wall. Way back in the corner there's Carmine, sitting on a barrel-size hunk of old pipe, his hard hat off. His head is shaved black stubble, he's mopping sweat off with a handkerchief.

Aren't you going to bundle up those tubes? I ask him. He waves at me to come nearer. "Sit down," he says, "take it easy."

I walk toward him, I realize this is his break corner, a place to hide from Gripper, the yard boss. Big pipes have been rolled back here to use as benches. I sit on a piece of pipe across from Carmine, it's about as cold as a block of ice. Carmine's looking through his jacket pockets for something, I ask him again about bundling the tubes. He gives me a hard look. "I'm going to tell you something," he says, "but it goes no further than you, okay?"

I shrug. Okay, I say.

"No," he says. "Give me your word."

My word, I say.

"You don't never want to be ready for the truck," he says. "You want to just start bundling when it pulls up. Okay?"

Okay, I say. Why?

He takes a big breath, lets it out, exasperated. "Look," he says, "if the job's all cut and bundled, it'll look like you ain't got enough to do."

Oh, I say.

"And word will get back to Gripper, believe me," he says. He's still looking through his pockets. Unzips his jacket and feels his shirt pockets now. "Besides," he says, "that ain't no rush job. A week from now it'll still be laying around. Then Gripper will tell me to get a truck and deliver it myself. They're always trying to put the rush on you down here." He looks me right in the eyes. "That's just part of this game," he says.

I'm nodding. He stands up, mumbles a curse, takes his jacket off, goes through the pockets again, finally pulls out a wisp of twisted paper, the remains of a thin marijuana cigarette. He looks at me for just a moment, then brings out a lighter, snaps the top, holds the flame to the joint until it's glowing, then brings it to his lips. I get that thick sweet odor that will always remind me of Vietnam.

Carmine's keeping the smoke down in his lungs, holds out the joint for me to take. I put up both hands to refuse it, Carmine chokes, lets out the smoke. Brings the joint to his lips again, almost burns them sucking in smoke, puts the joint out by gently tapping it on the pipe. Lets out the smoke. Coughs. "I thought you was over in Nam," he says.

That's right, I say.

Silence. He puts the joint back in his jacket pocket. Slowly pulls his jacket on again, closes the snaps.

"I heard the dope over there could send you to the moon."

I just nod my head.

"But I guess you didn't smoke dope or anything over there."

Sure I did, I say. But it made me sick, so I cut it out.

Long silence. I'm about to get up off the pipe and try to find *something* to do when Carmine says, "What were you over there, an officer?"

No, I say.

"You went to college and you wasn't an officer?" he says. I can see by his face that he has a hard time believing me.

I never finished college, I say.

"Oh," Carmine says.

Well, I say, ready to ask him what job to do next, but he cuts me off. "So you was a clerk over there or what?"

In Vietnam? I say. I was a trooper.

"What's that?" he says.

Cavalry, I say. I had to ride in helicopters.

Carmine thinks about that for a moment, sits back, like he's going to roll off the pipe. "Next you're going to tell me you carried a machine gun around," he says.

No, I say.

"What'd they give you, an M-16?"

I nod my head.

"You fire it much?"

Couple of times, I say. When I couldn't help it.

He just looks at me, and I know what the next question is, I can feel it coming. So I stand, put my hands in my pockets for warmth, and say, There must be another job to cut.

"No," Carmine says, and gives a big wave of his hand. "Sit down. I want to ask you some things."

I'll stand, I say. I'm cold.

"Were you really in combat over there?" he asks.

Combat isn't the word for it, Carmine, I say.

"What is, then?"

Absurd, I say. It was just stupid.

Silence. He's looking down at the floor. "So that's what

you think of it," he says finally. "Stupid." He looks up at me. I
nod. "Well, I wish I would've had my chance," he says.
"Missed it. Old lady and two kids at the time."

I don't say anything.

"I wanted to go for the Marines," he says, "but then I got
interested in the Army Airborne. I picked up all the bro-
chures and everything. I had it all figured out, with combat
pay and overseas pay and airborne pay, I could have made
enough to send home to the old lady. Especially if I made
sergeant and went to Vietnam."

Let him talk, Hollaran.

"You never was Airborne or anything, was you?" he says.

I shake my head.

"You never made no jumps at all, did you?"

No, I say. And I have to smile. No, Carmine, I say, I never
made that jump.

"Still, you was cavalry," he says. And then there's a silence. Except for Carmine's boot, scraping back and forth
across the floor.

Maybe we'd better get back and cut the next job, I say.

"No," he says, and pulls two yellow job tickets out of his
jacket pocket. "I'm spacing it out, don't worry." He looks at
the tickets for a long time, I'm stamping my feet with the
cold.

"Look," he says, all of a sudden. "Maybe you and me
could work together. What do you think? My old partner,
they got him in the hospital. He might be out two weeks or
maybe more."

What's wrong with him? I say.

"Some kind of pneumonia or something," Carmine says.
"I could get you in here permanent, set it up with Gripper."

I don't think so, Carmine, I say.

"I know what you want," he says. "Stainless or bar stock.
Because of the heat."

It is warmer in stainless, I say. A lot warmer.

"Yeah," Carmine says, "but it ain't always going to be
winter. And you get a lot of scam time in boiler tubes. Stainless there's eight guys and a foreman. You got to really work."

Carmine, I say, it's too cold in here to enjoy sitting around. I'll end up with pneumonia too.

"That guy didn't know how to take care of himself. He was in bad shape. You just come out of the army, man, you're in good shape. We could get along, I know it. I ain't such a bad guy, you'll find that out."

Just too goddamn cold down here, I say.

"Come on," Carmine says. "Let me talk to Gripper about it."

No, I say.

"That's all I need," he says.

What? I say.

"Spades," he says. "They're going to be hiring shines, that's what I heard. Government's making them. Everybody's got to hire them now. I'll end up, a spade in here with me."

Oh, I say. Oh, now I see.

"Boiler tubes you do everything," he says, still trying to sell me. "Even deliveries. You can get in the truck, make a quick delivery, sit around for an hour in a diner or gin mill."

Look, Carmine, I say, I hate that kind of stuff. It's easier just to work. I don't want to hide from the bosses or do any make-work projects or play any of those games. I've done enough of it, all right? I just want to keep busy, collect my paycheck, stay out of trouble.

"Until you can get another office job," he says, and I look at his face, angry, I realize he's just delivered his worst insult. His lips still snarled from pronouncing the words *office job*. So I go neutral. Shrug. Maybe, I say. I start to turn away, my mind on getting out of here.

I walk. Down the narrow, rusty passageway. He calls after me, "Hey, college boy." I keep walking. Out to the wide, slippery main floor. I hear him behind me, running. I cringe, ready for him to hit me from behind. Feel his hand on my shoulder, slowly turn to face him.

"I know guys like you," he says. "I know just what's going through your mind. You're going to make yourself look good by going right to Gripper. You're going to tell him that Carmine's a scam artist."

Okay, Carmine, I say, if you want to believe that, go ahead.

"Now I'm going to tell you something," he says, and pokes my chest with his finger. "I get any heat from Gripper, I'm coming to look for you."

You're threatening me? I say.

"Just remember," he says, and gives me the slightest push on the chest. "I know your kind."

He walks off toward his break corner, I watch him, then head right for the door. Out into the main yard and put up my hood, the sleet has turned to rain. Careful to watch my ᵁᵉᵉ under the asphalt are half-buried railroad tracks. When I get near the main warehouse I look up at the old control tower, cold hitting my face, somewhere up there, behind tinted windows, is John Johnson. My curses go out to him.

I'm knocking on the wired windows of the warehouse office, there's a girl in there, Bea, who hands out the paychecks and does the time cards, she comes over and unlocks the door for me. Mister Gripper in? I say.

"Yes, and your name? Aren't you the new fill-in? Hollaran? Yes, he's been wanting to see you."

Gripper? I say. Wants to see me?

She leads me over to a yellowish door with dirty handprints all over it, knocks three times, and pushes it open. Gripper's sitting there, long and skinny, his feet up on the desk. He's been reading something, he's just laid it flat on the desk, a racing form. Big drawing of a Thoroughbred on the cover. "What can we do for you, babes?" he says. "Oh, you're Hollaran. Bea, get that envelope for me, will you?" The girl leaves and Gripper takes one foot at a time off the desk and says, "Sit down." He's a young guy, curly hair, a gigantic nose, so big the sound comes out of it instead of his mouth. "How's things going out there?" he says, and before I can answer, "Yeah, it's pretty cold in that shed. That's for you," he says, and I see that Bea is holding a thin brown envelope over my shoulder. "Go ahead, babes," he says, "open it up."

A yellow piece of paper. I unfold it, a form, I read just the typed-in words. HOLLARAN, THOMAS J. COMPANY #1742 YOU ARE HEREBY NOTIFIED OF YOUR PERMANENT TRANSFER TO THE FOLLOWING DIVISION:

BOILER TUBE OPERATIONS
IMMEDIATELY
NO CHANGE
ASSISTANT WAREHOUSEMAN
F. T. GRIPPER, OPERATIONS SUPERVISOR

I read it over three times, four times. Then look at Gripper, he's got kind of a curl to his lips. Not exactly a smile, a resigned look maybe.

I can't work there, I say. That's what I came to see you about. I've got to get into some other— He cuts me off. "Boiler tubes," he says, and shakes his head. "Nobody likes it. We have a hell of a time keeping people in there. But look, you're new, right? Try it awhile. Then six months, a year, who knows, there's bound to be a better opening somewhere."

I stop short of telling him that I almost had a fistfight with Carmine. Because I don't want Carmine's words to come true. I say, I thought I was going to learn by being switched into all the departments for a while. . . .

"Look," Gripper says. "Take my advice, babes, don't fight it. This order came from way upstairs."

Johnson? I say. Gripper just nods.

Can I use your phone? I say.

"Knock yourself out, babes," he says. "But if you're calling Johnson, you're out of luck."

I've got the phone in my hand. Why? I say.

"Friday afternoon," Gripper says. "You worked up in the office, didn't you? What's the chances of him coming back from lunch?"

I dial anyway. Johnson's private number. And stand, listening to it ring. And ring. Leaned over Gripper's desk, waiting. No answer.

6

Flies in My Eyes

Eddie comes in the door with a white sack that smells of greasy onions and says, "Hey, what's this?" He points to the big pile of cooking utensils I've washed and set out on the sinkboard to drain, all my pots, pans, wooden and stainless spoons, colanders, knives, spatulas. I brought it from my apartment, I tell Eddie. We're going to start eating decent meals from now on.

"I got my supper," Eddie says, and holds up the bag, all grease stains on the bottom. It says WHITE CASTLE in black letters, along with a drawing of a castle, also in black. Eddie drops the sack on the kitchen workbench, which I've spread with a red-checkered tablecloth. "I bought enough for both of us," he says, and takes off his army jacket, black with oil stains, and hangs it over one of the barstools.

Look, I say, I could have been arrested sneaking home to get these pots and pans. Then I almost got crushed by fat ladies at the Italian market. Then I spent a goddamn hour making a good dinner from scratch. And you're going to eat greasy little hamburgers with dehydrated onions?

"Okay, okay," Eddie says. He's holding up his hands.

Sit down, I say. It'll be ready in a minute.

Eddie sits at the workbench and empties his top shirt pocket of pens, cardboard tags, Parkway toll receipts, screwdrivers, a miniature clip-on flashlight, two nuts, three bolts, a wire clipper, something that looks like a dentist's mirror, and

a jackknife that says, SID HARVEY'S . . . FOR OIL BURNER
PARTS . . . AND ACCESSORIES. I put a bottle of beer in front
of him and say, Here, have a Polish martini. He lifts the beer
and drinks. "The pause that refreshes," he says. "What are
we dining on tonight, Mister Chef?"

I'm rolling egg-coated strips of chicken breast in bread-
crumbs mixed with fresh-grated Parmesan. Chicken Satriano, I tell Eddie. And grind little white flecks of nutmeg over
the rolled chicken breasts. It's my uncle Anthony's recipe, I
say. If you went down to the restaurant tonight, this would
cost you four ninety-five. I take a knife and dot the chicken
breasts with raindrop-size pieces of butter. Then lift the cutting board and the meat slides into a broiling pan. I check the
top of the stove, water boiling furiously, and spinach with
mushrooms sautéing nicely in a cast-iron pan. I put a drop of
olive oil in the boiling water for luck, and follow it with a
handful of fettuccini. It'll be two or three minutes before I
can start broiling the chicken, so I get myself a beer, my third
or maybe fourth since I got off from work.

I take my beer and push through the swinging kitchen
door and into the living room, which is as bare as any room in
the house. My sleeping bag's in the middle of the floor, and
the only furniture is in one corner. A pair of long bench seats
Eddie salvaged from a 1953 Chrysler, and between them a
pine-plank table on two cinder blocks. Above that, hanging
from the ceiling by its black cord, is a mechanic's work light. I
added one thing this afternoon, my record player, my album,
and two speakers. I had to bring it because Eddie does not
believe in buying records or record players, not when there's
music on the radio, free.

I put on Glenn Miller, side three, turn the volume up,
wait through the scratchy static. Then all of a sudden the
locomotive sounds of "Chattanooga Choo Choo" come blasting out of the speakers. I push through the kitchen door and
see Eddie just sitting down again on the stool. "What the hell
is that?" he says. "I thought a goddamn train was coming
through the house."

I drink beer and smile. I know Eddie hates this music. I

shake my forefinger at him and sing along with the Modernaires. *Hi there, Tex, what you say . . .*

"Turn that shit off," Eddie says.

Now I'm singing Tex Beneke's part. *Step aside partner, it's my day . . .* I'm stirring the fettuccini, I slide the chicken under the broiler.

"Jesus Christ, at least turn it down," Eddie says.

Pardon me boy, is that the Chattanooga Choo Choo?

Eddie's shaking his head. "I should have ate at the White Castle," he yells. I snatch the sack of hamburgers off the table, throw it in the refrigerator, put out the plates, knives, forks. Go back to the stove and stir the spinach and mushrooms. *Dinner in the diner, nothing could be finer, than to have your ham and eggs in Carolina.* I take out the pasta, it's draining, I'm making a tiny amount of melted butter in a sauce pan, put in a piece of crushed garlic, some parsley, oregano, rosemary. Steam in the kitchen and it smells good in here. I check the chicken breasts and flip them over. The chorus is going, *Chattanooga Choo Choo-oo,* and this is my favorite part, the whole band wailing, Moe Purtill knocking out an offbeat rhythm, I'm shaking pasta in the colander. The end, glorious trumpets and a drumroll, and I've got the plates, I pile on the pasta, spoon on a little melted butter, lay down a bed of spinach, put the browned chicken breasts on top of that, add two lemon wedges to each plate, they're ready to go. One plate in front of Eddie and one plate opposite. I sit down and he gets up, pushes into the living room, cuts off "Johnson Rag" right at the beginning. He comes back, sits down, picks up his fork, and says, "Let's eat without noise."

I say, that isn't noise, Ed, it's music. The greatest music ever made.

"You're out of your mind," he says. "It's a bunch of blaring horns."

I'm cutting my chicken, it's just right, cooked white but still juicy inside. I take another piece, I'm satisfied, pick up a lemon wedge and squeeze it all over the pasta and chicken.

"So that's what you do with the lemon," Eddie says. He

the table, run water in the sink, cold, almost freezing. I keep forgetting, no hot water. Eddie turns it on every other day for a bath, but otherwise he says he can't afford it. So I fill a pot with water, put it on the stove, light the gas under it. Turn around and already Eddie's gone from the kitchen.

By the time I'm done with the dishes, he's back, sitting at the workbench, a book held in both hands. It's a library book, the title is *Welding Techniques for Shop, Home, and Farm.* Eddie, lost in concentration, turns a page.

He won't want to be talked to from here on. He'll read that book like he's in a trance, and then he'll go downstairs and lock the door after him. Then I'll hear a strange, continuous crackling sound down in the basement, there'll be an acid smell. Then maybe some miscellaneous pounding, long stretches of silence, a couple of thumps, then quiet again. He'll be down there until at least midnight, sometimes until dawn, then he'll go to his oil burner job on practically no sleep.

So I'm on my own for the evening. I take a beer out of the refrigerator, go quietly into the living room, sit down on the car-seat couch. Don't bother to put on the lights, this way I can see better out the windows. If I looked out the side there, and craned my neck, I could see a high chain link fence, and behind it the junkyard, and then a couple of blocks up, the JS&T office tower. But I've had enough of that place for one week, so I just stare out the big window in front of me. A road that's trucks in the day and deserted at night. Then a strip of rubble and dirt where there once were docks and warehouses. Then the Arthur Kill, filthy and foul, oily black, lit by floodlights from the Staten Island side. Tugboats over there somewhere, moored in the dark. Yellow lights of a truck depot beyond that, and that's as far as you can see from down here. I drink my beer and stare at the Arthur Kill.

And remember the night we came out of a basement at St. Peter's College and into the gray snow piles of a Jersey City street. Sandra and me. A bunch of badly printed pamphlets in my hand. And when the steel door slammed behind us, we started walking and Sandra said, Well?

That's the guy who's a friend of your family's? I said. He's not a lawyer, he's just a law student. And anyway he makes me suspicious. It's like he's got all the answers, ready-made.

Ready-made? she said. Of course they're ready-made. They've helped thousands of people already. You heard what he said, it's like the old underground railroad.

Railroad, I thought, that's the word, all right. But I didn't say that to Sandra, hoping maybe to save a fight. My mistake. We walked a narrow shoveled path through the snow and out to the parking lot. To our 1967 baby-blue Camaro, the one thing we owned. Or would have owned, with only twenty more equal payments to Sandra's bank.

I'll drive, I said when Sandra took out her keys.

No, I'll drive, she said. You're stoned.

So are you, I said.

But I can handle it, she said. And she got her key in the door before I did. See? she said. My reflexes are better.

I stood aside. My brain *was* pretty well twisted from the thin little joint the draft counselor had passed around, from him to Sandra to me. I guess I had expected a pleasant, mild high, something like the light-headedness of a quick cold beer. What I got was giddiness followed by confusion followed by paranoia.

Are you going to get in, or stand there in the cold all night? Sandra said.

I went around to the passenger side, got in, and for the first time since we bought the car, I buckled the seat belt around me. For some reason.

We do have choices, Sandra said, and started driving for the Turnpike. I think I like the idea of Toronto best, she said. I think we both could get good jobs up there.

Sure, I thought. Shoveling snow.

You heard him, she said, it's not much different there than it is in Chicago.

Silence from me. A long time driving.

What are you thinking? Sandra said when we got on the Turnpike. I know you, come on, what's in that mind of yours?

It is different than Chicago, I said. And the difference is, if I drive too far south from Toronto, they put me in jail.

So don't get in the car, and don't drive south, she said.

But maybe I'll want to go places, I said.

Like where? she asked.

I don't know yet, I said. Places. Anywhere. I don't want to be stuck up at the North Pole with a bunch of draft dodgers.

I'll be with you, Tom, she said. I can still, three years later, remember the sound of those words as they left her lips. And the brightness of headlights zooming past. I closed my eyes against them. And in the darkness of my mind I saw a witch and a walrus, and chased the images with thought. All about Sandra and Toronto. Because if she wanted to come home, what would stop her? A day's drive for her, a life's exile for me. But I never told her that in just those words. Another mistake.

I leaned forward against the seat belt and turned on the radio. Maybe two notes of music came out before Sandra snapped it off. I don't think you're taking this seriously, she said. If we don't do something, Tom, you're going to end up in Vietnam.

Or Germany, I said. Or Korea, or the Panama Canal, or maybe Kansas. They could send me anywhere.

You're fooling yourself, she said. I didn't realize, not then, that the woman was practically a prophet.

Even if I *did* go to Vietnam, I said, I wouldn't be in the infantry. I'd be a clerk or something, or maybe even a cook.

Sandra shook her head, bit her lips.

There's a lot of things we haven't talked about, I said. Like the reserves.

For rich people, she said.

The Coast Guard, I said.

Four years, isn't it? she said. Of going from one port town to another.

Maybe we'll get to live in California, I said. Or Florida. Who knows? They might even put me right here in New York harbor.

Tom, there isn't time to get into the Coast Guard, she
said. There's a waiting list, didn't you hear him say that?

Who? I asked.

The draft counselor, she said. Weren't you listening?

Probably I wasn't listening, not that I remember, really.
Because what I was doing was watching the law student,
Houlihan, or whatever his name was. The draft counselor. A
big blond guy, could have been a football player. Was I paranoid or did he talk too much to Sandra? Almost exclusively to
Sandra, if I remember right. He was looking at more than her
eyes, I caught that much.

I looked over at her, then, in the darkness of the car. My
wife. I had the dopey illusion there for a moment that she
belonged to me, no matter what. Because that was how I
understood things then. Everything in its place. Like a catechism where every question has the proper response. So if
you got drafted, you went off to the army. And if you were
married, your wife waited for you to come home. In the
comfort of thoughts like that, I closed my eyes. And dreamed
my own dreams. Had I been awake, I would have seen a
determined woman, driving.

I hear Eddie shut the basement door and lock it, then the
heavy one-foot stomp as he helps himself down the stairs.
Nothing for me to do but sit here and think. And it's thinking
that's driving me crazy. Sandra. Helicopters. Doctor Pyle.
Doctor Rhinehart. I wish I was back in Vietnam so I could do
it right this time. Do things different with Hoover. I can hear
the bastard screaming at me, Soldier! Soldier! Get in line!
And pain in my head, the helicopters so loud. Why am I
paying Doctor Rhinehart twenty-five bucks a week? I think it
all started with my old man, I really do. No, bullshit. I must
have started to go wrong at St. Veronica's, a Catholic educa-
tion warps the mind. Yes, I'm in Vietnam right now, wrap-
ping my head like an Indian with a big twisted-up bandanna.
Why, because my head hurts with the tension. And taking
the flashlight from Hoover. The noise of helicopters, but no
helicopters around. What did Doctor Pyle call this? Acute
anxiety. Which means it comes and goes. Like there's a

wrench tightening my guts and the back of my neck. Where are those tranquilizers when I need them? Shouldn't have dumped them, a stupid thing to do.

Up and walking around. Walk it off, Hollaran. Around the room in circles. Free-floating anxiety, that's what Doctor Rhinehart calls it. Attaches to anything and everything. Why, because I can't face it, whatever I'm really afraid of, she says. Oh, the hell with all of you shrinks, none of you has the answer.

Get a hold of yourself, Hollaran. Look around yourself, just look, there's no danger anymore. That's what you think. A fix of Glenn Miller, that's what I need. Go to the record player, crank up the volume all the way. Sit right between the two speakers and put on "In the Mood." Blasting away, eight to the bar. I get up, take two screwdrivers off the pine-plank table, I'm back between the two speakers, drumming on the floorboards. Beating with the handles. Eyes closed. I'm Moe Purtill, keeping the band together for Glenn. Who's up there on the bandstand, tough, shrewd, smiling, those wire-rim glasses. All of a sudden the music stops, I open my eyes, Eddie kneeling in front of me, he's lifted the needle off the record. "What the hell's this?" he says. "The Make-Believe Ballroom?"

It's bothering you? I say.

"It's a little loud," he says, "I got work to do."

Ed, I say, how about if you just dropped it for tonight? Suppose we went down to Lucky Leo's for a few. I need to get out.

He's shaking his head.

Come on, Ed, I say. I'll come downstairs and give you a hand, whatever you're doing. We'll finish early and then go to Leo's.

"It's a one-man job down there," he says.

Ed, I say, Leo's will be full of girls.

"I know," he says. "And that Laura bimbo will be there too."

So ignore her, I say. Come on, I need to, Ed, I'm going crazy in here.

"I'm all dirty," he says.

I'll wait for you to wash up, I say.

"It's going to be crowded," Eddie says. "We'll be lucky to get one drink."

Okay, I say. Be like that, Ed. I'll just get drunk by myself. On *your* vodka. And then I'll play Glenn Miller until four in the morning.

"Now wait a minute," Eddie says.

Then I'll start telling war stories, I say. I'm starting to remember some now. Did I ever tell you about the time we were surrounded by gooks out in the bush? We ran out of ammo and had to fight them off with the plastic spoons that come in C rations.

"I feel like I'm back in the smoking lounge," Eddie says.

I've got hundreds of stories like that, I say.

"Give me a minute to wash my hands," he says.

By the time we get to Lucky Leo's it's jammed body-to-body inside, the kind of crowd where you can't really walk to the bar, you have to almost swim. There's a blue haze of cigarette smoke, the smell of a hundred colognes and perfumes, Count Basie coming over the speakers. I manage to get myself two inches of bar space, then pull out a dollar bill. Hold it up, kind of in a Statue of Liberty pose. All around the bar there are dozens of college kids, holding up their dollars too. It's a trick to get Leo's attention, to entice him into moving a little faster, and it's become a tradition in here, even though it doesn't work. Leo ignores all the flapping dollar bills. He moves at the same speed whether there are two people waiting for drinks, or two hundred. Right now he's making four old-fashioneds, one at a time. He puts a teaspoon of sugar in the bottom of a glass, splashes in some club soda, drops in an orange slice, mashes it into the sugar with his fat fingers, adds ice, then a dash of bitters, a shot of whiskey, and club soda to fill. Tops it off with a cherry and then takes all four drinks to this big bony girl, puts them on a little tray for her, bows as much as a fat man can, and smiles. He's making conversation with the girl as he takes her four singles. All around him people are shouting, Leo! Hey, Leo! And holding out glasses and dollar bills. Leo's still talking to the girl, whatever he's saying is making her laugh. He's laughing too, wiping his hands on the front tails of his shirt, a big tent of a thing he lets flop over his pants.

Your chances of getting a drink in here would be almost hopeless if it wasn't for Betty, Leo's wife. She's as skinny as he is fat, and the joke is, Leo married the only woman who could fit in bed with him. Betty's older than Leo, in her mid-fifties somewhere, she's got short, boyish gray hair and cat's-eye glasses with gray rims. She's never still, and never more than three steps from a burning Pall Mall, and for every drink Leo makes, she makes five. She's got this system of making change, hardly ever uses the cash register, keeps dollar bills, fives, tens, and twenties folded long and thin and weaved between the fingers of her right hand.

Betty! Betty! I'm yelling, waving money. Finally she looks at me and I order quick, before she can turn away. I yell out for two vodka tonics no lime, two shots of Jack Daniel's, two draft beers. I get the beers first, sip a little out of each, fill them up again with the whiskey. I turn around and hand Eddie his vodkas and he says, "Shit. She's here. I knew it, goddamn it."

Relax, I say. Stay hidden. What do you think, she has X-ray vision?

"I'm done for," Eddie says. "I don't know why I let you drag me out here."

So we can have a good time, I say.

"Yeah," Eddie says. "So you can have a good time. You were drunk before we even got here."

So catch up, I say. Anyway, I've got a plan, Ed. What we've got to do is get real drunk first. Then we hang around until about quarter to two, when all the good-looking girls have been taken home. Then we look around the bar to see who's left desperate. We swoop in, how could they turn us down?

"You'd be surprised," Eddie says.

Leave it to me, I say.

"Yeah," Eddie says, "remember what happened last time I left it to you?"

What? I say.

"Remember, a couple of months ago in here, we went for those two bimbos? The twins, remember? They were built like bricklayers, the two of them were right over there, chewing gum ninety miles an hour, remember? Of course you don't remember, you were really blitzed. You told them I was president of a company that built racing cars. You asked them to come over for a swim in my indoor pool, remember that? You don't, do you? Well I do."

I shrug my shoulders. I'm too drunk right now to remember, I say. Look, Ed, why don't you point out this famous Laura? Let me get a look at her.

"I ain't going to point," Eddie says. "She'll see me. Just look for yourself. Over there near the corner. See the big dice? Well, one two three four to the left, that's her. The one with the drink up to her lips now."

What I see is a tall girl wearing a sporty blazer, three gold chains dangling outside a white blouse. She's got long brown hair and schoolgirl glasses, and she really is kind of pretty. That's a surprise, considering Eddie's taste in women, which just about matches his taste in food. Ed, I say, she's not bad at all.

"You don't know her," Eddie says. "All she ever wants is, take me here, take me there. Always some place where everybody's wearing suits."

So? I say. Maybe the girl's got some class. Slit open the mattress, take out a few bucks, buy a suit jacket.

"You think I'm made of money, don't you?"

I don't answer him, I'm busy staring at somebody, a girl, she's standing almost next to Laura. What made me stop and stare was her smile, she just looks, I don't know, pleasant. There's this little guy in a red shirt talking to her, cracking her up, her smile a laugh now. She's a blonde, hair parted in the middle and flowing over each shoulder.

Ed, I say. Two over from Laura. The blonde. The one laughing.

"Her?" Eddie says. "The one picking up her pocketbook now? I know that bimbo, she's Laura's buddy. Annie, that's her name. She's a nurse. They're all nurses, the whole bunch of them."

I'm watching this Annie, she slings a big brown pocketbook over her shoulder, then pulls some of her hair free from under the strap. I find myself in a hazy fantasy for a moment, it has to do with my hands and her hair. I say to Eddie, Annie what? Where's she from?

"What do I look like?" Eddie says. "An encyclopedia?"

I'm watching her, she's round, filled out but not fat, she's wearing jeans and a man's white dress shirt, the sleeves rolled up neatly. She's handing her drink to the little guy now. He puts his hand on her shoulder, says something into her ear.

Get your hand off her shoulder, pal, I say.

"What?" Eddie says.

Who's the guy in the red shirt? I ask.

"Him?" Eddie says. "The little guy? I don't know, but he's always hanging around with them."

Her boyfriend? I ask.

"No," Eddie says. "He's just one of those guys, you know. Hangs around with bimbos."

Look, Ed, I say, I want to meet that Annie. You've got to help me. We're going right up there and you're going to introduce me. Now don't give me a lot of shit, okay? I know you want to avoid Laura, but I need this favor from you. I've got to meet that girl.

"Then get your ass in gear," Eddie says, "because here she comes."

I look back and there's the guy in the red shirt, but no Annie. For a moment I feel sick to my stomach, then I see her, making her way through the crowd along the bar. I toss down one beer, take the other with me, I'm squirming through the crowd, pushing, protecting my beer with a little stiff-arm. For some reason I'm confident, everything seems to be working just right, I'm not worried about what I'll say, it's like destiny, maybe. I have this fantasy that I'll bump into her, perfect timing, I'll say just the right thing, we'll be out the door, arm in arm. That's my fantasy, but by the time I push my way into the tiny open space near the bathrooms, I see Annie's long blond hair and round moon of an ass disappear behind the ladies' room door.

Damn it, now I have time to worry. I try to come up with some good lines, come on, Hollaran, something clever. Mind going blank. I understand you're a nurse? Too stupid. Help me, I'm lonely? Too desperate. I'd like to run my hands through your hair? Too forward. I've got it. Tell me your phone number once, I'll remember it forever. Good. I practice the line. Gulp my boilermaker. The more I practice the line, the stupider it sounds. But I've got to say something. Jesus, I'm sweating like a hog. I want another drink. I practice the line.

Oh my God, here she comes, she's moving right by you, Hollaran, don't let her go. She brushes me with her shoulder, I say, oh, excuse me. Too quiet, she doesn't even look at me, she's slipping back into the crowd, I reach out, my hand touches, just touches, her shoulder, her hair. She turns. Tell me, I say. She's looking right at me and the rest of the line disappears from my mind. I'm sorry, I say. I know you don't know me, I don't mean to be a creep or anything, but I saw you over there, you're a friend of Laura Brighton's and see, she's a friend of my buddy's and I just happened to notice you and . . . I stop. Out of breath.

"Yes?" she says. That smile. Good white teeth. Green eyes.

Thomas Joseph Hollaran, I say. At your service. I bow. I would give her my hand, but my palms are sweating. I say, Your name's Annie, isn't it? I understand you're a nurse. I've always wondered about nurses, I mean, did you always want to, you know, when you were a little girl or anything?

"What?" she says. Smiling. She's almost laughing at me.

Tongue-tied, I say. Too many boilermakers.

"Try again," she says.

What I mean is, I'm celebrating something, I say. I'm celebrating something real important and I thought maybe you'd like to join me in some champagne. I mean I know you don't know me, but you're a friend of a friend, well, sort of, and I thought, you know, well, see, I'm really looking for somebody to celebrate with. I mean there's Eddie, but he's a guy. You know what I mean. I'm not talking very well, am I?

"Is it your birthday?" she asks.

Oh no, I say, nothing like that, see, I'm celebrating coming home. A year ago this month.

"Where did you go?" she says. "I'm really interested in travel."

Slow down, Hollaran, don't run off at the mouth. I take a deep breath and say, oh, I took this long, long trip on an airplane, to the other side of the world, actually. To find out what life was like on the other side, you know. And it's not very nice, except for the tropics part, I liked that, you could say it was an adventure, really, although I'd never, never want to do that again, and I'm glad as hell to be home and do you want to celebrate it with me? Champagne?

"Aren't you going to tell me where you went?" she says.

Oh, I say, well, I want to hear about your adventures, too. I mean you said you liked travel and everything.

"Oh, I don't have any adventures," she says. "I just meant that I was interested in traveling someday. I've hardly ever been out of New Jersey. Except for Maine."

What's in Maine? I say. Oh my God, she's got some big stud up in Maine. French lumberjack.

"Lobster dinners," she says. "Fresh sea air. Clear lakes. Woods. Wildlife." She smiles. "Mosquitoes. But I was up there for only two weeks. I could have used two years."

Oh, I say. Well, I guess that means you don't like your job. I thought it would be pretty interesting in a hospital, life and death and everything.

"I'm in the recovery room," she says. "The patients are out cold." A smile. "That's what I do, wake people up after an operation. That and watch the monitors and write reports." She shrugs. "Four years of college," she says. "It's not what I imagined it would be."

I'm trying to keep my eyes on her, pay attention to what

she says, and signal Leo at the same time. He sees me, a miracle, I yell for champagne, the biggest bottle he's got, with two glasses.

"But I don't want to talk about the hospital," she says. "Tell me about your trip. What kinds of places have you been?"

When a long, long time passes I'm suddenly aware that it's gray everywhere, and I've somehow lost track of the conversation. I'm cold. I realize I'm lying flat on my back on the floor of Eddie's living room. And the gray light is winter dawn. A single word, *loser,* is going around and around my brain. I sit up, I'm still fully dressed, I rub my head, God, I can smell myself. There's somebody in the kitchen, I hear the oven door open and close.

I groan and get up, stiff, my head like a bowling ball on my shoulders, my mouth practically glued shut. I hold my head in both hands, push through the kitchen door, there's Eddie, sitting at the kitchen workbench. In front of him is a small mound of White Castle hamburgers, a cardboard carton of orange juice, and a jumbo bottle of ketchup.

"You're alive," he says. "I don't believe it."

Juice, I say. Please. I sit at the workbench and drink right from the carton. I'm trying to bring back everything that happened at Lucky Leo's last night.

"Boy, were you putting the rap on that bimbo," Eddie says. He laughs, I start to sweat. I go cold.

"I never heard nothing like it in my life," Eddie says. "By the time I got over to you, you were giving her some rap about flies in your eyes."

Flies? I say.

"In your eyes," Eddie says. "You were telling her you had flies in your eyes, and that's why you couldn't see the flies in your eyes, because of the flies in your eyes. Something like that, anyway."

Oh no, I say.

"No sweat, she was laughing," Eddie says. "Where'd you get that rap?"

Out of a book I read in the Army, I say. *Catch-22.*

"So that's where you get your raps," Eddie says. "Maybe I'll start reading some of those books. I'm telling you, I was standing right over you for five minutes, and neither one of you knew it. You were talking and laughing like you were the only two in the world."

I remember her laughing. I think I do.

"But then you started talking crazy stuff," Eddie says. "So I figured I'd better get you out of there."

What do you mean? I say.

"Well, you made this big speech and told her how nice she was, and how pretty and all, and how you liked her right from the start. Then you said it was too bad you had to meet somebody like her when you were so fucked up."

That's what I said?

"Fucked up," Eddie says. "That's what you said. Then you said you hoped she'd understand, but you really didn't think you could do it all again."

Do what all again?

"Or go through it all again, something like that. That's when I tapped you on the back and said, 'Time to go.' I was ready to drag you out of there, but you didn't give me no trouble. You just put your arms around that bimbo and laid a kiss on her that lasted about ten minutes. And then you said you'd probably never see her again and you were sorry. We walked out of the joint, I had to hold you from falling over. You remember that part?"

Sort of, I say.

"Don't give me that," Eddie says. "I never seen you so out of it. I couldn't shut you up after I got you into the jeep. You kept saying the same thing over and over, all the way home. You don't remember, do you?"

Don't tell me, Ed, please, I say.

"Nothing to be ashamed of," he says. "You were pledging allegiance to the flag."

7

My Old Man

"Who is this Hoover fellow?" asks Doctor Rhinehart. "Have you mentioned him before?"

About a dozen times, I say to myself. I give out a long sigh, Doctor Rhinehart doesn't seem to notice. I say, Hoover was a lifer, you know, a guy with his head stuffed full of army crap and regulations. My platoon sergeant.

"Oh, your boss, then," says Doctor Rhinehart. "The one who was involved in your helicopter episodes."

Yes, he's the one, I say.

"And what did you want to do to him this time?"

Nothing, I say. It's what he did to me.

"Oh," Doctor Rhinehart says. And then it's quiet in here, an old moldy-smelling room filled with about a hundred plants, so much like a jungle that I keep waiting to hear the cries of tropical birds. But nothing, of course, just my own stubborn silence. I wonder, sometimes, just how much attention Doctor Rhinehart is really paying. I pick at a vine leaf that's growing on a pole near my chair.

"So tell me," she says, "what is it about this Hoosier fellow?"

Hoover, I say.

"Hoover, yes," she says. "And helicopters, yes. This much I remember. So tell me the rest. And indulge me with patience, please. You see, my memory is no longer so good. And I stopped taking notes many years ago."

Hoover, I say, was by the book. Do you remember me telling you that?

She nods her head. She's a tiny woman, pure white hair, about seventy or maybe older, a lined face that was once, I'm sure, really beautiful. She's sitting opposite me in a rattan chair, that's the only furniture in this rain forest of an office, two rattan chairs. "This is all quite familiar," she says. "A man is put in authority. So naturally he believes in the system that elevated him."

A believer, I say, that's right, that was Hoover. But it was worse over there, Doctor Rhinehart, because he had the power over us, you see? And this one time I'm trying to tell you about, well, see, at least in the Delta, the war had settled down. The government and the Americans had pretty much won by the time I got there, and just little guerrilla battles would break out at night. But the guerrillas would sometimes attack our airbase, see, so we were sent out in the daytime, sweeps, that's what we called them. We were looking for weapons or ammunition or even enemy soldiers that might be hidden in the rice paddies or the little peasant huts.

Most sergeants, they'd take it easy on a sweep. Why get somebody hurt? They'd treat it like a long hike. Check out a little hut here or there, but no big deal. But not Hoover. With him we'd stay for hours searching the huts and fields.

So this one day, there we were. Inside this mud and straw house where only this grandmother was home. Dirt floor. She didn't speak a word of English, and none of us had more than a few phrases of Vietnamese. We did it by the book, somebody pointed a rifle at her, everybody else searched the house. Stomped on the floor for hollow spots. Tapped the walls. Shook out the bedroll. The lady had one of those ornate Oriental chests, her only real furniture. Hoover himself went through that chest item by item, the old lady looking on. I remember she had this strange, fixed smile.

Of course, we didn't find a goddamn thing. Except that this lady had a bomb shelter dug right there in the one big room. They all had them, somewhere to hide when the shooting started at night. They were dug in this hard, reddish clay-mud, always in the shape of an L, because shrapnel or bullets couldn't turn the corner.

Anyway, we took turns searching those tunnels, and this one was mine. Hoover handed me the flashlight. I took off my shirt, I don't know why, maybe to keep it clean. I wrapped a bandanna around my head like an Indian. To relieve the tension, my head felt like it was being squeezed. Meanwhile, Hoover kept trying to talk to the old lady. To find out whether anything or anybody was hidden in the bomb shelter. But the woman was frozen with fright, an M-16 pointed right at her. Finally, Hoover said, Okay, lady, if there's anybody down there my man's going to blow him away. She had no reaction but a smile. Hoover handed me his pistol, a big brown forty-five. Do your duty, he said.

I got down on my knees in front of this hole, and crawled in. The flashlight turned on, the pistol in my right hand and cocked. Moved myself along with my elbows, very slow. There were little roots coming all through the mud walls, I remember that. It was only about eight or ten feet to the corner of the L.

Of course, when I got to that corner, I stopped. And tried to convince myself there was no chance at all that there were two or three Viet Cong right around the corner with their fingers on the triggers. Because they *could* have been there. And then one thing started going through my mind. What if that old lady isn't scared stiff because she's looking down the barrel of an M-16? What if she's hiding the VC down here? And she knows what's going to happen the minute I turn this corner?

So real, real slow I put my left hand forward, with the flashlight in it, switched on. I kept thinking, what's a hand? So what if you lose a hand? But when it was stretched all the way out there, the light shining into the hole, nothing happened. Not the slightest sound or movement, and believe me, I was so keyed up I would have felt a hair move at fifty paces.

So I put my right hand out there, too. The forty-five ready to go, and those things have sensitive triggers. Bump them and they'll go off. The pistol was stretched out, too, all the way, and still no movement or sound.

I kept wishing there was some other way to do it. Because I was all alone down there, no room in the tunnel for anybody but me. So I did what I had to do, which was put the tiniest part of my head around the corner, and then pull it back, quick. Nothing, so I waited, listened, tried to *feel* if anybody was around there. Then finally I just stuck my head out, very, very slow, until I could see just a little bit into the hole. Nothing. Just the beam of flashlight on a mud wall. But I still couldn't see all the way in, I knew I'd have to move up. I just *made* myself put my head out all the way. I still don't know to this day, Doctor Rhinehart, what kept me from pulling the trigger. Eyes, that's what I saw in the beam of my flashlight.

Very small. Very small eyes. In the split second it took me to focus I realized it was a little girl, and in that same split second she burst out crying. I mean a tiny girl, Doctor Rhinehart, four, five, I don't know, a baby. I pointed my forty-five toward the sidewall and let the hammer down easy, then I crawled forward into the big mud-wall room. The kid was screaming her brains out, hysterical. I remember she had a white dress on, all muddy, no shoes, socks, underwear, anything, and she was just sitting there, shrieking, her back to the wall. So I grabbed her, made a cradle out of my arms, put her in there, and backed out of the tunnel. Of course, when I got near the entrance a couple of guys grabbed my feet, they always did that, to help pull you out. And there I come popping out of the tunnel with this baby in my arms, she was still screaming and crying. And nobody was saying anything, not even Hoover. And I went over and gave the little girl to her grandmother. Who hadn't moved an inch, her face still a frozen smile. And the grandmother took the girl in her arms, soothed the kid, patted her, talked to her, and in the meantime was actually thanking us, *Cam on, cam on*, nodding her head, smiling, acting grateful. Like we had saved the baby and were great heroes. I can't tell you what I felt like, Doctor Rhinehart.

"Try," she says.

I felt like a fool, Doctor Rhinehart. And I felt something change inside me. Because, Doctor Rhinehart, if I had pulled that trigger, the stain would have been black on my soul forever. But just on mine, do you understand? Because nobody in America would have known or cared. That's what I realized when I came out of the tunnel, that's what changed inside me. I knew I was on my own. And I realized the Viet Cong wasn't my only enemy.

"Good!" she says. "I'm proud of you. Who did you find was your enemy?"

I sigh. Maybe Hoover? I say.

Doctor Rhinehart's face wrinkles up, a look of disappointment.

Maybe everybody who was back here, I say, I don't know.

She still looks disappointed. "So," she says, "if it's everybody in America, how will you take your revenge?"

Revenge? I say.

"Come now," she says, "isn't that what is really in your heart?"

Look, Doctor Rhinehart, I say. And then just shuffle my feet and shift in the chair, silent.

"Wasn't that whole episode concerning Hooper and the helicopters—"

Hoover, I say.

"Wasn't that episode about revenge?"

I know exactly what she's talking about, a story I told her the first day I came in. A story I haven't told anybody else. Out of shame, I think. It happened between me and Hoover one night, there was a helicopter hovering right over our heads.

"But you see, it's only natural," Doctor Rhinehart says. "Everyone's first thought is revenge. So I repeat my question. How will you take your revenge?"

On who? I ask.

"On those who have done you wrong."

And who is that? I ask.

"Didn't you just say?" she says. "Everybody in America?"

How can I take revenge on a whole country? I say. It's too big. Who am I supposed to single out and blame?

She smiles. "Haven't you already done that?" she says. "Your episode with Hoover? Your urge to strike out at middle-aged, middle-class businessmen? The hostility you show toward authority? You see, Mister . . ." she says, and then stops, mentally gropes for my name.

I'm angry. I wonder, sometimes, if I'm wasting my money, a shrink who spends half of every session lost in space. Hollaran, I say. Doctor Rhinehart, I say, can't you even remember my name?

Two blue eyes staring at me. Blue the color of the sky. Not angry, not hurt, but peaceful, and just staring at me. "Mister Hollaran," she says, "I am old, it is true. But that is not the only reason I have trouble with names. It is because I have heard the same story so many times. Of hurt and anger and revenge, and then more hurt, more anger, and more revenge. A terrible cycle. And believe me, only the names ever change." Blue eyes still staring right at me. "I have been sitting in this chair a very long time."

But revenge comes naturally, I say. You said so yourself.

"Mister . . . Hollaran," she says. "May I ask you? Do you believe in God?"

I used to, I say.

"I, too, had my doubts at one time," she says. "But the years and my practice have convinced me otherwise."

Oh no, I'm thinking. She's going to tell me to get down on my knees and pray.

"Do not be worried," she says, "I am not about to lecture you on piety. I do not believe that the mere existence of God means that mankind is saved. Quite the contrary. Because the existence of God is the heaviest of all human burdens. I see you are puzzled, Mister Hollaran."

Yes, I say.

"If there were no God," she says, "then it would be a much simpler world. The most brutal would rule by sheer force, nothing would matter but the welfare of the most powerful, and the value of an ordinary human life would scarcely equal that of . . . perhaps a horse or an ox. But suppose with me for a moment that there is a God. And that a spark of this Supreme Being exists in every person, no matter how weak or low. That would mean that all persons would have to be treated fairly, with respect and dignity. That every wrong, every abuse, every insult, will have to be made right before there can ever be peace."

Then it's hopeless, I say. Because in getting revenge, another wrong is done, and the cycle goes on and on.

"Exactly," she says. "But still, if you have been wronged, you must do something. You will have to become even somehow."

How am I going to get even without taking revenge? I say.

"Become even," she says.

Okay, I say. Become even. How am I going to become even without taking revenge?

"That," she says, "will be your challenge, Mister Hollaran. What will ultimately come from Vietnam? Good or bad? It is now up to you."

All right, I say. Suppose I go along with your idea. Who's this enemy I'm supposed to become even with?

"Think," she says.

Hoover comes right to my mind, but I dismiss that. I tried to take revenge on him once, but I failed, and even that caused me nightmares. So if not Hoover, then who? Sandra? Wolpenheimer? Johnson? Carmine? I can only guess.

Maybe it's my old man, I say to Doctor Rhinehart. Our relationship has never been too good.

She sighs. She seems annoyed, like this is another story she's heard too many times. "All right, then," she says. "Tell me, how would you even the score without hurting him?"

I would like him to understand, I say, just how I feel about Vietnam. And everything I've told you today. Because, see, he thinks it's a great thing that I went over there. Something to be proud of. I've got a couple of things I'd really like to tell him.

"Practice on me," she says.

A few minutes later I'm out on the porch, buttoning up my army jacket against the cold. This office building has a porch because it's really an old rooming house, converted a few years ago when they put up the big white six-story addition to St. Elizabeth Hospital, right across the street. When this place was a rooming house, one of my St. Veronica's teachers used to live here, along with a lot of guys who looked like old winos, and a psychic reader named Sister Roberta. She used to have a sign out, right here facing Broad Street, it was blue, with stars and a drawing of a crystal ball. That's been gone a long time, and now there are carved-wood signs for a chiropractor, a nurse-practitioner, a gynecologist, and Constance Rhinehart, MD, Practice Limited to Psychiatry.

Up there in the windowless sixth floor of St. Elizabeth's, that's where they do operations, and where Annie Rogers checked in for work, just about an hour ago. I can picture her in white stockings. I can picture her taking off those stockings. Later, Hollaran, you've got your work cut out for you now.

I put my hands in my jacket pockets and walk up Broad Street, it's just half a block to St. Veronica's grammar and high school. Three stories of sooty brick, topped off by what look like gun emplacements, and surrounded by a corroded green iron-spike fence. If it had a moat it could be right back in the Middle Ages. And every time I walk by, I'm surprised at how small it is. And that everything that was said and done here once seemed so important. What a narrow little space I lived in, really. Just three blocks from here to home. The most familiar three blocks in the world.

Somehow this walk home reminds me of the ninth grade. With my first bad report card. I'm going home with another one, now. Civics F, Economics F, Marriage F, Veterans' Bonus Points, Zero. The kind of bad report card that started in high school.

And what was that about, anyway? Resistance to authority, I guess. Resistance to a life planned out for you. The jacket and tie, the catechism, the religion classes, five days of that and then confession on Saturday, mass on Sunday. And you'd better be there or the nuns would send your name up to the Loving Creator who would run you down with a Mack truck and send your soul to burn, no mercy, in Hell.

All I can remember now is a summer Sunday at the lake, probably I was fourteen. We had been on a family vacation, and it had rained the whole week, or at least it seemed that way. The sun came out on a Sunday morning. And there I was in the backseat of the Hollaran station wagon, headed for Sunday mass. While other kids were screeching and running and swimming at the beach. And girls I knew, pretty girls, were lying on the rafts practically naked. I remember that one station wagon ride in particular. Holding my *St. Joseph Daily Missal*. My big sister Joan beside me, her sour look. She elbowed me and said "Stop squirming." And in turn I elbowed my little sister Theresa, who started whining. And my father in the front seat, driving like a madman to make the mass on time. Because if you got there after the Introit, it was a mortal sin. My mother beside him, silent.

I turn on South Street, and walk past the schoolyard where the nuns, as bad as any drill sergeants, used to form us into neat squads for marching to church. Past the basketball court, for the training of future school heroes. Past Liberty Street, where for some reason there's a row of about eight black families, with no relationship to the neighborhood at all, except for mutual ignorance.

Around this corner and up a block, that's where Sandra and I had our first apartment. I stop to look at it. It was pretty hard on us both, I guess, when we first got married. Neither one of us wanted a church wedding, but that's how it turned out. We needed the big reception, really, for the money in it. We put it down on a new car. I was still in school at the time, working one or two little part-time jobs. Sandra had dropped out already to take a full-time job as a teller.

She brought home less than seventy a week, and we

were living from payday to payday, barely. A couple of times
the landlord had to come knocking for the rent. As bad as it
was, the future looked worse. Because I was almost finished
at Union College, and would have to transfer to Rutgers.
With a big increase in tuition. It didn't seem like it was going
to be possible, living like that for two and a half more years.

The thing that saved us, for a while, was that we were in
love, or thought we were. It was strictly a physical thing, now
that I look back on it. And there was no way it could have
survived once the war started. I don't mean the Vietnam
war, I mean the one between Sandra and me.

The other thing that helped, for a while, was the cabin. It
was a romantic place, but more than that, it got us out of the
apartment on weekends. And gave us something to look forward to besides bills and cheap meals and alarm clocks.

I remember one weekend, winter out there, an ice
storm so thick we couldn't see the lake. We sat in the cabin,
drank a lot of vodka, and hatched a plan. I worked it all on my
accountant's columnar pad, but Sandra came up with the
original idea. The answer to our problems.

I would register for spring semester at Union, but would
only show up for the first few classes, to protect me from the
draft. Then I would get a full-time job, we took it for granted
that I'd make twice as much as Sandra. It would be August,
maybe September, before the draft board brought me in for
a physical, and if necessary I could use delaying tactics.
Meanwhile, Sandra would get pregnant. Simply stop taking
her little pills and let nature have its way. By the time the
draft board got around to me, I'd be a father, and exempt.

Wasn't that a good idea? We'd save money all spring with
both of us working, we wouldn't have tuition to pay, we'd
beat the draft, we'd have a baby and didn't we want one? I
was weak, and agreed to everything.

I registered for school and went out on what I figured
would be a practice job interview. It was at JS&T, sales
trainee, some college preferred. They were paying $140 a
week for the training period, with a raise later to $165.
Which sounded good to me at the time.

There was only one part that didn't work, and that was the important part, the baby. Giving us a baby was a promise Sandra never did keep.

I cross the street now so I don't pass too near Satriano's, might get tempted to go in. The place smells pure and sweet, like when you first drop a garlic clove in hot butter. Keep moving, Hollaran.

Turn the corner and onto Washington Street, a liquor store and then nothing but houses. I'd better start working on my speech, don't want to blank out when I face the old man. Because I'm already nervous that he knows about Sandra's cabin, won't be surprised if he calls the cops the minute he sees me.

Speech. Practice. Now look, I'll tell him. You listen to me for a change. I've been listening to you for twenty-five god-damn years, and . . . no, Hollaran, bad. Already you're practically foaming at the mouth. Keep it cool. Keep it reasonable. Okay. Try again. And slow down, don't walk so fast.

Dad, I've been meaning to have this talk with you for some time now. About our family history. Your father came here to make a little money and work on the railroad, right? And he still had the dirt of Ireland on him when they put him on a troopship and pointed him at Europe. He got there, what, two months before the armistice? And for the rest of his life, his ears rang from the shelling. Drove him almost crazy, didn't it? The constant ringing.

That was to end all wars, or so they said at the time. But when you were seventeen they had a repeat performance. Another Hollaran, another machine gun. And then your own brother, wounded in the chest in Korea. Aren't you starting to see a pattern there?

Why us? Every goddamn time it's the Hollarans. Can't you just see these bozo big shots, sitting around in their offices? Saying, let's see, who can we get to do our dirty work this time? Give that mick a rifle and that nigger a shovel and that wop a mortar shell, Democracy's in danger. Put that Polack in a tank and that rebel in an airplane, somebody's got to fight this war. And when they come home, why, we'll call them heroes and have a parade and give them little specks of bronze to wear on their chests. They fall for that one every time.

So when are the goddamn Hollarans going to wake up? And say, enough, you bozo bastards. We've bled enough, we've sweated enough, we've humped rifles around every miserable swamp in the world, get somebody else next time. Get them out of Harvard and Yale and Stanford, see how those guys like being shot in the chest. Let them get leech bites and ringworm and trenchfoot, let their ears ring for the rest of their lives, let them walk into an ambush in a rice paddy and see how the hell they like it.

But no, we'll never do that, will we? Because we're the Hollarans. And Hollarans have always been fighters. And proud of it. Proud of the medals and wounds and the flags taken off coffins. There we are, the whole crowd of Hollarans, marching along with the VFW on Memorial Day. Because it was the most glorious time in any Hollaran's life, wasn't it? The only time he went anywhere, or did anything worth talking about.

Stop. The corner of Boyle Place, yellow-and-black sign that says DEAD END, I grew up here. A deep breath and let it out, smoky cold. This street so narrow it's hard to imagine kids using it for stickball, but we did. This house on the corner is where Eddie grew up, his folks still live here, their shades always pulled down all the way, it runs in the family. Next here is Marianos', a big manger scene on the front lawn, they put it out every year at Thanksgiving. Lucky Leo used to rent out the basement apartment, I have no idea who lives there now.

Up a tight little alley, this is the house where I grew up, open the side door, never locked. Dark, though. Fumble at the door, open it into the kitchen, my old man sitting with his back to me, doesn't move or startle. He's wearing a sleeveless undershirt, his white lieutenant's shirt with its gold badge hangs over one post of the chair, under that a brown holster dangling the weight of a .38 Police Special. My old man's

drinking coffee and reading the Elizabeth *Daily Journal*. He
finally looks up.

"Tommy," he says. "Oh, I thought it was Theresa coming
in from school. Sit down," he says. "Have some coffee."

I take a chair out and sit right across the table from him.
If he's heard anything from the cops, he's not showing it,
although my old man's always been a terrific actor.

"Here, let me get you a cup," he says, but doesn't start to
move from his chair.

I don't want any, I say, it'll keep me on edge all night.

"Did you eat anything?" he says. "How about some bacon and eggs? Let me get up and make them for you." He
doesn't mean that, really. That's the Irish way of saying,
there's bacon and eggs around here somewhere, but don't
ask me to get up and cook them for you. I know my old man,
he'd stand over the stove frying bacon about as soon as he'd
bring a hobo home for dinner.

"You've got to eat something," he says, but he won't look
me directly in the eyes. He turns a page and pretends to be
scanning the news. But I know better, my old man really
takes the paper for the obituaries.

"I see the Mets traded Shamsky," he says, his eyes still
focused on the paper.

Oh, I say, I don't follow that stuff anymore.

"Baseball?" he says, and looks at me for the first time.
"*You* don't follow baseball?"

Couldn't tell you who's on first, I say.

It takes my old man a few seconds to recover from that
one. "Well," he says, and looks down, turns the page. "Shamsky was a bum anyway."

My old man never says that word *bum* without growling
the *m*. There is no lower word in the vocabulary of a railroad
policeman. My old man's worked his whole life chasing bums
from the big railroad yards of Weehawken and Hoboken, but
for every one he's rousted, twelve have come in on the next
freight. To him, the world is a struggle of the decent people
versus the bums, and he's proud to be a soldier for the good
side. He's come home many times with scratches, bruises,

cuts, cigarette burns and even bites he's gotten from bums. When we were kids, he used to roll up his sleeve or pants leg and show them to us.

My old man reaches back around him, takes a silver pen out of the pocket of his lieutenant's shirt, uses it to underline two names on the obituary page. *Brennan. O'Hanlon.* This weekend he'll attend the wakes, even though he's never met the deceased. Brennan and O'Hanlon will no doubt turn out to be Irish Catholic males of somewhere near my father's age. There is something about the rites surrounding death that has fascinated my old man ever since I can remember. He used to take me, and then my sisters, along to the wakes, until my mother finally put a stop to it. But here's how I remember my old man the best, at the parlor of some funeral home, taking the hand of some bewildered widow he'd never seen before, and saying, Joseph Hollaran, ma'am. I'm terribly sorry.

"There's plenty of coffee," my old man says, and pushes his chair back, gets up and goes to the sink, rinses his cup, reaches for the percolator. "You used to love your mother's coffee."

I don't want to talk about my mother's coffee, I say. I realize I've said it very loud. A bewildered look from my old man. A retreat. He goes to the refrigerator, slops too much milk into his coffee. "I know something's been bothering you," he says, and turns around, puts the milk carton back in the refrigerator. "The cops were here the other day."

I feel like a wave of heat just flashed through my body.

"They had a warrant," my old man says, and puts his coffee down on the far end of the kitchen table, starts drying his hands on the front of his undershirt. "I told them I haven't seen you in five years," he says. "I said the last I heard, you were in Venezuela." He sits down, far across the table from me, puts his lips down to the rim of the cup and slurps. "I can't help you with the city cops, you know. They can't just rip up a warrant."

What kind of warrant? I say.

My old man shrugs. He will not look at me. I'm all of a

sudden aware that the refrigerator is humming. The only noise.

"You give any more thought to going back to college?"

No, I say.

"How long's the GI bill good for?"

I'm not going back to that college, I say. Period.

"I was just thinking out loud," he says.

Here it comes, I'm thinking.

"It's the accountants and lawyers who run this world, Tommy," he says.

I've tried accounting and it's not for me, I say.

"You got A's," he says.

But I didn't *like* it, I say.

"Nobody *likes* it," he says. "You think I like my job? It's nothing but aggravation."

Anthony likes his job, I say.

"Your uncle Anthony?" he says. "Prancing around a kitchen, cooking spaghetti? Is that any way to make a living?"

Silence from me. This is what it always comes down to. If I push it any further, my old man will accuse Anthony of being a queer, and then drag out twenty-seven years' worth of complaints about the Satrianos. Who according to my old man are a bunch of good-for-nothing lazy dagos, with the singular exception being my mother, who he practically elevates to sainthood when he's not ordering her around. It's like it's all stored on a record somewhere, the Hollaran family album, I can take it out and play it anytime.

I actually find myself with my head in my hands, listening to my old man sip coffee. And wondering how old I can ever be in this house. And realizing that things here will never change.

"Have you seen anything of Sandra lately?" my old man says, and tries to make the question sound casual.

I take a deep breath. As a matter of fact, I say. Then I stop. As a matter of fact, I say, that's probably what the cops were here about. See, I went up to the cabin last week, and Sandra came by and called the cops on me.

"I think you ought to know," he says. "She pressed charges."

So you do know what the warrant was about, I say.

"Breaking and entering, criminal property damage, and malicious mischief," he says. "I sneaked a look at the papers."

I suppose you want me to turn myself in, I say.

"If the judge finds out you're planning to go back to college," he says, "it'll just be a fine."

But I'm *not* planning to go back to college, I say.

"Then you'd better have a talk with Sandra," he says, "or you might find yourself in jail."

A talk with Sandra?

"This is all a misunderstanding," he says. "You can't just *leave* a woman like that. If you'd go back to her and try again, I'm sure she'll drop the charges."

No, I say. You really don't understand.

"I understand that she's a divorced girl. Whatever happened between you two, it can be patched up. Believe me, marriage is a rocky road, Tommy."

Look, I say. And then just swallow. What's the use?

"I know I've been harping on this lately," he says, "but if the two of you would get together and go see Father Dennis, then maybe with the grace of God . . ."

Sure, I say. The great moral leader Father Dennis. It's all right to shove a rifle down a rice peasant's throat, but don't you dare get divorced.

"Don't be sarcastic about the Church," my old man says, and puts the coffee cup down hard enough to rattle the spoon.

Typical, I say, and shake my head.

"You're making a mess out of your life."

Maybe I want to, I say. And you stay out of it.

"Then what did you come home for?" he says, loud.

I forget, I say. I get up from the table, walk past him. I should have known better, I say. And stomp down the stairs and slam the outside door.

8

Happy Memories
Fresh and Clean

I'm standing in Eddie's kitchen, trying to shout down through the locked basement door. What did you say? I yell.

"The welding book," Eddie shouts up from the basement. "It's in my room somewhere."

Okay, I yell down, I'll find it. I walk away from the door and that noise starts in the basement again, bong, bong, bong, a hammer hitting metal, it's been going on since dinnertime. I go through the living room, Christmas Eve but you'd never know it, not a sign of it in here. Up the stairs, bare creaky wood, dark handprints along the wall. Ever since we were kids, Eddie's had kind of a phobia about letting people into his room. He must need that welding book pretty bad.

Push open Eddie's door, grope for the light switch, flick, I recoil from the glare of a couple of hundred watts. Bare walls, no curtains, Eddie thinks they're frills. On my left is a big gray wall locker, the kind they give you in the army, with its door thrown open and uniforms, underwear, dungarees, piled in two cockeyed stacks. The rest of the room is taken up with dozens of buckets, boxes, pails, and cans, all open at the top, most filled over the rim with brass fittings, or rags or papers and pamphlets or nuts and bolts or rolls of electrical wire. There's no bed but an army sleeping bag laid over an army air mattress, both olive drab. The only piece of furniture is what Eddie calls his "hot seat," he brought it down and showed it to me once. It's a hardwood chair with a bed pillow strapped to its seat, and its legs cut off so that it fits right on top of the radiator.

I look around for the book, pick my way over the boxes and pails, looks hopeless to find anything here, sit down on the sleeping bag, there it is, right in front of me, on top of a box. I pick up the book and notice underneath it is a heavy, olive-colored flight suit, like the ones they used in Vietnam. I hold it up by the shoulders, a big one-piece overall, the name SADOWSKI still stitched over the pocket, the Spec. 5 rank still in place on the left shoulder.

There are more flight suits in the box. Two, three, four. I lift them all out, underneath is a flight helmet, microphone attached. Beside that there's a thick olive-colored binder that says in black letters, *Procedures, Maintenance, United States Army Rotation Wing Aircraft.* A thousand yellowed pages of maintenance bulletins inside. And wedged beside the binder is another book, a photo album, on the cover is a drawing in faded gold leaf, a water buffalo with a peasant plowing behind it. I bring the album out and open it to the middle. Bong, bong, bong, the hammering going hard and heavy downstairs.

Pictures of Eddie, a skinnier Eddie, a shirtless Eddie, half the time with a burning cigarette stuck in his mouth. In one big black-and-white picture he's standing next to a motionless helicopter, one arm hung casually over the protruding barrel of the machine gun.

I'm startled by a muffled shout. "Hollaran!" Eddie yelling from the basement. "You find it?"

I answer him with a shout, take both the album and the welding book downstairs with me. When I get to the kitchen, I call out, "I've got it, Ed."

"Do me a favor," he shouts up, "just leave it by the door."

Okay, I yell, and drop the book right by the corner of the door. Then I sit at the workbench and open the album to page one. No photos there, but an American-style promo, printed in yellow and blue. A big crude drawing of a round smiley face, and beneath it some ad copy written by a Viet-

namese with only a half grasp of English. It says, *Direction:*
Happy memories fresh and clean, it keeps the photos safe
from filthy or scratch. Following that there's more lousy art-
work, showing just how to lift the clear plastic from the pages
and stick in the snapshots.

I start through the album, going slow until I get used to
Eddie's photographic style. Most of the photos were taken
from the air, shot after shot of green jungle mountains as seen
from a helicopter. A lot of times there's part of a machine
gun, out of focus in the foreground of a scenic shot. Once in a
while there's an out-and-out bad photo, the back of a pilot's
helmet, the inside roof of a helicopter. Eddie never could
stand to throw anything away.

I go quick through the last few pages, a gallery of my
least favorite machines, Slicks, Kiowas, Chinooks, Loaches,
every kind the army had, photographed from every angle,
some nosing up for takeoff, others hovering, others motionless on a runway. The last thing in the album seems to be just
a square of white cardboard, until I realize it's a photo turned
facedown. I lift the plastic from the page, peel the photo
gently away from the sticky gum. It's a blurry shot, out of
focus and off center, a Vietnamese peasant in a sampan on
brown water. He's an old man, looking almost straight up at
the camera, waving his arms.

There's thumping on the cellar stairs, Eddie making his
way up, I think about hiding the album, decide not to. I leave
it open on the workbench, don't bother to turn that last
photo facedown again, I want to find out what it's about. I
stand in front of the cellar door as Eddie undoes both bolts
and pushes it open. He sees me, moves like a cat out of the
doorway, slams the door.

"What the hell are you looking at?" Eddie says.

What makes you think I was trying to see downstairs? I
say.

"Nothing," he says. "I'm talking about there on the table. You getting nostalgic over your old war pictures?"

Actually, Ed, I say, they're your old war pictures.

"What!" he says, and takes two off-balance strides for the

workbench. "Why you son of a bitch," he says, "they are mine. How'd you get them?"

Ed, I say, you *told* me to look around in your room.

He slams the album shut, picks it up, waves it around. A photo falls to the floor, Eddie doesn't notice. "This was in the bottom of a box," he says. "You had to dig around to get this out." The photo is lying on the floor faceup, it's the one of the peasant waving his arms. Eddie sees it, squats to pick it up, glares at me. "Son of a bitch," he says, and slips the photo back in among the pages of the album. "You can't leave nothing alone, can you?" He puts the album under his arm.

I just wanted to look, I say.

"You seen it, didn't you?"

That picture? I say. Yes, but I still don't know what it is.

"Good," Eddie says. "Because it's none of your business."

Look, Ed, I say. I'm tired of everybody being quiet about Vietnam. And trying to forget it all. The least we could do is talk to each other for God's sake. Because you know, Ed, that's just what the bozos want. They want us to shut up. Fuck them, talk about it, shout it out, holler it in the goddamn streets, don't let them ever forget it.

"That's you, Hollaran," Eddie says. "That ain't me."

So you're going to hide those pictures the rest of your life? I say.

"Leave me alone, will you?"

Come on, Ed, I say. Tell me something.

"Ain't you got no decency?" he says.

No, I say, let me see that, you're going to talk about it right now.

"Get away from me," Eddie says. I'm grabbing for the album, he turns and tries to pull it away but I grip it, rip hard, yank it free, hold it behind my back. Eddie looks at me, hatred in those gray-green Polack eyes. He comes at me, I'm backing into a corner. He's breathing deep. "That's my property you got there," he says.

Tell me about that picture, I say, and I'll give it back to you.

"You're asking for it now, Hollaran," he says. He makes a

lunge for the album, I sidestep him. I'm in the middle of the kitchen now, album behind my back, I'm up on my feet like a fighter. He's coming at me, I push him away with one hand. "God damn you," he says, "all right." And goes into a crouch, steps toward me, swings, I duck. "Come on," he says. I back away, push backward through the kitchen door, backpedal through the living room, Eddie after me, fists up. I back to the Chrysler couch, circle it, keep it between me and him. We go around, he grabs for me, I twist out of the way, we go around again, stop, look at each other, breathing hard. Slowly we start to circle again, then Eddie puts both hands on the couch and shoves it out of the way, charges at me, trips, lands hard on his elbows, scrambles up, I'm running for the stairs, take two at a time, I'm at the top, miss a step, grab for the bannister, Eddie's behind me, he grabs my ankle, I'm falling. My hands spread out, the album gone, I'm sliding backward, headfirst down the stairs, Eddie falling with me, I hit my head on the landing, the album's right near my face, I grab it, turn on my stomach, lock it to my chest like it was a football. Eddie's on top of me, there's a knee in my back, hard.

"You going to give it to me now?" He's panting.

No, I say. Never. Fuck you, break my ribs, go ahead.

The knee comes out of my back. Eddie's standing on the landing now, all I see is work boots. "Go ahead, keep it," he says. His bad foot hits the floor hard as he turns away. "Look at it all you want," he says. He stops at the kitchen door, comes limping back toward me. Grabs the bannister, brings his good foot back, kicks me in the thigh. "You lousy bastard, you," he says. I'm clutching the album still. He thumps his way back into the kitchen.

I roll over, feel my lower lip, blood where I've bitten it. Sit on the stairs and rub my thigh, the album closed on my lap now. I look down at it, what have I won? I realize I've done a lousy thing. I take the album and push through the kitchen door, there's Eddie, sitting on a stool, the leg of his green work pants rolled up, he's feeling his calf where it's bruised and scratched, his bad leg, he won't look at me. I drop the album on the kitchen table. Here, I say. No reaction from

Eddie, he's fixed-focus on the back window, staring out at nothing but night.

I apologize, Ed, I say.

He doesn't even blink.

I was wrong, I say. Definitely wrong, here, take it back, I'm sorry, it's none of my business, I'll never ask you anything about it again, case closed. Okay?

"You bastard, you," Eddie says, without moving anything but his lips. "Now you got me thinking about it."

Ed, I say, I'll never bring it up again. I swear to you. Here, I'll make you a drink, okay? Half and half, right? Eddie doesn't indicate yes or no. I make him the drink anyway, half a styrofoam cup of V-8, vodka to fill it, stir it around with a spoon. Then I make myself a vodka, straight with just ice cubes. Here, I say, and hand Eddie his drink. He reaches out his hand without looking at me, then just sets the drink on the floor.

Come on, Ed, I say, a toast. To old soldiers. To forgetting everything.

"Yeah," Eddie says. "First you want to dig up the old dirt, then you want to forget it."

Now I don't know what to say, so I keep quiet.

"You want to know what sandbagging is," he says, "well, that's a picture of it, the old guy, waving his arms around. He's waving his arms because we're going to drop a sandbag on him."

I sip my drink. Eddie still hasn't looked at me, he's waiting for something. Finally I ask. Why?

"Just for the fucking hell of it, that's why," he says. I don't say anything.

"You know how on a Slick you cover the floor with sandbags sometimes? You're coming back from a mission, you don't need those sandbags no more, right? So you fly up and down the river, real low level, and you find some papa-san poling his LDB along, you buzz him, scare the shit out of him. Then after you done that a couple of times, you hover right over him, drop a sandbag, boom, it goes right through the bottom of his boat. Next thing you know, papa-san's in the water, hanging on to what's left of the boat, trying to swim it to shore."

Silence. I wait through it. Eddie finally looks at me. "I figure you could understand it, Tom," he says.

Sure, I say. The old papa-san was probably a VC anyway.

Eddie gives me a hard look. "No, no, no," he says. "You don't understand at all, do you? Them papa-sans weren't nothing, just old fishermen, that's all."

Then why did you sandbag them? I ask.

"I been asking myself that lately," he says, and takes a Winston out of his pocket, lets it dangle from his mouth. "You know how lousy I am at talking," he says, and lights the cigarette. "See, the first couple of times we done it, I felt real bad. Even though I was laughing like the rest of the crew, I really didn't take no part in it. But then once I kicked out a sandbag myself. Just to be one of the boys, you know. Then pretty soon I was taking pictures of it and everything. Just like I was a bozo."

So you realized that too? I say.

"Not until a long time later," he says. "Not until I went to see this old buddy of mine from the unit, he was in jail on Long Island. Drugs. Anyway, I hadn't heard from nobody in the unit all the time I was in the hospital, so what this guy told me was a surprise. He told me I was the only one who lived through the crash, but I knew that because some nurse told me in Saigon, the first hospital I went to. What I didn't know all that time was how I got to the medics. I just naturally figured it was by medevac, you know. But he told me some old fisherman had picked me up, bleeding and all, put me in his sampan, and poled me downriver to the base."

Ed, I say, that's great. Don't you realize? We're talking about the same thing. Because when I was over there I started to think that maybe the VC wasn't the real enemy. It got so bad, a couple of times I was ready to jump, right from the chopper.

A puzzled look on Eddie's face. "Was it flying okay at the time?" he says.

Of course, I say.

"Then why did you want to jump?"

Ed, I say, practically shouting. How could you not understand after what you just told me? I had to get out of it somehow. I couldn't stand being in those helicopters.

"But why blame it on helicopters?" he says. "What was it brought you guys hot Alphas out in the field. Roast beef and mashed potatoes and all. Tell me."

Helicopters, I say.

"And what was it that brought you beer and soda and mail every day, no matter what?"

Helicopters, I say.

"And when you guys were going to be inserted somewhere, what was it that flew in first and sprayed the shit out of the bush for you?"

Okay, I say, I admit it. Helicopters.

"Then what have you got against them?" he says. "They were the best things that ever happened in my life. If it wasn't for helicopters, I probably would have been a grunt. This way, I got to fly, hundreds of hours. And a couple of times, believe it or not, Tom, they let me sit in the copilot's seat and handle the controls. I was flying then, actually flying them things myself."

I just look at him. It's strange how you can know somebody for twenty years, and still be seeing things for the first time. I guess we'll never agree about helicopters, Ed, I say. But hell, here's to it. To disagreements. I lift my styrofoam cup.

We drink for maybe two hours, and with little silences in between, we tell stories about Vietnam. But only ordinary little stories, things we can agree on. Like, how the officers hoarded the Budweiser and left the enlisted men to drink Black Label. Or how many times a week the cooks served the dreaded roast beef. Or how everything rotted in the monsoon season, including your skin. We even compare the lowest-priced whore we'd ever heard of, me a dollar, Eddie seventy-five cents. By the time we get near the bottom of the vodka bottle, we're down to the pettiest kind of griping. How they never had any decent movies, how the malaria pills were too big to swallow.

Well, I say, and lift my glass toward Eddie. We made it, didn't we? It's all behind us now, Ed, and here's to another Christmas, our second one home.

"Don't remind me about Christmas," Eddie says. "I ain't even bought any presents for the old man and the old lady yet. It just slipped my mind this year."

Ed, I say, with Christmas music all over the radio, how could you forget?

"I don't listen," he says. "It makes me sick, dingdong, bells ringing and all. As soon as I hear the first Christmas music I turn off the radio until spring. I could have even had a date tonight, but I couldn't stand the thought of Christmas music."

A date with who? I ask.

He hesitates, like he's not sure he should answer. He takes a drink. "Laura," he says. "She wanted me to go to midnight mass, and then there's a whole bunch going back to her house for supper."

Ed, I say, is Annie Rogers going to be there?

"Sure," he says, "ain't I told you? They're roommates, the two of them."

And you waited until now to tell me this? I say.

"Yeah, why?" he says. "Don't get upset. You wouldn't want to bump into Annie in church, would you? You wouldn't stoop that low."

What time is it right now? I ask.

"Late," Eddie says.

It's never too late to get a little religion, I say.

"You're crazy," he says.

Come on, I say, please, be a good guy, I'll mention you to the Pope, come on, Ed, please, midnight mass, the place is already filling up, we'll never get a seat, *please* just do me this one favor, revert to Catholicism for one measly hour, come on, Ed, I know it makes you sick, I'll do anything, I'll wash the jeep for you, I'll buy at the White Castle all month, I'll replace every drop of vodka I ever drank on you, Ed, I'm desperate, I'm begging you.

Eddie takes on the resigned look of a suffering Polish saint. He sighs and reaches into his pocket for a Winston. "I don't know why I let you talk me into these things," he says.

Between arguing and pleading, and me taking the fastest bath of my life, and Eddie trying to find a pair of corduroy pants without any grease stains, it's almost midnight by the time we're out the back door. Snow. Two powdery inches over everything and still coming down. I ask Eddie could he knock off the jeep's warm-up time just this once, and he gives me a solemn no with a shake of his head, and gets in the driver's side. "Don't track in no snow," he says.

I'm shuddering in the jeep, but sweating under the arms, thinking of nothing but Annie. The sooner I see her again, the easier it will be to make things right, that's what I'm telling myself. And I'll apologize and tell her I was terribly drunk, that's all. But you can't blame it on the booze forever, Hollaran. I know, I know, leave me alone. I've got all the complications I can deal with right now. Ed, I say, isn't this goddamn thing warmed up yet?

We're off in the silence of the snowy night. And a fresh snowstorm can make even this neighborhood look good, the piled-up cars in the junkyard look as natural as any hill, the Arthur Kill looks like a picture-book frozen river, not a running sewer. I could be lulled into certain things during a snowstorm. And it's dark here in the jeep.

Hey, Ed, I say, I'm going to tell you something, okay? One last thing about Vietnam and then I'll never mention it again. I've only told this to one other person in my life, a doctor. It's about this guy, Hoover. A lifer, I've told you about him. How he made us really search the tunnels and all? Well, one night, a really spooky thing happened, Ed, and I really don't understand it. Maybe you can. See, we were called out. Middle of the night. Some chopper pilot had been flying back to base, and thought he caught the glimpse of a VC in his landing lights, in a little swampy area just outside the barbed wire.

Well, you know how it is to get called out at night. Spooks you. Hoover came down the aisles knocking on bunks with his rifle. The lights went on, everybody jumped into their clothes, started strapping on ammo, you never knew what was out there. They took us out to the wire in a deuce-and-a-half, everybody smoking cigarettes. That was all you could see in the back of that truck, the orange lights of all those cigarettes.

We got out of the truck, helmets, flak jackets, the works, we're dressed to kill. Hoover used his hand and foot to hold the barbed wire open, patted everybody on the ass as they went through. Behind us on the flight line a helicopter took off.

We had to pick our way through about fifty feet of concertina wire. And I started wondering whether some doped-up tower guard was going to think we were the NVA and open up on us. Finally we were through the barbed wire and on the bank of this narrow river. The helicopter was up over us, no lights on but you could hear it.

The place we had to search was a swampy island, weeds three and four feet high. We waded the river, it was deeper than we thought, almost up to our armpits, and the bottom was a foot of slimy muck. It was all you could do to keep your balance, keep your weapon up over your head. And every time you pulled your foot up out of the muck, there was a big sucking noise.

So we got to the opposite bank all right, but wet. And who knows whether muddy ammo will jam in a sixteen? Hoover made us form into a line. We were just supposed to walk straight across the island, one pass, and flush the guy out.

Of course, there was no way of knowing whether there was one VC or twenty, or maybe none, the pilot could have been stoned, you know that, Ed. So we started walking. And way above us, the chopper lit up, it was a firefly. You've probably flown them yourself, Ed, big spotlight in the door, and a machine gun behind it. And the swamp was lit up wherever the spotlight aimed. And I mean lit up, intense white, brighter than day.

So there I was walking, slow, my sixteen held up waist-high, my finger on the trigger, I could actually feel my hair rise up and stand on end. Every step through the weeds I kept expecting somebody in black pajamas to pop up, it would be him or me. And the more I walked, the more I thought, the crazier my thoughts became. And I was thinking, maybe if somebody pops up I won't fire. Maybe I'll freeze, face-to-face, a coward. Or maybe it will be easier, just to die that way. And be out of it once and for all, Eddie, I'm telling you, I wanted out so bad. I was walking more and more like a robot. I wasn't even looking. Something took over my mind and my body, and I knew death was right around. And I realized I was all alone, Ed, lost in the tall weeds.

And then the chopper came down. To mark where I was and get me back to the unit. It hovered right over me, a horrific noise. And the light from it, I couldn't see a damn thing. And the prop wash was blowing all the weeds flat, and that's when I saw Hoover, making hand motions at me. The chopper lifted a little, and I heard Hoover screaming, Soldier, soldier, get in line.

What I did, Ed, was turn on him. My sixteen pointed at him. And I saw the future like a rapid-fire movie in my mind, I actually saw bullets from my rifle ripping through his chest. But the last shred of sanity or whatever kept me from twitching my finger. But it was hard, Ed, I had to strain to keep my finger still, because, and I know this is crazy, Ed, it was like I had been taken over by some force. I mean, I wasn't myself anymore.

Silence. The jeep moving up Bayway, deserted in the snow. The humming of the engine, the slap of the windshield wipers.

I know it's crazy, Ed, I say. I don't really expect you to understand.

"Are you kidding?" he says. "I heard plenty worse than that. I knew a couple of guys who actually pulled the trigger. And one who bragged about it."

You understand? You know what I'm talking about?

"Sure," he says. "The only thing I can't understand is what you got against helicopters."

I find myself laughing.

"Don't laugh," he says, "I'm serious."

But I am laughing, almost hysterical, so hard that tears come to my eyes and my stomach hurts and I have to hold it. Eddie's retreated into silence. We turn the corner onto South Broad, and I'm trying to get control of myself.

All around St. Veronica's there are cars, parked tightly block after block, and Eddie cruises about five miles an hour for a space. I'm getting worried now, it must be after midnight. We're prowling, I'm starting to squirm, no spaces anywhere, finally I just say to Eddie, let's drive out a couple of blocks, park and run back.

"Why?" he asks.

We'll never get a seat if we're late, I say.

"That's what you're worried about?" Eddie says. "Why didn't you tell me?" He speeds up a little. "I got an idea," he says. We're moving a lot faster now, coming up on the old lit-up Gothic church, Eddie turns up the driveway, stops the jeep, flips the four-wheel-drive lever, hits the gas, we're over the curb, climbing a small snowy hill, the church lawn, we're on top of it, Eddie grins at me and shuts the engine off.

Excellent, Ed, I say, and open the jeep door, church organ playing, I'm half running through the snow, Eddie behind me. I get to the path, floodlights, nobody around, in back of me Eddie says, "I swore I'd never come to this church again."

Me too, I say. Eddie's right behind me, we're at the big oak doors. "They're always wanting money," Eddie says.

I pull open one door, a wall of people, their backs to me, jammed together. I stand on my toes and look, mass hasn't started, but there isn't an inch of breathing room inside. Excuse me, I say, could I squeeze in here? Mean look from a tall young stud and his wife in new matching leather jackets. Organ starting up "O Come All Ye Faithful." I'd like to get in, I say, would you move so I can hear mass, please, somebody?

An old lady in a purple flowered hat looks at me, looks away. Nobody moving. I'm still holding the door open with one hand. Movement on the right, a gray-suited guy, big old Italian, head of hair like a monk's. Looks at me, looks past me to Eddie. He's an usher. I'm all of a sudden conscious that we're wearing old army jackets.

"Could you boys move in or move out?" the usher says. "But shut the door, please?"

Could you horn us in somewhere? I ask.

He gives us a long stare, looks past Eddie, then at me. "Does that vehicle belong to you?" he says.

Which one? I say.

"The one that happens to be parked on church property," he says.

No, I say, it's not mine, can't you get me in here, please, ask some of these people to move?

"Is that your vehicle, sir?" the usher asks Eddie.

"The jeep? Yeah," Eddie says.

"Would you remove it from its illegal parking spot, please?"

"There's nowhere to park," Eddie says. "Don't worry, it ain't hurting the snow any."

"Excuse me," the usher says to me. "I need to talk to this gentleman outside." I step back and let the door close. The usher, me, and Eddie on the stone steps in the snowstorm.

"Are you gentlemen parishioners here?" he asks us, arms folded across the stomach part of his gray suit. He looks from one of us to the other, no answer. "If you were," he says, "then you'd appreciate that this organization runs by the rules, and that the church property belongs to everyone."

"I know," Eddie says. "That's why I parked my jeep on it."

The usher's face sets. "Remove that vehicle," he says. Silence except for the organ inside. The usher and Eddie trying to stare each other down. The choir starts, *O come all ye faithful, joyful and triumphant* . . .

"Look, pal," Eddie says.

O come ye, O come ye, to Beh-eh-thlehem.

"I could call the police and have it removed," the usher says.

Come on, Ed, I say, they don't want us here.

Eddie takes a step toward the guy. "Look, bozo," he says, "I'll run that jeep up and down the main aisle if I want to."

"And you'll spend Christmas Eve in jail," the usher says, "both of you." He turns and opens the door, gives us a look, closes it.

"Let's get him," Eddie says.

Ed, I say, all I need is the cops. Let's get out of here, okay? I'll get to Annie some other time.

Eddie turns and limps down the stairs, I follow him to the jeep, knock some snow off my shoes, get in. Eddie revving the jeep engine high. "That bozo's going on the list," Eddie says. "Right near the top."

9

Psycho-Cybernetics

Two black guys ahead of us in an old blue Oldsmobile, both taillights busted, license plate missing, sparks flying as the muffler drags along the asphalt. For blocks the car's been swinging in and out of lanes, and now it spurts ahead with a cloud of black smoke, only to come to a screeching, clanging, sparking halt at the next traffic light. Carmine makes sure to stay well back from that Oldsmobile. "Look at them spades," he says to me. "Driving like they're in a circus."

I look down at my book. I've taken to reading a lot on these delivery runs with Carmine, but it's hard to focus on words when I'm bouncing in the seat of a JS&T truck. "What the hell do they even give them licenses for?" Carmine says. I try to ignore him and concentrate on my book, *Psycho-Cybernetics*. It's a self-help book written by Maxwell Maltz, a famous cosmetic surgeon. I'm just starting the chapter called "Do-It-Yourself Tranquilizers That Bring Peace of Mind." I'm reading this sentence for about the third time, it says, *Our own feelings do not depend on externals, but on our own attitudes, reactions, and responses.* Suddenly I pitch forward, put my hand up, it smacks the windshield, the book drops, Carmine's cursing, we're stopped just inches from the bumper of the Oldsmobile. Already horns are blowing in back of us. The Oldsmobile's door opens and the driver, tall and skinny in a brown plastic jacket, slips out, drops to one knee, starts looking under his car. Trucks and cars are whizzing past left and right. We're too close to steer around the Oldsmobile, so Carmine blows his horn. The black guy doesn't look up, he's on both knees now, studying the underside of his car. Carmine hits his head three times with the palm of his hand. "What do we got here," he says, "a spade garage?" He looks in the rearview mirror, a line of traffic in back of us, no chance to back up. So he rolls down the window, sticks his head out into the cold air, and shouts, "Hey, you're messing me up here."

Without even looking up, the black guy just waves him off.

Carmine gives the truck gas, high revs. "Look," he says to me. "Is that a bottle of wine sticking out of his pocket, or ain't it? Eleven in the morning, and they're drunk already." He's racing the engine, kicking down the gas pedal, letting up, kicking down, letting up. Car horns are blowing all over the highway now. "Hey," Carmine yells out the window. "Move that piece of shit. Or I'll move it for you."

The black guy gets up off his knees, carefully brushes his pants with both hands, takes two steps toward the truck. There *is* a big bottle of wine in his jacket pocket. "I was dragging something, man," the guy says to Carmine. "If you don't mind."

Carmine's shaking his head, he looks in the mirror, the traffic behind us has all gone around, he shoves the gearshift into reverse, backs up ten feet, slams the gears into first, zooms around the Oldsmobile, practically sideswipes the guy, his face goes right past my window.

"Check the load," Carmine yells at me, and runs the truck through the gears. I look back, my big job on this truck is to check the hundred and some boiler tubes chained and staked in the flatbed, to make sure they don't shift or move or slide off. I check the load real quick, then look for the Oldsmobile, I see the driver get in, the car jerk forward. Here they come, I say to Carmine.

"You think I'm afraid of a couple of drunk niggers?" he says. Then he checks the rearview mirror. A traffic light turns red in front of us, Carmine zooms through. But he has to stop at the next block, there's a traffic light at every intersection, and you can never make more than three or four greens in a row. This is the road that separates the two main parts of Newark, the Italian junkyards and the black slums. All around us are hundreds of low, lousy Newark houses, porches sagging, plywood over half the windows, alleys full of trash. I'm real glad when the light turns green, I give a glance over my shoulder, the Oldsmobile's in the left lane, way back there.

"Just don't hit them in the head," Carmine says. "That's all you got to remember about a nigger. Their heads are like a rock, that's how thick their skulls are."

I look back at the Oldsmobile, it's gaining.

"This town was something," Carmine says, and shifts a gear, "really something before the niggers moved in and ruined it. But once in a while, we get them back." He grins at me.

Maybe it'll just be an argument, I tell myself. I try to ignore everything, I don't want any fights with anybody. I'm trying to concentrate on this book. *The biggest secret of self-esteem, it says, is this: Begin to appreciate other people more; show respect for any human being merely because he is a child of God and a thing of value.* I look at Carmine, there must be exceptions to the rule. He's driving for the fourth light in a row, doesn't make it, we screech to a stop, I hear the boiler tubes sliding in back of us, boom, they hit the cab, my ears ringing.

"I thought you chained them things tight," he says.

I didn't know we were going to run the Newark Grand Prix, I say.

He shakes his head at me, then looks in the mirror. "Uh-oh," he says, "here comes the spademobile."

I turn around and see the blue Oldsmobile coming fast, my stomach cramps up, my crotch tingles, feelings I last had in Vietnam. The light in front of us turns green and Carmine moves out, heavy on the gas. The Oldsmobile gains on us, it's near our tail, pulling up on the left, the bald-headed young guy in the passenger seat rolls down his window, makes a motion with his hand, he wants us to pull over.

"Yeah, sure," says Carmine. He floors the gas pedal. "Right in the middle of spadetown."

The Oldsmobile rocks back on its springs, a roar comes from under the hood and the car cuts in front of us. Carmine stands on the brakes, boiler tubes bang the cab. He whips the wheel left, rams the gearshift into second, powers around the Oldsmobile, swings into the right lane. The Olds, tires squealing, roars up from behind, makes a run like it's going to ram us, then cuts in front of us again. Carmine turns left hard, we go over on two wheels, thump down again, slam to a stop, my hands braced on the dashboard, we've clipped the Olds on the back fender. Both guys are out of the car at once, Carmine grabs the door handle. "Come on," he says.

No, I shout. Get out of here.

He gives me a split-second look of disgust, shoves the gearshift into reverse, backs up hard, one black guy coming for each door. We're going backward, losing them, Carmine slams the truck to a stop, rams the gearshift into first, we're going toward the two guys, Carmine aiming at them, the bald guy dives to the right, the skinny guy steps to the left, then leaps as we go past, he's on the running board, holding on to the mirror, he's got a knife. Carmine swerves hard, the guy swings on the mirror, knife clacks against the window, falls, Carmine swerves again, the guy jumps off, lands running, falls on his hands right on the yellow line. Carmine zooming through the gears, I realize there's been a series of metallic bongs, boiler tubes sliding off the truck bed in twos and threes, then I'm watching helpless as the whole load slides off, a big roar, twenty-footers rolling all over the road, stopping traffic in back of us, then from a side street red flashing lights, Newark police.

"Great," says Carmine, "just what I fucking need." He stops the truck in the right lane, the cop car pulls up behind us. Just one guy in there and he gets out, a big bull of a black guy, he puts his cap on, holsters his nightstick. I've got my hand on the doorknob, I'm thinking nothing but jail.

"Have you got trouble with your hearing?" the cop says when Carmine rolls down the window. "Or is it your eyesight? License and registration."

I look back for the Oldsmobile, it's nowhere I can see, just traffic all backed up, nothing passing us, cars trying to find a way around the mess of boiler tubes splayed across four lanes. Some drivers are getting out to kick them aside.

"Weren't you aware," the cop says as he writes Carmine's name and numbers into a notebook, "that you were spilling your load all over the highway?"

"Yes, sir, I was, sir," Carmine says.

"Any particular reason you didn't stop?" the cop asks.

"Yes, sir," Carmine says. "We were riding along minding our own business when this car cut us off, a big blue Oldsmobile. Then when we pulled up at that light back there, the driver pulled a gun."

"Oh," the cop says. All I can see is his face, perfectly shaved, framed by the window.

"Ain't that right, Hollaran?" Carmine says.

I don't make any answer at all.

"Cat got your tongue, there, Mister Helper?" the cop says. "Did either of you happen to notice the license number of this purported gunman?"

Carmine shakes his head. I shrug.

"Did this purported gunman fire any shots in your direction?" the cop asks.

"Two," Carmine says. "But he missed."

"My, you *are* lucky," the cop says. "And I suppose it was this alleged assault that caused you to speed, drive recklessly, and fail to maintain control of your load."

"Yes, sir," Carmine says, "that's right."

The cop gets out his ticket book. "So you admit to speeding, driving recklessly, and failing to maintain control of your load."

"Hey, wait a minute," Carmine says. "You're not going to give me a ticket."

The cop just looks at him, and starts printing in the ticket book.

"Hey, buddy," Carmine says. "My company don't pay my tickets. That's going to come right out of my pocket."

"I would strongly suggest," the cop says, "that you refrain from calling me 'buddy.' "

"Why don't you look for those two guys in the Oldsmobile who shot at us?" Carmine says.

"Oh, now there were two gunmen?" the cop says, and smiles.

Carmine just looks at me. "Ain't this hot shit," he says. "Newark police."

The cop backs away, his hand goes to his nightstick. "Step out of the cab," he says, "you and your partner."

Shit, Carmine, I say under my breath. I get out, walk around the front of the truck.

"Now I want the two of you," the cop says, "to put your hands on the hood and lean, all right?" I'm leaning, hands on the hood, Carmine next to me. "Now, if either of you moves or talks, I'm going to summon some of my co-workers. And they're not all gentlemen. Do you understand?" No answer from either of us. "Good, I knew you would," the cop says.

The cop slowly, methodically writes out the ticket, looking up at us every few seconds. Cars have gotten past the boiler-tube logjam somehow, they're whizzing by, the occupants looking. I'm actually praying that the cop won't ask for my ID, won't check it on the radio, won't find there's a warrant for my arrest. I keep my eyes off the cop now, stare directly at the dull red paint on the hood of this truck, saying every prayer I can drag up from my childhood.

"Lift your hand precisely one quarter of an inch," the cop says to Carmine, and when Carmine obeys, the cop slips the ticket between hand and hood. "Careless driving," he says, "I let you off easy."

"Now can I talk?" Carmine says.

"Certainly," says the cop. "But watch your manners."

"Look here," says Carmine, and points down to the truck's bumper, it's pushed in at one corner, the red paint streaked with blue. "See?" Carmine says. "I'm telling you the truth about that blue Oldsmobile. But nobody's going to believe me now. And my company fires anybody who gets into an accident. I'm going to have to get this bumper fixed myself, before my boss sees it."

"That sounds like a personal problem to me," the cop says. Carmine just tightens his lips and shakes his head.

"Now I'm going to tell you a story," the cop says. "Once upon a time, there was a police officer in Newark. And this officer could have caused a lot of trouble for a certain truck driver and his helper. But the police officer refrained from causing that trouble. And do you know why? Because that police officer did not want to stand out in the cold, directing traffic while a city road crew took all day to pick up a load of pipes. So this is what happened. The police officer sat in his car with the dome light flashing, keeping traffic away. Meanwhile, the driver and his helper quickly picked up the pipes they had so thoughtlessly spilled on a public roadway. Now, that's a gentlemanly way to end a story, don't you agree?"

Yes, I say. I'm nodding. Carmine doesn't answer.

"May I suggest," the cop says, "that we begin?"

Five hours later my muscles are still aching, arms, shoulders, legs, everything aching as I plop my laundry bag down at the Coin-O-Rama. My head hurts, too, from listening to Carmine all afternoon, about how he was going to get the ticket fixed, and how he had that cop's badge number, and how he'd pay that cop back if it took the rest of his life, and how there was trouble coming in Newark someday, when the white people would stand up and fight back. There was no sense in arguing with him, really.

I've got two bottles of Rolling Rock with me, and a cheeseburger from Jersey Joe's Drive Inn, and my copy of *Psycho-Cybernetics*. I put it all down on a yellow plastic chair, get out a quarter and a dime, buy a little box of Cheer from a vending machine. Near the machine there's an old lady, kerchief over dirty white hair, a grayish mustache, she's wrapped in a soiled, buttonless black cloth coat. She gives me a hostile look, like I'm barging into her private Laundromat.

It's quarter to six, dark out already, she's the only other person in the place.

I open one of the big front-loading automatics, fill it with damp, foul-smelling uniforms, underwear, socks, blue jeans, I'm doing my stuff and a little of Eddie's. I've been coming here to Wolpenheimer's Laundromat for a couple of weeks now, my original idea was to confront him right on his own territory. I wanted to show him that I'm not just some clown who got suckered into going to Vietnam and leaving his wife alone. I wanted to show him that I'm a real live person, and that he took advantage of a situation where I was helpless, and Sandra was vulnerable. I wanted to push my finger right in his face and tell him that he's a weak lousy fat whoremonger, and that the only way he can get a girl is by waving money at her. But now I don't know, he never seems to be around, no matter what time I come, and all I end up doing is giving him my money.

I put two quarters in the coin slide, dump the Cheer into the soap vent, select hot wash, hot rinse, at least that will drive up his electric bill. Of course, I've already dealt with the idea that he might call the cops the minute he sees me, but it's a chance I'll have to take. And anyway, Wolpenheimer might not even recognize me, at least not until I begin telling him off, I mean he's never seen me in a good light, he'd probably walk right past me on the street.

I slide in the two quarters, get no movement, no sound, nothing. I jiggle the coin slide, still nothing. Shit, I say. Come on. Kick the washer, bang the coin slide, come on, you bastard, nothing. Hey, I shout. I bring my foot up and ram the washer door, jam the coin slide in, pound it, nothing, cursing, defeat. I throw open the door and dig out my clothes, slap them to the floor, kick them, pick them back up again, put them in another machine, slam the door, two more quarters. I go over cursing for another box of Cheer. The old lady says, "Watch out for that dryer, too." She points. "Number four," she says. "I lost twenty-five cents in there." She's shaking her head. "The guy who owns this place is getting rich off me," she says.

I know the feeling, lady, I say.

I walk back and dump in the Cheer, this washer works. I sit down and pick up my book, open one beer, unwrap my cheeseburger, the cheese is like a wad of half-dried yellow glue, I take a bite, disgusting, I chew it anyway. I'm reading, trying to ignore the taste in my mouth, this lousy Laundromat, the dirty old lady, everything. This chapter's called "How to Remove Emotional Scars or How to Give Yourself an Emotional Facelift."

Many people have emotional scars, the doctor writes, *who have never suffered physical injuries. And the result on the personality is the same.* How can I concentrate in here? It's the old lady, complaining to some imaginary audience, something about the dryer not putting out enough heat.

Back to the reading. The doctor's prescription for people like me is thought control. Hell, if I *could* control my thoughts, I wouldn't be in the shape I'm in today, always stewing about Hoover and helicopters and Carmine and the warehouse and John Johnson and my old man and Wolpenheimer and Sandra and everybody. I look at the back of the book, there's a picture of the author, smiling, he looks like the nicest man in the world. A renowned doctor and certainly a millionaire. I wonder if he ever imagines people reading his book? I wonder if he can imagine it in the hands of a guy in greasy clothes in a Laundromat in New Jersey.

"Have you got a quarter for two dimes and a nickel?" It's the old lady, standing in front of me, two graying bras draped over her arm. No, I shake my head. I've only got enough change for myself right now, I say. I go back to my book, hear her shuffle off.

Let's see, where was I? Here, a subchapter called "Forgive Yourself as Well as Others." I read, *Not only do we incur emotional wounds from others, most of us inflict them upon ourselves. We beat ourselves over the head with self-condemnation, remorse, and regret.*

We beat ourselves down with self-doubt. We cut ourselves up with excessive guilt. Remorse and regret are attempts to live emotionally in the past.

How well I know it, Doctor. Because of how much time I spend in the past. Trying to relive it. And do it right this time. There are lots of days I wish I could live over, and I remember one especially, it was the last time I could call Sandra my wife. That was in Monterey, California, just south of Fort Ord. Sandra had come all the way across the country just for a weekend. At a seaside motel with an old, cracked pool.

Why Sandra came out there was kind of a puzzle to me, at first. Because I was in my fifth week of infantry school, and if she had waited three more weeks, I would have been home on leave, airfare paid by the army. But I didn't ask too many questions at the time. Because after weeks of marching and machine-gun drills and life with thirty grubby guys, just the thought of Sandra made me feel warm and wanted. Even the sight of her handwriting on a letter could make me horny.

But they didn't give out weekend passes at infantry school, that was the problem. Maybe they were afraid we'd be reminded of normal life too much. Anyway, I had to go AWOL. It was as easy as taking a bus downtown.

We made love practically at first sight, on one of the narrow single beds, ocean sounds coming in the open screen door. After two hours naked we decided to get dressed. Sandra went into the closet and came out with civilian clothes for me, and when we were dressed we looked almost alike, in blue jeans and tie-dyed shirts. Except that my army-stubble haircut gave away that I was a soldier.

We walked out to this pier they have in Monterey, and ate dinner at a fish-and-chips place. We sat in the loft and the guy raised the dinners to us in a basket attached to a rope. We thought that was funny and romantic. From up in that loft we could see the crescent of Monterey Bay, and out on the rocks, seals lying in the late afternoon sun. For a while there I forgot about being AWOL. In fact I forgot the army entirely. And fooled myself into thinking I was a tourist in California.

We were like honeymooners all weekend. Slept with our arms around each other in one of the single beds. Talked about friends, neighbors, and family like we hadn't seen one another in years. On Saturday morning we didn't come out of the room until almost two, then took a walk down Cannery Row. Which, I should have known, is lined with trinket shops and T-shirt stands. I bought her a sweatshirt that said CALIFORNIA GIRL. She bought me a brass peace symbol on a leather cord.

We didn't argue at all until Sunday afternoon. In the pool, nobody but us there. I was sitting on the steps at the children's end, up to my waist in green water, facing the sun and the sea. Sandra swam laps and then floated over toward me.

What are you looking so sad about? she said.

I just kind of smiled and shrugged. Nothing, I said. Actually, I had been thinking about what was out there, across the ocean, past the blue curve of the Earth. For just a moment there I was facing the future, and it scared me. A lot. I remember thinking over and over, Maybe they'll make me a supply clerk, maybe I'll somehow end up a cook.

I hope you're not thinking about going back already, Sandra said.

I have to, I said. I've got guard duty.

When? she asked. Anger in her voice.

Tonight, I said.

Why didn't you tell me? she said.

I didn't want to spoil it, I said.

She stood up in front of me. A flowered bikini, thin but strong arms and legs, red hair dripping water onto her shoulders, she blocked out the sun.

What do you have to guard? she said.

I don't know, I said, whatever they tell me to guard.

That's ridiculous, she said. She was looking down at me, her face got hard, her eyes got narrow and mean. I flew all the way out here, she said. And now you're going to make me spend Sunday night alone in this motel? With you a few miles up the road?

I don't like it either, I said.

But you're already AWOL, she said. What's the difference?

You don't understand, I said. Missing guard duty is differ-

ent. You could go to the stockade for that. As it is, they're
going to fine me a month's pay and put me on two weeks KP.
And, Sandra, I really don't want to stand out too much, if you
know what I mean. Because if you make trouble, they put
your name right on the list for Vietnam.

She walked past me, splashing up the concrete steps, and
out of the pool. Stood there at the edge, and when I turned
around to look she had her hand held out toward me. I've got
something to show you, she said, give me your hand. She led
me away from the pool.

We got inside the room and Sandra closed the drapes, sat
me down on the bed, everything was in gray shadow, or
seemed that way after all that sunlight. You just sit right
there, Sandra said. And went to the closet.

She came back with a suitcase, opened it on the bed in
front of me. It was packed tight with clothes, hers and mine.
Sandra dug under them, came up with her cosmetic case,
unzipped it, put something in my hand, money. A bundle of
it. I held it in my lap and riffed through it. All twenties. My
first thought was that Sandra had stolen from her own bank.

I've got the bus schedule to Vancouver, Sandra said. And
here's two tickets.

Where did you get this money? I asked her.

Are we going, Tom? she asked. I want to know.

First tell me where you got this money, I said.

I forged your signature, she said. I sold the Camaro.

Grind of the machine changing cycles and I realize
where I am, how long ago that all happened. What can I do
about any of it now? I look down at the book and keep
reading.

"Give Up Grudges (Like) You Would a Gangrenous
Arm," that's the title of another subchapter. Forgive and
forget, you'll be better for it. I'm really starting to wonder
about this book. Flip past a couple of chapters to "Ingredients
of the Success-type Personality and How to Acquire Them."
In this chapter, the doctor gives his formula for being a suc-
cessful person.

S-ense of direction
U-nderstanding
C-ourage
C-harity
E-steem
S-elf-confidence
S-elf-acceptance

I guess that leaves me out on pretty much every count. I close the book, open my last Rolling Rock. Just staring at my clothes in the washer and I realize there's something wrong, the laundry's going around but there's no water. I jump up, yank open the washer door, buzzer goes off, rinse cycle, clothes still smelly and dry and dusted with Cheer, Jesus Christ! Why do I come here? Why do I do this to myself? This lousy dump, cigarette butts all over the floor, smells like bleach and vomit, half the machines leak, the other half don't work, dregs of the city in here, walls plastered with rules and regulations, plastic furniture cut with knives and burnt with cigarettes, I've lost a buck and my clothes are still dirty, what am I doing here? Wolpenheimer. Fuck Wolpenheimer! I kick his machine, kick it, kick it, kick it, damn it all, foot hurts now, I rip the clothes out of that machine, jam them into the next one, if this doesn't work I'm going to throw something right through that big front window.

I search my pockets, only one quarter left, I kick the washer door closed, need another quarter, call out to the old lady, have you got change of a dollar?

"My last quarter went into the dryer," she says. "I'm on Social Security, you know."

I run out the door, past a hairdresser's, jump a mound of bulldozed snow, dark icy parking lot, slip, fight for balance, run into the fluorescent-lit Big Bargain, push through the turnstile, make a semicircle, get in line behind a lady in pink stretch pants, express checkout, I'm huffing. On the conveyor belt the lady puts Toasty Hashbrowns, a carton of Benson & Hedges, an eight-pack of Diet Pepsi, two pillow-size bags of Big Bargain Brand Imitation Potato Chips. A cigarette stuck between her bright pink lips, ass as wide as the checkout lane, the lady talks to the girlish cashier like they were old friends. "They're still coming in," she says. A long ash falls from her cigarette and lands on the big slope of her blouse. "Must have been a terrible Christmas," she says. "Nobody got what they wanted." Her whole body shudders with a smoker's cough, but the cigarette stays in her mouth. "Twenty-two years I've worked down there, and this is the worst I've seen it," she says. The cashier's busy bagging the purchase, making change, she forces a brief sour smile as she hands the lady the bag. "Bye, dear," the lady says, and waves.

The cashier doesn't answer but turns to me, black eyebrows plucked to the width of a thread, black hair weighted down with hair spray, she's a serious gumchewer. Can I have change for a dollar? I ask.

"For the cigarette machine?" she asks.

No, I say, for the Laundromat.

"Sorry, sir," she says. "We don't give change for the Laundromat." Her mouth moving with the wad of gum, she's already looking past me.

Okay, I say, it's for cigarettes.

"I'm sorry, sir," she says, "but you have to make a purchase." I have a split-second fantasy, my hands squeezing her skinny neck. "Sir, these people are waiting to check out."

I look around the cash register, there are razors, *TV Guide*s, a big display of the latest filter cigarette, *National Enquirer*s, butterscotch candies, gum. What kind of gum do you use? I ask.

"Me, sir?" the cashier asks. "Are you talking to me?"

I hand her a dollar, pick up a pack of Wrigley's Doublemint, get three quarters dumped into the palm of my hand. I flip her the pack of gum. Here, I say, chew on it.

I run back toward the Laundromat, don't want to leave clothes for long, they'll steal anything in a neighborhood like this. Inside, I drop in the two quarters, give the coin slide a shove, a little green light goes on, I wait, the sound of water gushing. I sit down, might as well skim the rest of the book, go to the index, look up the subject of forgiveness. All of a sudden a blast of cold air makes me shudder, the front door's open, a vacuum cleaner being pushed through, a fat man behind it, Wolpenheimer! I cover my face with the book. Sneak a look around the side. The bastard in a felt hat, little red feather stuck in the band, tweed overcoat down to his fat knees. He gives a disgusted look around, shoves the vacuum cleaner toward the back. Takes his overcoat off, folds it, brushes one of the folding tables clean, lays his coat down, pats it, unbuttons his suit jacket. New clothes, the bastard didn't miss a beat.

"Are you the owner?" It's the old lady, coming out of a chair at Wolpenheimer.

"Yes, lady," he says. Big deep voice.

"Well, I want you to know," the old lady says, "I lost two dollars in your dryers this afternoon."

"Two dollars?" Wolpenheimer says. He looks, there's only one dryer busy, just a few garments tossing around in there. "Is that your load, lady?"

"Yes," she says. "I'm on Social Security."

"Lady," Wolpenheimer says, "how could you possibly have lost two dollars on a load that small?"

"I put two dollars in there," she says. "Don't you tell me I didn't, young man. Two dollars and got nothing out of it. Right there, number four, see for yourself. It doesn't work." She goes over to number four, clicks the control knob, keeps clicking it. "See?" she says.

Wolpenheimer is laughing. "Lady," he says, "you lost a quarter in number four, I'll give you your quarter back."

"No," she says, "I put two dollars in there."

Wolpenheimer breathes out hard. I've lowered my book, I'm just staring now, I hear faintly the noise of helicopters.

"Lady, don't try to fool me," Wolpenheimer says. He looks around the place, sees me. Raises his eyeballs as if I should sympathize with him, then turns to the lady and says, "It's not possible. Why would you put in one quarter after another?"

I feel a wave of heat go through me, he hasn't recognized me at all, still it's everything I can do to sit here and keep from zooming out the door. I'm holding on to the seat of my chair with both hands, my jaw clamped shut. The old lady's yelling at him now. "I'm going to report you to the Better Business Borough," she says. Wolpenheimer's walking away from her, coming toward me, the noise of helicopters getting louder in my brain.

"Nothing, lady," Wolpenheimer's saying over his shoulder. "You yell at me, nothing." He comes by me, bends over, picks an empty detergent box up off the floor, "Slobs," he says, to nobody in particular. I've locked my leg muscles, I could kick him right in the face now, I command my legs to stay still. Wolpenheimer throws the detergent box into the garbage can next to me. I start to talk, I'm so tight inside the words are just squeaking out, I stop talking, squirm in the chair, take a breath, Wolpenheimer staring at me. "Did you say something?" he says.

Another deep breath. "You shortchanged me," I say. "Your machine."

He breathes out hard, like the whole world is nothing but frustration. "Washer?" he says. "Which one?"

I panic, jump up, it's like a helicopter's hovering right over me, light, noise, Wolpenheimer just staring, I circle him, my fists up, come in at him. "Hey! Hey! Hey!" he's saying, he takes a step backward, another one, bangs into the pay phone, hands up in front of his face, "What's the matter with you?" Backing up, still backing up, he's near the door now, my fist going forward, my whole body going forward, fist bounces off his palms, deflected, I ram him with my shoulder, he goes backward into a dryer, my fist hard in his stomach, a sound like he's going to puke, he falls into a chair, it cracks, tips, he's on the floor, holding his stomach, no more noise of helicopters, I'm standing over him, breathing like a maniac, I see the old lady looking over the next row of washers. "Hit him again," she says, "kick him."

Wolpenheimer making dry-heave sounds from deep inside his stomach. It just begins to occur to me, very strange, I'm in a Laundromat, Wolpenheimer is on the floor, somebody must have hit him, me. I grab my laundry bag, fling open the washer door, scoop out wet sudsy clothes, run for the door, I look behind me, a trail of wet socks and underwear, my copy of *Psycho-Cybernetics*.

10

A Room Full of Bozos

"Would you care to see the wine list, sir?" It's the waiter, black tie for the evening, addressing Eddie and bowing just slightly. Eddie seems to think for a moment, then says, "Why don't you just tell me what kinds you got?"

I break in and tell the waiter, please, bring the wine list, thank you.

"What kind of fancy joint is this anyhow?" Eddie says. He's sitting in a white antique chair directly across the table from me. "One guy greets you, another guy sits you down, another guy comes over and asks you about wine, I ain't used to this."

I don't say anything. I just smile at Annie, my cool smile, my isn't-Eddie-a-riot smile. The candlelight makes the smooth skin of her shoulders and neck seem summer tan. She's in a green dress, her hair's been put up, tiny earrings reflecting gold light. I realize I'm staring. I tell her, I'm going to order champagne again. But not so much of it. She just grins. Coming from the ballroom downstairs there's Big Band music, very faint.

I look over at Laura, she's got her hand on Eddie's arm. "I'm very impressed, Edward," she says. "You're full of surprises. I didn't think I'd ever see you in such a nice suit."

"Yeah," Sadowski says, and shoots me a look, eyes hard with resentment. "Me neither." Only the socks and underwear are Eddie's. The blue pinstripe suit, powder blue shirt, dark tie, and wing-tip shoes are all mine, a legacy of my salesman days. "You both look very nice," Laura says. "Real gentlemen." She smiles at Eddie. He starts tugging at the knot of his tie, her smile disappears. "Ed, stop that," she says. "You've been pulling at that ever since we sat down."

"I'm choking," Eddie says.

"If you were choking," Laura says, "you wouldn't be able to talk."

Eddie gives me his now-you-see-what-I've-got-to-put-up-with look, just as the waiter puts the wine list in his hands. It's red leather, held together by a white tassel, and in gold script it says *The Brass Door*. Eddie's got it open, Polack eyes roaming up and down the page. "They got all kinds of wine in this joint," Eddie says. "It could keep a Frenchman soused for months." He pokes the wine list between the candle-sticks. "Here, Hollaran, you figure it out."

I turn right to the champagnes, pick the best I can afford. Moët, I say, and close the book. Is that all right? I look around the table.

"Let me see that again," Eddie says, and I hand him the wine list. I know he's going to look at it for price. "How do you spell that?" he says. I tell him, and when he finds the price he whistles. "Hey," he says, "you're kidding! That's some grape juice."

I give Annie a quick smile. Ed, I say, it's imported champagne.

"How many oceans did it have to cross?" Eddie says.

I smile like I used to when I was a salesman, the same tight, hard, unnatural feel of the face muscles. Ed, I say, we'll discuss it later, okay?

"How many glasses you get out of one of those bottles?" he says.

Ed, I say, it comes once a year. Loosen up. Relax.

"Even if we got thirty-six glasses," he says, "that'd still be a buck a glass." He looks over the wine list again. "How about this? Almaden Mountain Chabliss. Nine-fifty, a better buy."

Ed, I say, my voice rising. Champagne, okay? I want it. I'll pay for the bottle myself, all right?

"That ain't the point," Eddie says.

Then what the hell is? I say.

"Would you excuse me?" Annie says, and stands up. "Laura, I'm going to the ladies' room, do you want to come?" Laura grabs her pocketbook from under her chair, gets up. I watch Annie walk away, a full-length dress, bare shoulders, a natural rhythm to her. She and Laura are past three rows of crowded tables before I'll say anything.

Thanks, pal, I tell Eddie. You showed no class at all, zero. I wouldn't blame her if she played sick and asked to go home.

"Good," Eddie says. "We don't belong here anyway, dressed up like educated apes, the whole room full of bozos. And why? So you can impress this one good-looking bimbo and get in her pants, that's why."

Ed, I say, listen. I want things to go right tonight between me and Annie. It's New Year's Eve, time to get off to a new start, and you're right, I want to impress her. I don't even know why she agreed to this date, maybe she just wanted something to do tonight. But I want to make up for babbling like a crazy man the night we met, and this is my chance. Okay? Now let's act civilized.

"I can tell right now," Eddie says, "this bimbo is going to lead you right to bozoland. You really like this shit, don't you? Champagne and all, guys running around taking your orders."

Ed, I say, where did we spend last New Year's Eve?

"Last year?" he says. "At my house drinking beer. Why?"

And who was with us? I say.

"Nobody, just us two."

Right, I say. And what happened New Year's Day?

"Nothing," he says. "We just got up and puked our brains out and went down to the White Castle."

So isn't this better? I say.

"No," he says. "Look around you, look at them all, it's enough to turn your stomach."

Forget the bozos for one night, I say. We're here to eat and drink and have a good time.

"Yeah," Eddie says. "This is what was going on the whole time we was over there, Tom. They was drinking champagne and eating oysters Rockefeller and dancing the tango and all, and nobody gave a damn what we were doing. They were having too good a time being bozos."

I know that, Ed, I say. But what can I do about it now?

"What can you do about the bozos?" he says. "Plenty. Give me another couple of weeks, you'll see." He pulls out a Winston and a kitchen match, sticks the cigarette in his mouth, a busboy comes running over, holds a plastic lighter out, flicks it, flame, Eddie draws his head back, looks at the kid, looks at the flame, finally allows the light to take hold, sucks in. The busboy leaves, Eddie lets out smoke. He smiles, the smile widens to a grin, all his crooked teeth show. "That's something," he says. He looks around, sees the busboy lighting another diner's cigarette two tables away. He shakes his head like he can't get over it. "That's luxury," he says, "I never seen nothing like it in my life."

I look over and see Annie and Laura just coming out of the ladies' room, Eddie sees them too, his look changes, he's serious and confidential now. "I found out something from Laura," he says. "She likes you."

Laura? I say.

"Annie," he says, trying not to move his lips.

"Don't stop talking just because we're here," Laura says. I watch Annie sit down, I feel a new kind of excitement. Possibilities. "Ed," I hear Laura say, "must you?"

"Yeah, I must," Eddie says.

"I can't tell you," Laura says, "how many smokers I've seen wheeled into the OR."

"Yes, you can," Eddie says, "you done it plenty of times already."

Laura grimaces. "You're incorrigible."

"Thank you," Eddie says.

"What were you talking about?" Laura says. "Women? Were you discussing us, Ed?"

"Bozos," he says. "We were discussing the problem of bozos in modern society."

"Bozos?" Annie says. "Clowns?"

"Sorta," Eddie says.

"Edward has this theory," Laura starts, but she's cut off by Eddie.

"It ain't no theory," he says. "It's facts. Bozos are people who just care about themselves."

"Well, isn't that everybody?" says Annie. "People have got to take care of themselves first."

"Yeah, but a bozo, he takes advantage," Eddie says, "he acts like there ain't nobody else."

"Edward's theory," says Laura, "and it's only a theory"—she looks at Eddie, puts her hand over and rubs the arm of his suit coat—"well, it has to do with—"

Eddie cuts her off. "With who gets stuck with the dirty work," he says. Talking just to Annie. "Like at the hospital. Laura told me all about that place. I'll tell you, if it was up to me, I wouldn't pay them doctors nothing. They're learning how to get rich off people's troubles, right? So why not make them work for free now? And pay good money to the nurses and all, and them old bimbos that mop up the blood and guts."

"I'm starting to like your theory, Ed," Annie says.

"Don't," Laura says, and holds both hands up. "Don't encourage him, please."

A silver ice bucket appears on Eddie's left. "Did you order champagne?" Laura says.

While you were all talking, I say.

"Delightful," she says. The waiter's showing the label around, Eddie deliberately looks away from it. There's a pop, pale bubbly wine flowing into four chilled glasses on the table. Eddie leans over and sticks his nose practically into his glass, gives a long suspicious sniff. "I'll tell you what, chief," he says to the waiter, "you got any Schaeffer's back there?"

"Certainly, sir," the waiter says. "One bottle?"

"Yeah," Eddie says. "And a clean glass."

The waiter turns for the kitchen and Laura picks her champagne glass up, using three correct fingers. She takes a delicate sip and says, "Well, this is very nice, isn't it?" Eddie raises his eyes in exasperation. "Shall we have a toast?" she says. "To whatever we'd like the New Year to bring us. Tom?"

I pick up my glass and say, To a lot of forgetting. To new and better things for everybody. Of course, I mean that specifically for Annie, but I avoid looking into her eyes.

"I'd like it," Laura says, "if Ed were to go back to school after the New Year." Eddie's face turns bright hot red, and he opens his mouth to protest, but Laura speaks first. "Annie?" she says.

"Oh," Annie says, and flushes a little. "I don't know. I think I'd like to go somewhere."

Where? I ask.

"Just somewhere different," she says.

I'm staring right at her, I have to fight the urge to stand up, grab her by the wrist, and take her out of here, to somewhere different.

"What's wrong with New Jersey?" Eddie says.

"Nothing, Ed," she says. "It's just lately, things . . . I don't know," and she ends with a mysterious, sad little smile. Laura cuts right in, "Now, Ed, it's your turn."

Eddie looks around, sees the waiter coming with his beer, and says, "Hold on." The brown bottle and frosted glass are delivered, and Eddie unfolds his dinner napkin, uses it to wipe the glass free of frost. Then he pours the beer in, a big foamy head. He lifts the glass. "Down with the bozos," he says.

"Edward," Laura says, "be more civilized, please."

"This is the year they're finally going to get it," Eddie says.

"Get what?" Laura says.

"Everything they deserve," Eddie says. "All it will take is one guy to start it off. One guy with a mission. Then it'll spread everywhere, like a revolution."

"What are you talking about, Ed?" asks Annie.

"Getting back at the bozos," he says. "The retired generals, the tax accountants and lawyers, the doctors, the stockbrokers, the car repossessors, the bankers, the insurance salesmen, the foremen, the union bosses . . ."

"Ignore him," Laura says, "he's just prattling."

"What's wrong with insurance men?" Annie asks.

"They're the worst there is," Eddie says. "Ask Tom."

They *are* bozos, I say.

Annie looks from me to Eddie and back to me. "Why?" she asks.

"Because they take something from you and don't give nothing back. They make suckers out of you. We seen plenty of that, Tom and me. Over there."

"Over where?" Annie asks.

"They're talking about Vietnam," Laura says.

Can we please toast? I say. Before we get into an argument.

"No, wait," Annie says. "I don't understand, really. What do bozos and insurance men and Vietnam all have to do with each other?"

"Annie," Laura says, "believe me, they're not seriously blaming the war in Vietnam on insurance men."

"The hell we ain't," Eddie says.

"Edward!" Laura says.

"They're bozos, ain't they?" Eddie says. "Then they're to blame."

"Unfortunately," Laura says, "Ed has found it impossible to identify those who did promote the war, so his fantasies of retaliation . . ."

"They ain't no fantasies," Eddie says.

". . . have become focused on an entire class of individuals," Laura says.

When you come back from over there, I tell Annie, you feel used. The ultimate sucker. Why? Because you believed and risked your life and were a fool, for nothing, for a lie, for a sales pitch. When you realize that, you start to see it all around you, the lying, the using, the manipulation. And all the manipulators, the managers and insurance men and so forth, well, your first urge is to do *anything* to get back at them.

"Hear, hear," Eddie says. "A toast. A happy New Year and down with the bozos."

Down the hatch, I say, the whole glass now, everybody drink up or it's no good. We drink, all except Annie, who kind of halfway lifts her glass, then puts it down without sipping. Her face has sort of a hollow, sad look to it. Annie, don't you like that champagne? I say. Do you feel okay?

"What's the matter?" says Laura, and leans toward Annie a little, gives a nasty stare at Eddie, then me. "You're upset aren't you?"

Annie shakes her head yes. Laura shoots me the look of a stern schoolteacher. It's the kind of look that's supposed to tell me something, only I have no idea what.

Annie gets up from the table. "Excuse me, I'll just be a minute," she says, and turns, hurries off.

"Tom," Laura says, "if I were you I'd go after her."

I go around tables, tray stands, rushing waiters, I squeeze past chairs, follow Annie, almost running, through a wide doorway into a dark foyer, past the coat-check room, down stairs, she's a little clumsy going down them in high heels, I put my hand on her shoulder just as she reaches the big brass door. She won't turn her face toward me. Annie, I say. Nothing from her. The smooth sound of the swing band behind us, I know that tune. Annie, I say. "Please," she says, but doesn't look at me. She pushes through the brass door and I follow her out into the freezing air, out on the floodlit steps. Men in heavy overcoats, women in stoles getting out of Buicks and Chryslers right in front of us, parking valets in ski jackets running all over the lot. I put both hands on Annie's shoulders, cold goose bumps already perked up there. Tell me what's the matter, I say.

Her back still turned to me. "I'm just . . ." she says, and trails off. "I'm just in a bad mood," she says.

Why did you run away? I ask.

"I just get depressed sometimes," she says. I know that's not it. I let go of her shoulders, walk around her, down two steps, look in her face, there's anger. "I don't think it's right," she says all of a sudden.

What's not right? I ask.

"You and Eddie are up there putting down this guy and that guy . . ."

Eddie gets carried away sometimes, I say.

"You said it too," she says.

Said what? I ask.

"You were picking on people," she says. "Not everybody's what you think."

What are you talking about? I ask.

"My father worked for an insurance company," she says. "He was a manager, too. And he was a fine man, a good man, not some bozo."

Oh, I say. And breathe out. Angry at myself, my own stupidity. My own self-centeredness. Come on, I say, we'll both freeze out here.

"You don't have any *right* to sit up there making judgments," she says. "I know you were in Vietnam and I know it was rough and I'm sorry. But you don't even *know* the people you're calling bozos."

All I can feel is tight muscles across my face. I become aware that I'm nodding. Well, I say, if you want to go home now, I'll drive you.

All she does is kind of search me with her eyes.

Please, I say, come inside. I take her by the hand, with my other hand I grab the brass door. Come back, okay? I say.

The door closes and we're standing in the foyer, she's holding herself, rubbing her arms for warmth. I realize what's playing down in the ballroom, it's "Moonlight Serenade." Not exactly as smooth as Glenn Miller, but close enough. I reach out for Annie, just touch her cheek. I apologize, I say. And look square into the deep green of her eyes.

"I just lost my father," she says, and looks away.

I'm sorry, I say.

She shrugs her shoulders. "How were you supposed to know?" she says. We end up looking at each other again, the music playing. I say, you wouldn't want to dance or anything, would you?

The next day, early, Eddie's griping as we knock at the back door of Lucky Leo's. "You should have used your brains," Eddie's saying. We're both knocking loud at the same time. "No way two bimbos, roommates, are going to do something like that."

The door pushes open and there's Leo, smiling, sweating, a blue workman's bandanna tied around his thick neck. "Where were you boys last night?" he says.

"Mister Brilliant here," Eddie says as Leo holds the door open and we step in, "he had the idea of a double date that cost us seventy bucks each, and at the end of the night we didn't even get our noodles wet."

Leo laughs, his enormous stomach shakes under a thin, sweaty gray T-shirt.

"Leo, you're a man of the world," Eddie says. "You could have told him. You can't get laid after a double date, not when the bimbos live together."

Nothing out of Leo but a smile. He locks the door behind us. We walk up a stairway to the main barroom, empty of people and well lit for cleaning, stools overturned on top of the bar. Eddie and I each take a stool down, Leo pushes a big industrial vacuum cleaner out of the way, starts making our drinks.

"You should have seen this joint we went to," Eddie tells Leo. "All the way up in Summit, you ever been there?" Leo nods his head, drops a handful of ice in a glass. "Chandeliers hanging off the roof, enough silverware on the table to start a mint, they even had Puerto Ricans that come around to light your cigarettes. And bozos! I never seen so many in one goddamn place. A bomb dropped in there would have done a lot of justice, let me tell you."

Leo puts the whiskey and beer in front of me and starts talking to Eddie, but I'm losing the conversation. I take a tiny sip out of the shot glass, the whiskey goes down and makes me feel a little sick, no breakfast to cushion it. I'm having a little remorse this morning, but it has nothing to do with last night's champagne.

I wake up with these ideas sometimes, I really don't

know where they come from. Like this morning, I woke up in a panic. Still dark out. With the picture in my mind of Wolpenheimer, doubled up, moaning, holding his stomach in the Laundromat. But it wasn't the grown-up Wolpenheimer, it was a kid, a fat boy. Then, in a flash, I realized something very simple. That on the inside, Wolpenheimer the well-dressed businessman was a weakling. A fat boy. The kind of kid that gets picked on in every schoolyard.

Of course, as soon as I realized that, I knew I had done wrong, hitting Wolpenheimer. Even if he did deserve it. Because Wolpenheimer's not my worst enemy, that's for sure. And if he deserves it, what about Sandra, Carmine, John Johnson, Hoover? The list could go on and on. And it shows a lousy trait in me that I picked on the weakest. Because that's what being a bozo is all about.

I get hauled back to the conversation because Eddie punctuated his last sentence by banging his glass on the bar. "The whole country's lousy with them," Eddie says, and I see at a glance how frustrated, hung over, and horny he is. "You go to the hills, they're building ski lifts. Go to the shore for a little surf casting, they're putting up condos. Go out on the lake and they swamp you with their powerboats. They're everywhere. Making houses out of wallboard and cars out of plastic and clothes out of chemicals, and everybody dressed up in a three-piece suit, wanting to run the show."

"True," Leo says, "and getting truer all the time."

"How do you put up with it?" Eddie says.

"There's ways," Leo says.

"Well, Tom and me," Eddie says, "got a plan." He elbows me. "To get the bozos back for everything."

We? I say. *We* have a plan?

"Okay, it's my plan," Eddie says. "But you're in it. You got to be, you drank to it. Right here in this bar. What I want to see," he says, and takes a Winston out of his top pocket, "is the look on the face of the first bozo that gets it."

I want to talk to you seriously about this, Ed, I say.

"No backing out now," Eddie says. "I'm depending on you. Who's going to get the bozos if we don't?"

I look to Leo for help. He's smiling, like he doesn't take Eddie very seriously. But then Leo hasn't heard the pounding and banging and scraping and crackling coming from Eddie's basement every night.

"You boys wouldn't be human if you weren't angry," Leo says. "I know, because I got back myself in fifty-three. Of course, it was a little different, the Korean war. But it opened my eyes just the same. Because I came back from murder and mud and mayhem, and I saw that everybody here was just having a swell time."

Eddie just looks at me.

"Took me years to get over it," Leo says. He sips at this big drink he's made himself, a shaker glass with club soda and half a lime. "That's when I lived in your neighborhood. I was just hiding out. I didn't want anything to do with anybody. Except kids, like you boys were then. For years I could only bring myself to trust kids." A big drop of fat man's sweat rolls from his temple and all the way down his cheek. "Plus I ate. All junk food." He shakes his head. "What a loser. No job, no money, no girl, no friends, not an ounce of self-respect. He shrugs. "Hey," he says. "I'm going to fill you boys up." And he bends to make our drinks. Even that effort gets him sweating, he takes the bandanna from around his neck and mops his face. "Now I've got to go," he says, "I've got a lot of work to do in the back room."

"What?" Eddie says. "Something bust? You need a hand?"

"No," Leo says. "I've got plans."

"Oh ho," Eddie says, and looks at me. Leo walks out from around the bar, picks a big toolbox up from the floor, holds it out in front of his stomach, both hands. "Got to get busy," he says, and disappears into the back room.

Eddie's still looking at me. "Don't tell me Leo's getting to be a bozo, too," he says. "I can't take it no more."

11

Hole in the Wall

Full-moon night and what looks like a city up ahead is really the Bayway Refinery, pumping and burning and stinking, a red-orange glow surrounded by thousands of little white lights. Annie next to me, she's fallen asleep, her head against the window. Glare of headlights as a trailer truck passes, then a Greyhound, then a rattling empty car-carrier. Big green sign, ELIZABETH AND STATEN ISLAND 3 MI.

And right along here the runway of Newark Airport. There's the old terminal, I remember the dirty little waiting room inside there. I remember the day Sandra was standing beside me biting her lower lip. Me in my uniform. With one hand I was holding on to her waist, and in the other hand was a big brown envelope, my military file. Which I was to bring with me to Oakland and Vietnam.

Outside the waiting room windows a big white helicopter was warming up, blades moving slowly. They called for passengers over the loudspeaker, New York Airways, service to Kennedy. I held her, she would not cry. I kissed her and looked her in the eyes, and outside the noise of the helicopter picked up, roaring, I kept looking for something in Sandra's eyes and when I couldn't stand it anymore I kissed her again. As a way of breaking it off. I'll write you the minute I get there, I said. Don't worry, please? I touched her face. Goodbye, Tommy, she said. I kissed her and ran. Last call for the helicopter.

And when I got on there were only aisle seats left. From where I sat, next to a businessman, there was no way to catch even a glimpse of the waiting room, or Sandra. The engines started to howl, the helicopter lifted, and all of a sudden I was afraid.

I was trembling, actually, and the businessman next to me was staring. I tried to keep my face turned away from him. For something to do I opened the envelope, took out my file. Tried to concentrate on it. Anything. The first piece of paper was my AWOL punishment, an Article Fifteen, explaining my crime, the exact days and hours of it, and saying that I had pleaded guilty and so accepted the fine, the extra duty. Underneath that was my infantry school record, pages of it, claiming I was trained in machine gun, in map reading, in ambush technique, in fire-team tactics, in hand grenades, land mines, and the newest in plastic bazookas. Underneath that was basic training. I'd run the mile in 7:52, eight seconds under the absolute minimum. And did not distinguish myself in any area of combat competence. Marksmanship awards, none. Leadership qualities, blank.

Finally I could feel a change in how the helicopter was flying, and I looked up from my papers and tried to see out the window. We had crossed the Hudson and were landing on top of the Pan Am Building. Where the guy in the business suit got off, and a Marine sergeant got on, took his place. I kept my aisle seat. Slipped my records back in the envelope. Closed my eyes and pretended to sleep all the way in to Kennedy Airport.

Here's the exit and I put on my turn signal.

Annie's head moves, her body shifts in the seat. I pay the toll. I'm hoping, in a way, that she won't wake up until I get her home. So I don't really have to face her. Because I feel like this date's been a failure. It cost me fifty bucks, and at matinee prices, to find out she's not impressed by Broadway. Or at least she didn't seem it. Because all afternoon I had the feeling that Annie was being very polite, and trying hard to have a good time.

Drive out on the ramp and there's JS&T's control tower, lit up, on a Saturday night it must be cleaning people in there. Down the ramp and onto Bayway, into the city. Glare of orange streetlights. Red glow of tavern signs. I stop at a traffic light, Annie coming awake. Reaches for my arm. "Oh, almost home," she says.

The touch of her hand does something to me, even through layers of coat, suit jacket, and shirt. Makes me horny, but that turns right away into fear, sweat breaking out on my palms. Because the big moment's coming up when I'll have to walk her to the door. Don't think, Hollaran. Drive.

Down Bayway and through the circle in silence, turn on Washington Street, don't even look when I pass Boyle Place and the old homestead. Just drive. Red light, Washington and South. The lights on in Satriano's and it looks warm in there, dinnertime. Do I smell garlic, yeast, tomato sauce, or is it my memory?

"That place belongs to your family, doesn't it?" Annie says.

My grandfather started it in the thirties, I say. It was strictly a meatball-and-spaghetti joint until he retired. Then my uncle Anthony took it over.

"He must make good food," Annie says, "I've seen lines outside sometimes."

Well, there are only twelve tables, I say. Green light, I get the Volks moving again. But Anthony has a loyal following, I say, that's for sure.

"Interesting," Annie says, and turns her head to watch the place as we go by. "Maybe we should have gone there for dinner."

What? I think about the twenty-four bucks I shelled out for drinks and steak sandwiches in a Manhattan restaurant, doorman and everything.

Didn't you like that place? I ask.

"It was okay," she says.

Just okay? I say. I think about how short I'm going to be on gas and grocery money, I hope the anger doesn't show in my voice.

"No, it was fine, really," she says. I take a right on Pear
Street, maybe a little too fast, driving right for the big white
hospital.

"It's just New York restaurants in general," she says, and
stops talking, a reluctance there.

What about them? I say.

"Well, the food's not that great, usually, and the waiters
are rude and somehow I always feel out of place there."

Oh? I say. And shoot her a look.

"See, I've been there a lot," she says.

Oh, I say. I'm trying to stay cool. But for some reason I
feel jealous, excluded, possessive. A stupid feeling comes
over me, I'm angry that she went to New York with anyone
else, ever.

"You don't really want to hear this," she says, "but I had
this boyfriend, all through college and high school. His family
had a little money, and when he took me out it was New York,
New York, New York. Which, when I was a high school girl, I
was really impressed. But . . ." She doesn't finish.

Go ahead, I say. I pull up near the hospital gate. A high
fence built around the nurses' quarters.

"He treated me like a princess in a fairy tale," she says.
"But he wanted to control me too. What I did and who my
friends were, and even my thoughts sometimes. And he
wasn't very affectionate. So we broke up, after all those
years." A silence. Cold in this car but somehow I don't make a
move to get out. "The last time I saw him was at my father's
funeral," she says. "And he was very nice to me. I think he
half expected us to get back together. But Tom, I learned
something when my father died." She looks right into my
eyes. "That life can't be a fairy tale, no matter how hard we
want it to be."

I think I know what you mean, I say. I kiss her, we get out
of the car. I take her hand, we walk along the fence to the big
locked gate. She digs keys out of her little black purse.
"Would you like to come in for a cup of coffee?" she asks. For
some reason I notice her eyes. Something gentle in there,

windows of the soul, they say. Sure, I tell her, I could use a cup. She unlocks the gate.

Into a quadrangle of nurses' quarters, two-story brick barracks, lots of lights on in the windows. We get to her door, she puts her key in. Don't be afraid, Hollaran. How can I help it? She leads me into the apartment, it really looks more like a hallway, a wide one with sink, stove, counters, and cabinets running along the left. And almost blocking the right side is a Formica-top table, a sleeping body collapsed at it, Laura. Her long brown hair splayed over reading glasses and an open textbook. Annie, finger to her lips, asking for silence. She walks around the card table, puts one hand on a doorknob, holds the other hand out toward me, crooks her index finger twice.

We're in her bedroom, I shut the door quietly, Annie's busy hanging my coat and hers in the closet. I can't help but make a quick study while her back is turned, blond hair loose and straight brushing her shoulders, frilly white blouse, plain black skirt that doesn't even start to hide the roundness of her ass, pale stockings and all I want to do is strip them from her legs, stroke her legs, I imagine them, bare and smooth. "I'll go put on the coffee," she says, and bends a little to take off her shoes. "Sit down."

She's gone and I look around the room. Two chairs, a desk, a big bed, that's the basic furniture, with one whole wall a complex of closets and drawers and dressing tables. Two big windows, thick with burglar wire, look out on the courtyard. I sit in one of the chairs, gray Naugahyde, institutional modern. I can see why she wants to get out of here, it's only a little more than a dorm room, really, with the big white hospital looming a half block away. I unbutton my suit jacket. Hate these things, but sometimes you've got to wear them, maybe Eddie's right and I'm getting to be a bozo. My jacket's off, I'm loosening my tie when Annie walks in.

"A few minutes," she says quietly, and sits across from me, on the edge of her bed. "I could put on music," she says, "but we'd have to keep it really low. Laura's supposed to be studying her sociology, but I know she needs the sleep." She looks toward the door like she wants to be sure it's closed, and then says, "She's been hoping Eddie would call or come by."

He's been really weird this week, *really* weird, I say. He's all nerves. He called in sick at work and he's been down in the cellar day and night, the noise down there's been tremendous.

"He's not really sick or anything, is he?" she asks.

I smile, that's a nurse for you. No, I say, he's just got things on his mind.

"Oh," Annie says, and I see she's distracted, looking at her alarm clock. It's seven-forty now, she has to work at eleven. "I'm going to check the coffee," she says, and I'm alone again in the room.

I stand up, go to the windows, look out past the burglar wire, a definite feeling in this place of being enclosed. Brick barracks, white wall of the hospital, asphalt courtyard with just a few rows of hedges as an excuse for nature. I have to bend my head and twist my neck and look almost straight up to see the moon and stars.

Annie's hand on my arm, I must have been off in space there, staring at the moon. "It's going to be a few more minutes for that coffee," she says.

Oh, I say. And shrug, flap my arms. I can wait, I say. Her hand still on my arm, her lips coming for mine, soft, warm, I put my hands on her waist, I'm beginning to sweat, I can feel it.

"Tom," she says, and that's all, I kiss her for a long time, standing, my arms all the way around her, my hands stroking that hair, the warm soft feeling of her breasts pushed against me, she rubs me a little with the hard part of her pelvis, I can hardly breathe. Pull myself away a little. Coffee's going to scorch, I say.

"I turned it off," she says.

Tight feeling in my head, stomach tensing. You did? I say. That's all I can say.

"We can have it later," she says.

Well, I say, see, I . . .

"I'm on the pill," she says.

That wasn't the problem, I say, see, it's, well . . .

"Don't be afraid of me, Tom," she says.

I can't help it, I say. It's just, I don't know, I've been hurt.

"Tom," she says, "so has everybody."

I take a deep breath, put my arms around Annie, but I *feel* like it's Sandra. I kiss Annie to get it out of my mind. But what comes in is no better, a series of five-dollar business transactions with Can Tho whores, my .45 always loaded and an arm's reach away.

"Is there something the matter?" Annie asks. She backs away from me, puts her hand out, holds mine, brings me right to the edge of the bed. I'm falling somehow. In the bed, her lips warm and moist, my tongue in her mouth and she takes it, I smell flowers and herbs in her hair, my eyes shut tight, I seem to be sinking. My hand moves from her face to her neck and on to the frills of her blouse, down the front of one breast and then the other, undo a button, my hand still a little shaky. Buttons undone, blouse open, I run one finger up over the soft smooth contours of her face. Kiss her face, her lips, her mouth opens, tongues in and out, we're pressed together now, hard. I roll off, she lifts a little, I take off her blouse, snag the hooks of her bra, she reaches back and releases them, the bra drops away, first thing I do is kiss her breasts. She unbuttons my shirt, cuffs too, I help her by wriggling out of it. My hands at the zipper of her skirt now, she's on her back, lifts her hips off the bed a little, with both hands I'm taking down her stockings, underwear, loving the touch of smooth warm skin, down over thighs, knees, calves, feet, she's naked, I drop the tangle of clothing to the floor and take a long look. "Come here," she says, and holds out her arms to me, and I know I'm in for something sweet and gentle and good.

It's about eleven-fifteen when I kiss Annie at the main hospital entrance and watch her run, in whites, through the big revolving door and toward the elevator. And when she's gone, I feel more alone than ever, walking back to my Volkswagen. But not lonely, just alone. I drive away from the hospital, hardly watching the road, but looking in the rearview as the big white building fades block by block. I shiver, it feels colder and colder, someday I'm going to get around to fixing the heat in this car. Downtown now and Broad Street juts left, my last backward glimpse of the hospital. I know what I need, a cup of coffee.

I drive under the big stone railroad arch, bumping along, patches of this street worn down to cobblestones and trolley tracks. Past the low-rent stores, the newspaper building, the big post office, everything dark for the night. Pull up at the Union Street Diner, the only place there's any light or life. In for a cup of coffee and right out again.

Cardboard cup in my hand, I'm standing out on the street, taking deep breaths of cold air, sipping coffee, hot and burning and satisfying. I can't remember the last time I felt this good, a man worthwhile. I have an odd, tingly sensation, a feeling that the world is all right, a good place to be. Happy to be alive. I'm trying to enjoy it, taking deeper and deeper breaths of smoky New Jersey night air.

I feel stupid even thinking it, but in a way I miss Annie already, I wish I were telling her a story or making her a meal, or maybe just lying in bed next to her. But I want to be alone, too. To get things straight in my mind. Besides, I don't really know her. That's all I need, is to fall in love with Annie. Because the mess I got in with Sandra, it cost me my money and my sanity and almost my life. But Annie's not like Sandra at all, is she? I mean, I've been through a lot in the last few years and learned some things, haven't I? I'm smarter and a better judge of things. I think. Besides, women aren't all like Sandra, are they?

I spill the dregs of my coffee on the sidewalk, throw the cardboard cup in the gutter, get in my Volkswagen, start it up. Driving back toward Eddie's and somehow I've lost that feeling of joy. Past the hospital now and I don't want to look at it, or think about Annie. Worry. My brain in overdrive again, sweat on my palms, muscles tightening around my skull. And I don't know what's wrong except a feeling of disaster coming, very strong, I want to pull to the side of the

road, and stop just to breathe, I'm fighting myself just to keep
driving. Something terrible about to happen, what? I stop at
the light on Bayway, revving my engine all the time, the
impulse to just shoot through, drive until I'm out of gas, then
run until I fall from exhaustion. Running from what, Hollaran? Breathe deep, says Doctor Rhinehart. Let it come
upon you fully. It's only a feeling. Breathe deep and relax.
What's the feeling, Hollaran? I don't know, I'm just afraid. Of
course you are, and who isn't?

I'm feeling much more normal by the time I turn in at
Eddie's driveway, but just as I get alongside the house,
there's an explosion of noise, a roar that lasts a few seconds,
then dies out with a whine. I shut off the Volks and get out,
ready for just about anything. I creep to the corner of the
house, look around carefully.

The garage doors are closed, but somehow light's coming out of the cellar. I look up and there's its source, a big
rectangular hole in the wall, just above the garage doors. I
take a couple of steps toward the doors and there's another
blast of noise, by instinct I flatten myself on the ground. I
recognize the noise now, coming from inside the garage, it's
a mechanical growl, a big engine of some kind, with no muffler. The noise fades to a whine and I get up, creep toward
the doors, they're closed, I get down on my stomach. There's
a crack at the bottom and maybe I can see in. "Ha ha ha," I
hear Eddie say. He's not laughing, he's saying it. The bong of
a dropped wrench. "All right, you bastard," he says, "I got
you figured out now."

I crawl right up to the crack and look in, blinding yellow
light, a big *something*, can't see Eddie, just something huge
and high as the ceiling, an egg shape with something black
tapering back sharply from it and ending with an oh my God
it's a helicopter. Plexiglas bubble, an exposed engine in back,
then a tapering latticework of steel tubing, ending with a
red-and-yellow tail rotor. Something missing, though, and I
can't figure it out. Skids? No, it's on three wheels. What's
missing? Off to the side I hear the shuffle of Eddie limping,
the bang of tools on a workbench. "Son of a bitch," he shouts,

and pounds on the workbench. Stay down, Hollaran, you're dealing with a madman.

"All right," I hear him say, "All right, let's give this son of a whore one more spin." He shuffles into my view, picks up a vodka bottle from among tools scattered on the floor, turns his back to me, takes a long swig, looks at the label. "This is good shit," he says, and takes another drink, puts the bottle down. "Okay, bozos," he says, and claps his hands. "Look out. We're coming." He walks around the chopper, pats it everywhere, stops to spin the tail rotor. Lights a cigarette, walks around the other side of the chopper, crawls under it. Rolls over on his back, cigarette pointing straight up from his mouth. He pulls on something, wiggles something else. "Oh, you're ready to fly, ain't you?" he says. He elbows himself out from under the chopper, stands, dusts off his hands. "What time is it?" he says. "Where is that goddamn Hollaran, anyway?"

I'm shifting around to get a better view, lying full-length on the ground, I'm starting to feel like chilled meat here. I watch Eddie take another impatient tour around the helicopter, looking everywhere, touching everything, bending, crouching, kneeling, checking from every angle. Finally he stands up straight, jams his hands in his pockets, starts pacing, stepping over tools, talking to himself, mumbling, I can't hear. Then he stops pacing, looks around the cellar, and says, "Nah, I can't wait no more." He takes an oily rag from his back pocket, picks up the vodka bottle, wraps the rag around the neck. Takes a wobbly step toward the helicopter, raises the bottle over his head like an ax. Looks up at the bottle, brings it down to his lips for a long drink, raises it again. "I now christen you the *S.S. Bozo Bomber,*" he says, and breaks the bottle, glass flying everywhere.

"There," he says, "it's done." He throws the rag and bottle neck against the wall, looks at his right hand. "Damn it," he says, and makes a fist, holds it. With his left hand he starts patting his work pants pockets. "Where's the goddamn keys?" he says. Still patting his pockets, he goes to the workbench, runs his hands over tools and wires and parts, rummaging, lifting, spreading, his right hand dripping blood. Then he stops, snaps his fingers and says, "Oh, yeah." Turns to the chopper, looks into the bubble. "There they goddamn are," he says, "been there all the time." He slips into the hole in the bubble, sits in the pilot's seat.

He's facing me now, maybe twenty feet away. Glare from the bubble, but I can see his face. He puts on a flight helmet, the kind with a microphone out front. Adjusts the helmet a couple of times and now it looks like he's talking into the microphone. He reaches up to the top of the bubble, throws a switch, throws more switches on the instrument panel, there's a series of loud clicks. Then a low whine, the engine building up momentum, has he flipped out? What's he going to do, try to take off from the cellar? The engine catches now and roars, a noise that's a high tweet and a low rumble all at once, it's head-splitting now, I'm holding my ears, oh my God here he goes, and then I realize there's something strange about the sound, something missing, and there's no wind, either, no prop wash, I look for the main rotor and there isn't one, just the mast sticking up from the engine compartment, perfectly still, and I look at the tail rotor and that isn't moving either.

Inside the bubble, Eddie's looking serious, twisting dials, throwing switches, scanning the instrument panel, he looks to his right, a vacant seat, he gives it the thumbs-up and grins. His left hand pulls on something, the noise is out of this world now, I can feel it in the nerves of my teeth, Eddie with his right hand moves the control stick, of course the helicopter doesn't move an inch. Eddie looks to his rear, his left, his right, looks at the vacant seat, says something into the microphone, leans forward with the stick like he's taking off, glances down and to his left, leans his whole body left, looks up through the bubble, pulls back on the stick, leans right a little, looks all around him, settles back into the seat and grins.

Like he's flying. Up there grinning and really happy. He's actually looking down like he can see a landscape below him. Then after maybe a minute his left hand starts moving a lever down, the engine noise drops to just ear-busting level, he's looking all around him again, leaning backward, nodding and talking into the microphone, the engine noise drops suddenly, like he's landed. The engine dies, a ringing silence, Eddie taking the helmet off, switches all thrown, he steps out of the chopper and pats the bubble. Walks all the way around the helicopter, slowly, an inspection. Stops near the pilot's bubble hole and says, "Done. Perfect. Now where's my drink?" He looks around on the floor and then says, "Oh, that's right." Limps over toward the wooden stairs that lead to the kitchen, starts climbing them, stops halfway up to admire the helicopter. "Polack know-how," I hear him say. Then one, two, three hard gimpy footsteps, and the kitchen door opens and then slams.

I get off my belly slow. Quiet, Hollaran. I can hear Eddie above me, opening and closing cabinet doors. I stand, legs shaky, holding on to the garage door handle, the door pulls open a foot. A surprise because Eddie never leaves it unlocked. Without moving the door or making a sound, I squeeze into the cellar.

I take one step toward the helicopter, stop, I'm practically gagging on exhaust fumes, I put my hand over my nose and mouth. Take slow, careful, silent steps to the helicopter, put my hand up on the bubble. Inside it, black leather seats, an instrument panel with dozens of switches and dials, steel pedals coming up from the floor. Above me I hear Eddie shout, "Hey!" and I freeze. Has he seen me? The Volkswagen? Then I hear stomping, a short-legged jig on the floor, he's dancing, maybe he found another bottle.

I walk around the chopper, picking my way, stepping over all kinds of tools and gadgets and machines, they're everywhere, a jumble of wrenches and hammers and bolts and nuts, rolls of wire and solder, steel rods and tubes, all scattered on a green tarp that covers the whole floor. Around the back of the helicopter is a semicircle of machinery, a big drill press, a band saw, a welder with tanks, a whole cabinet of electronic meters. Eddie still stomping around above me, I'm looking, amazed, at the main workbench, a landscape of

small metal parts, and stuck in there, a book, a red one, I pick
it up. It's one of those things you can buy in Woolworth's, a
daybook, this one says 1969. I open it to the middle, July 12,
just a blank lined page. July 13 and 14, blank, no notes. I flip
to October and November, all blank pages. No writing at all
until December 17, and then just a simple printed acronym,
DEROS, which is army talk for the day you were scheduled
to leave Vietnam. That's it? That's the only note he made the
whole year he was over there? I flip to the front of the book,
nothing, flip to the back and there's a list, hand-printed in big
blockish letters and spread over two pages. On top of one
page is a big black capital *B* underlined five times, and then,

AUGGY MORELLI, KENNEDY BLVD. J CITY
J. DOMBROSKI ELIZ, SIX HOUSES PAST HOSP.
L. KING, SKILLINGTON, PENNSY.
WORTHINGTON, MENASHA, WISC.
TRUMBULL, 1ST AV? FORT HOOD?
JOHN JOHNSON, 411 SUBURBAN CIRCLE,
WESTFLD

On the other page there's the word *WHY* printed big
and dark, and under that,

AUTO PARTS. BANDIT. PAYCHECK
VA CLERK. DISABILITY
CHU LAI!
LIFER PILOT
LIFER
FOR HOLLARAN

The book in my hand, I walk around the other side of the
helicopter, looking at it, thinking. I practically trip over the
main rotor, there it is, red and yellow, fifteen feet long, lying
on the tarp. I step over it, walk to the front of the helicopter
and look into the bubble again. Trying to imagine what's
going through Eddie's mind. Inside the bubble, all that

catches my eye is the flight helmet, army green, SADOWSKI stenciled across it in black. I walk away from the bubble, follow the trail of fresh blood drops to the bottom of the stairs. "Hollaran!," I hear Eddie shout. "Hey! You home?" I stop with my foot on the first step.

"Tom," he yells out. "You up there? You left your car lights on."

I wait in silence, I can hear my own heart thumping.

"Hollaran, come down for a drink, I got something to show you."

I make myself shout out, Ed!

"Where are you?" he yells.

Down here, I shout.

The door opens, light at the top of the stairs. Eddie coming down, army boots, work pants, flight jacket with Americal patch, face spread in a smile. "You seen it?" he says. "You seen it, didn't you?" I step away from the stairs, the book's in my hand behind my back. Eddie's right in front of me now, eyes glazed. "Well?" he says. "You seen it. You ain't saying nothing."

Ed, I say, what the fuck is this? I hold out the red book.

"It's a helicopter," he says, like he doesn't even see the book. He gives out kind of a drunken giggle. "I built it all by myself," he says.

I can see that, I say. But what's this? I wave the book in front of his eyes.

"The only bad mistake I made," he says, "was the height. The mast is too tall to get out the door, that's why I had to knock a hole in the wall."

Ed, I say, this. I open the book to the back, and put the list right in front of Eddie's eyes.

"That's just bozos," he says. "Tomorrow, I'm going to start putting the rotor on." He walks past me and toward the chopper. "It'll take a week to test it and balance it and all, and then we can take off."

To where? I say. For what?

He turns and looks at me. "You known all along, ain't you?"

Known what? I say.

Big grin. "Come here," he says, and grabs me by the arm. "Come on, come over here." He practically drags me over to the helicopter, starts pushing me into the copilot's seat. Will you stop pushing? I say.

"Just sit in there," he says. "Come on, I been working on this for months, sit." I let him push me into the seat. In front of me is a duplicate instrument board, a curved control stick. A nasty sweat breaks out all over my body.

"Buckle up," Eddie says, and holds part of the seat belt out for me. "I'll run you through the basics."

Ed, I say, and hold the book up. Explain to me what this is.

"Give me that," he says, and snatches the book out of my hand, flings it across the room, it lands on the workbench where I'd found it. "I'll tell you all about that later," he says. "Now, here, put your hand on the collector."

I don't think I want to do this, Ed, I say.

"It ain't that hard, believe me," he says. "The collector's kind of like your throttle, but it does other stuff, too. Now, this thing between your knees," he says, and wiggles the curved stick, "that's your cyclic. You got to move that in combination with the collector."

Ed, I say, listen to me, please. I hate helicopters. Hate them, don't you understand?

"Sure," he says, "that was in the army, though. This is different. This is ours. Now, you see them pedals down there? They're your rudder controls."

Get out of my way, I say. Let me out.

"Don't panic," Eddie says. "It's easy. You'll love it once we get in the air."

12

THERE GOES ANOTHER ONE

"There goes another one," says Doctor Pyle, "just like a dream." He's swiveled around in his chair, looking out the window and across the Turnpike where a bright orange jet rises out of the flats of Newark Airport. "Just like a dream," he says, shaking his head, a lost tone to his voice. "I'm sorry," he says, and swivels around to face me. "What were you saying?"

That I've already made up my mind, Doc. To just forget about Vietnam, and go straight. Like you've been telling me all along.

"What brought on such a quick change of mind?" Pyle asks.

A friend of mine, Doc, I say. I think he's going off the deep end. From fighting the war in his mind, if you know what I mean.

"I see," says Pyle, but I have the feeling he's not really paying attention. There's a silence and he just stares at me.

Doc? I say.

"Yes!" Pyle says, and comes to attention.

There is one other thing, I say. See, I've been dating this woman, she's been real nice to me.

"Oh?" says Doctor Pyle. He's looking over his shoulder toward the window. An Eastern airliner rising into the rare pure blue of a Newark sky. "You're not going to invest your emotional well-being in one woman, are you?" Pyle says.

She's a good woman, I say.

Pyle shrugs. "You must have felt the same way once about your wife," he says. "And she turned on you. Viciously."

I look down, like there's an answer on the floor, or on the tips of my greasy work boots. I am afraid of that, Doc, I say. Of getting tangled up in it, and hurt again.

"Of course," says Pyle, so loud it startles me. He leans forward across his desk. "They're fickle, these women, that's what they are." He seems to realize he's talking too loud, and sits back in the chair. Pulls a cigarette out of his vest pocket, manicured fingers reach across the desk for his Gucci lighter. Flick, flame, smoke.

"Let's be rational about this," he says. "You know, of course, that there is a shortage of men in this area. It's quite well publicized. There are literally thousands of desperate women out there."

Can't prove it by me, I say.

"Statistical fact," Pyle says, and points his cigarette at me. "Personally, I've found it highly rewarding to date a variety of women. It's stimulating, and reduces the vulnerability factor to the minimum."

But I don't want to date around, I say.

He looks at me, anger and impatience there, a hard look coming over his face. "What do you want, Mister Hollaran?" he says. "Do you really know?"

I want your advice, Doc, I say. On going straight. On getting a better job, and getting out of this mess I'm in with the cops.

"You want my advice?" he says.

I nod.

"All right," he says, and stops for a moment like he's thinking. "I believe I can help you, Mister Hollaran," he says. "Now that you're finally receptive." He swivels his chair a little, stands, jams his hands in his pockets, starts pacing behind the desk. "It's interesting, this police predicament of yours," he says. "I've got a friend, a lawyer, downtown." He stops to tap his cigarette in the ashtray. "His specialty is keeping cases out of court. His methods are brutal and simple. Your ex-wife has pressed charges against you, correct? What my friend the lawyer would do, for a fee, is to discover unpleasant facts. Which he would then use to force your ex-wife to drop the charges."

You mean dig up dirt on Sandra and this Laundromat guy? I say. They're not doing anything illegal.

"The idea," says Pyle, "is to embarrass them. To make them afraid of a public trial. To blackmail them with the dirty facts of their own lives. Who could stand up to that?" he says, and reaches into his suit coat, pulls out his wallet. His hand's shaking as he gives me a little brown card, *Shuster and Houlihan, Attorneys at Law.*

"There is one problem," says Pyle. "Margolis R. Shuster does not work cheap. But he might take monthly payments, if you mention my name. And if you were earning a decent salary."

That's the other problem, Doc, I say. I've decided I've just got to make more money, no matter what.

"Now you're thinking straight," Pyle says, and turns back toward his desk, but stops at the window. A red-tailed airliner leaves the runway and angles for the sky. "Just like a dream," Pyle says, and shakes his head. "This time of year they're all going to Florida," he says. "Imagine." He digs for another cigarette, lights it, keeps staring out the window. "Beautiful," he says.

I'm trying to put together some ideas on making more money, I say.

"Oh, yes," says Pyle, and comes around to sit in his chair. "Very good. I have an idea I'd like you to consider. I guarantee," he says, and sits back, blowing smoke, "that it will produce results. Who is your immediate supervisor?"

A guy named Frank Gripper, I say. The yard boss.

"Describe your relationship with him."

He hardly knows me, I say. He treats people in sort of an offhand way.

"Good," says Pyle. "Excellent, in fact." He folds his hands over his vest. "You see, this indicates that he is isolated, alone, possibly fearful that others despise him. An authority figure, you understand, is the recipient of a great deal of hostility. So your strategy should be to get a promotion by simple friendliness."

Be friendly? I say. To Gripper? I hardly ever see him.

"Seek him out, then," Pyle says. "Ask him for little approvals. Solicit his advice. Let him know you value his opinions. And you will see how quickly he adopts a new attitude toward you."

I don't know, I say.

"Don't be a child," says Pyle. "It's done all the time. Soon after you become friendly with this Gripper fellow, you'll undoubtedly find ways to make him look good to *his* boss. Eventually this will earn you a promotion, probably to some minor administrative post. There the opportunities to make him look good will be even greater. Sooner than you think, they'll be calling you management material."

That's what you think, I say. There's still Johnson, the big boss, and he's out to get me.

"Nonsense," says Pyle, and puts out his cigarette, waves his hand at me. "It's the other way around. Are you familiar with the psychological theory of projection? Vastly simplified, it means the patient will deny his faults, his unacceptable feelings, by attributing them to other people. Usually people he fears, loves, or hates. In your case, it's your own hostility that you attribute to your boss."

I blame him for faults that are really my own? I say. That's what you're telling me?

"Yes," says Pyle. "In reality, this Johnson fellow would probably be quite pleased to see you become a cooperative worker. It's likely he would view it as a personal achievement, attributable to his own management skill."

But, Doc, I say, I don't know if the steel business is really for me.

"You already have the experience," he says. "Besides, the bosses would love to say that one of their managers had literally worked his way up from the warehouse. Really, conditions are quite favorable for your advancement there, if only you would realize it."

Silence. My mind working like a calculator. "Think about it," says Pyle, and gets up, goes to the window. For what seems like a long time, he stares and I'm silent.

Doc, I say, sometimes I think I should do the kind of work I was cut out for. Maybe cooking in a restaurant. If I could just get that first job. My uncle Anthony's got to know somebody who's looking for help.

No response from Pyle. I realize he hasn't been listening.

"You're a young man still, Mister Hollaran," Pyle says suddenly. "Youth has its dreams. I was very good in science at school. When I was young, flying was still a new thing. And I wanted in the worst way to be a pilot. I made a hundred model airplanes, out of wood, my own designs. I saved up five dollars when I was in ninth grade, it was a lot of money then, and used it to pay for a sight-seeing flight around Manhattan. In a biplane. It was the thrill of my life, I couldn't imagine being higher than the Empire State Building." He's staring out, silent now, I'm sure he can see, a few miles east of the airport, the Empire State Building sticking up out of Manhattan. "But nobody knew, then, whether there was any future in flying. And besides, the world was starting to fall apart, terrible things happening in Europe. So I went to medical school. As it turns out, it was a safe thing to do. I was a student for the whole war. Many of my high school classmates died in that war, a few of them were even pilots. You see, Mister Hollaran, the world . . ." He stops talking, turns away from the window, hands in his trouser pockets, a lost and almost lonely look on his face. "But I'm not unhappy," he says. "Yes, I'm cooped up in an office all day and, if I may be frank, this job can be tedious and sometimes even frightening. I still wonder from time to time what my life would have been like had I made another choice when I was young. But I live a comfortable life and drive a fine automobile and I've made some very sound investments." He walks around behind me, pacing the room now, he ends up at the window, looking out, his back to me. "You found out in the service, didn't you,

Mister Hollaran, that the real world is a frightening place. That's precisely why so many people choose to insulate themselves. It's natural. It's inevitable."

I stand up to get a look at the clock on Pyle's desk, just what I thought, three minutes over, another rush to get back to work.

"Most people's lives are nothing but compromise," Pyle's saying.

I'm at the door already. I've got to get back, Doc, I say.

"Good-bye, Mister Hollaran," he says absently, still staring out the window. I pat my pocket for the car keys and open the door.

"There goes another one," he says. "Just like a dream."

Running down the corridor, I'm always running down this green tile corridor, I don't want to look in any rooms, too many ugly secrets hidden in there, the human wreckage of every war within memory, mutilated men, drug-dazed, spread after all these years into the exact shape of their wheelchairs, they never get out of pajamas and bathrobes, all clustered around the blue glow of TV, smelling of cigarettes and medicine and pus. Keep running, Hollaran, don't look to either side.

Out into the parking lot, huffing, pain in my side, running between rows of cars, my Volks, it starts right up, thank God, can't afford to be late anymore, drive.

There's something to what Pyle said, that I'm sure of. Because I can't continue this way, a good job, that's what I need for starters. Can't stay in boiler tubes much longer. Something with a future. No need to be a grunt all my life.

Out on the Turnpike, step on it. And will you look at this sorry mess? Not even a mild, sparkling midwinter day can make it look good, an industrial swamp, pools of petrochemicals, streams of sludge, built over with junkyards and smokestacks. At one time, so everybody says, it was a beautiful meadow, alive with beavers, ducks, plenty of fish. Something's wrong, Hollaran, something's just plain wrong.

Drive. Lift my ass off the seat, go for my wallet, what's that lawyer's name? Drive with one hand, trailer trucks swooshing past, not even a dollar in this wallet, thumb through the papers, there it is, the brown card. I'll give him a call. Now, as a matter of fact. Before I lose my determination. SERVICE AREA ONE MILE. I'm pulling in.

Bank of phone booths, I'm out of the car, searching my pockets for change. Into the booth, cold phone up to my ear, I put two quarters up on the gray metal shelf, drop one in the slot and dial. I can barely hear the ringing for the sound of trailer trucks roaring by. Hello? I say. No, still ringing. Come on. A voice, faint. Hello? Hello?

"Hello, law office." The voice sounds like it's in Singapore.

May I speak to Mister Margolis R. Shuster, please? I shout, reading from the card.

Some kind of answer that sounds like the buzz of a dying bee.

I can't hear you, I shout. I'm on the Turnpike.

"Mister Shuster," the voice shouts back, a husky woman's voice, "is in conference at the moment."

Well, I need to talk to him, I say. I've been referred by a friend of his. Doctor Pyle.

"Doctor who?"

Pyle. P-Y-L-E.

"One moment, please," says the voice, and all of a sudden I'm listening to Christmas music, a month late, a country version of "Jingle Bells," with steel guitar. Waiting. Trucks going by with a loud, low gargle. Tapping my knuckles on the glass, come on, lady. A loud click on the line, mechanical voice. *Please deposit ten cents for the next three minutes.*

I just put a *quarter* in, I say. Of course, it's hopeless, dealing with a machine. You miserable bitch, I say. And drop in the other quarter.

Thank you, the voice says. I kick the booth for revenge.

"Hello, sir?" says the woman's voice, "may I take your phone number and have one of Mister Shuster's associates get back to you?"

I don't have a phone, I say. And then I realize how broke that makes me sound. I mean, not one that works right now, I say. It's out of order. Please. I'm in a phone booth. I'd like to speak with Mister Shuster himself.

"Sir, he is the senior partner."

I've been recommended, I say.

"It would be a very long wait for an appointment with him, sir," she says. "Just a moment, please. I have another call." Click, I'm cursing. A song, "Let There Be Peace on Earth, and Let It Begin with Me." I'm cursing Shuster, his secretary, the phone company, cops everywhere, all lawyers, all judges, Sandra . . . "Sir? The best I can do is an appointment two weeks from today."

I spell my name for the lady, the mechanical voice breaks in and starts asking for another dime, I just hang up. One more call to make and no more quarters. Kick the booth again, hard. Hurt my toe this time. Limp out to the car, I'm desperate for a dime. Lift the floor mats, no silver under there. Hand under the seats, two lousy pennies. Two fingers into the ashtray, I used to keep toll money there, under a layer of Eddie's Winston butts, something round and hard, a nickel. Dig, nothing but ashes. Rip out the ashtray, dump it on the pavement, ping, another nickel, the gods are with me. Back to the phone booth, dial. I recognize the voice of Jerri the receptionist, I don't want her to give me away, I talk very low trying to disguise my voice, and ask for John Johnson.

"Ringing for you," Jerri says.

Click. "Hello, Johnson here." Very relaxed. I find myself stammering, recover, take a deep breath, start again. Mister J, I say, Tom Hollaran, sorry to bother you, but I really need to meet with you this afternoon, it's important.

"Well, Tom," he says, "I had the afternoon booked fairly solid."

Mister J, I say, it's kind of urgent. And personal. I mean, I need your advice on something.

"You what?" Johnson says.

I'm making an important decision right now, I say, and I've always kind of . . . I pause to let a big truck roar by . . . I've always kind of respected your opinions, Mister J.

A pause on the phone. My stomach feels like it's trying to turn inside out.

"Well," Johnson says, "I suppose if you came in right after five I'd still be around."

Thanks, Mister J, I say, you won't be sorry, I've got to go now and get back to work, see you right after five.

I jump in the Volks, hang on to the steering wheel, breathe out hard, I've done it, feel better now, it's all over. A breeze from here on in, just do what I'm told, a member of the team. Drive, pedal to the floor.

It's after dark by the time I cut my last boiler tube of the day and run through the pipe yard, toward the office building, the elevator. I'm standing outside it, bong, the door opens, out come secretaries and an accountant with an unlit cigar in his mouth, they all walk wide around me, I realize how greasy I am, out of place on wall-to-wall carpet. I ride the elevator alone, it wobbles, this thing, so nicely paneled and carpeted but is anybody inspecting the workings? I hope I'm not in it the day it gets stuck. Or falls. I've got to relax, that's what's the matter. I shove my hands in my pants pockets, I want to be casual when the door opens, Johnson might be right there.

Elevator stops with a jerk, door slides open, lights on everywhere, nobody around. I walk quietly across the polished tiles to the frosted-glass door, JOHN JOHNSON, V.P., OPERATIONS AND SALES. Laughter coming from inside there, not Johnson's, though, I stand at the door, trying to get myself to knock. "And then he says to me"—it's Gripper's voice, he laughs again—"he says to me, 'Grip, how am I supposed to know three-oh-four stainless from three-sixteen stainless?' And I says, 'Bite it.'" Laughter from Johnson and Gripper. I'd better not get caught eavesdropping, but I can't seem to knock. But some things you have to make yourself do. I either knock now or forget it. Quit. Turn around. Go out and be a bum.

I find myself tapping on the door. "Come in."

Gripper's sitting back in a chair, long thin legs crossed at

the ankles, hands clasped behind his head, elbows spread.
Johnson's behind his desk in the big chair, his tie loosened,
pulled down two inches. "Have a seat, Tom," he says. "How
you doing, babes?" says Gripper.

I sit. Same spot where I sat when Johnson kicked me
down to the warehouse. But now it's night, the window behind Johnson like a picture postcard of lower Manhattan in
lights.

"How are things going down there, Tom?" asks Johnson,
and I realize I've been quiet a while. Feeling lost. I try to
think. Think about what Doctor Pyle told me, make Gripper
look good to his boss. Fine, I say, just fine. I look at Gripper
and he's nodding. No complaints at all, I say.

"Good," says Johnson. "I'm glad to hear that. So." He
leans back in his leather La-Z-Boy. "What's on your mind?"

Well, I say, and look at Gripper and hesitate.

"Anything you can say in front of me," says Johnson,
"you can say in front of Francis."

Oh, I know that, I say. Then I feel my throat closing up.
You liar, Hollaran. I put my hand up in front of my mouth and
clear my throat. Excuse me, I say. Something caught in my
throat. I cough. Hard. Oh my God, am I going to heave right
here? Stars orbiting in front of my eyes, close my eyelids,
shake my head, clear it. I'm okay, I tell Johnson, and cough
again. Excuse me, I say. And clear my throat. You see, I came
up to tell you that I understand now why I was demoted.

"Oh?" says Johnson.

Yes, I say. Because I was uncooperative. And unreliable.
Gripper and Johnson just look at each other.

And frankly, Mister J, I say, I'm glad I went down there,
because it's made me appreciate what I had before.

Johnson's just looking at me.

If you know what I mean, I say.

Johnson nodding, very serious. Gripper with a tight little
smile, his arms folded. I'm trying not to squirm in the chair, I
take a deep breath. And so, I say, I was kind of wondering,
you know, if there was any way I could sort of regain my old
position.

Silence. I find I'm sitting far forward on the chair, looking from Gripper to Johnson. What are they thinking? Why
don't they say something? I find myself babbling to fill the
silence, the warehouse is well run, I say, and it's been interesting to see what goes on down there and I'm sure it will
make me understand the business better, it's just that, I don't
know, I feel I'm capable of doing, well . . .

"Better things," Johnson says.

Yes. I'm nodding.

"What'd you have in mind, babes?" says Gripper.

Oh, I say, maybe I could help you out in the office. Ship-
ping and receiving or something. I look at Johnson. Or
maybe, I say, junior salesman or I'd even take inventory
clerk, anything.

Johnson swivels his chair a little toward Gripper. "Have
you got anything down there, Francis?" he asks.

Gripper spreads his hands. "Nothing open," he says.

"Things are pretty tight up here, too," Johnson says to
me, and shakes his head. "Right now the damn Japanese are
kicking our butts. Especially in stainless and exotics. I could
very well envision a no-growth year ahead for us, Tom."

I'm nodding. I've got to say something, what? I understand, I say. But your voice is trembling, Hollaran. Look,
Mister J, I say, I wonder if you could give me some, well,
direction on how I might resume my sales career with, say, a
company of similar quality.

Johnson picks up his half glasses from his desk, twirls
them, just sits there, twirls them.

You see, lately, I say, I've considered all my alternatives,
and I've kind of decided to try for a career in management.
Sales management, to be exact. I think it's a goal worth working for. And see, your advice would mean a lot to me, and so
would, well, a recommendation of some sort.

Johnson leans back, looks at the ceiling, like he's contem-
plating something. Gripper's arms are folded tight, one foot
moving, work boot tapping impatiently on the carpet. Johnson comes forward now, elbows on his desk, hands folded, he
rests his clean-shaven chin on them. "You've always im-

pressed me, Tom," he says, "as a young man of a certain intelligence and promise. And I realize you haven't had the easiest of times lately." I shift in the chair. "Be that as it may, I think your relationship with this company is certainly salvageable, don't you, Francis?"

"Oh, yeah," Gripper says, his arms still folded, head nodding now. "Absolutely, John."

"Of course," says Johnson, "Francis and I would have to talk it over, to find just the right spot for you. Something where you could prove yourself, grow in responsibility, that sort of thing." He stands up, that's my cue to rise too, my legs shaky and numb. No handshake, Johnson just nodding. "Come see us next week," he says. I back toward the door, I'm saying thanks, thanks, thanks, until Johnson puts his hand up like a traffic cop and says, "Tom." I stop. Johnson looks at Gripper and shrugs. "Sit down a minute," Johnson says.

I'm back in the chair, Johnson comes from behind his desk, sits on the side of it, right between Gripper and me. "I'll tell you a little something in confidence," he says. "There's no special secret to management, not at all. Ask Francis, he'll tell you."

Gripper's nodding.

"The key is loyalty," says Johnson.

"That's it, babes," says Gripper. "Whole thing in a nutshell."

"It's a little like being in the army, Tom," Johnson says, "and we're both veterans, so we can understand that." He moves his fist out a little, almost like he's going to chuck me on the shoulder. "There are times," he says, "when loyalty requires you to put your feelings aside, and suspend your own judgment, and just do your duty. It's as simple as that."

"All there is to it," says Gripper.

13

COMBAT ZONE

Bong, I drop another boiler tube onto the pile in front of the big hissing boiler, from the ceiling there's another shower of white dust. It comes down, cruddy asbestos snow, and settles in my hair, in Carmine's stiff black crew cut. He's standing at the small barred window, a highway of rusty, rag-wrapped pipes just over his head. "How many's that?" he says.

Sixty, I say. Half the load.

"Time for a break," Carmine says. Which annoys me, because he's been on break for the last twenty minutes, just standing down here in the school basement, watching me bring in tube after tube. I mean, if there's anything I want this week, it's to stay out of trouble while Gripper and Johnson decide what to do with me. But now I've carried in one too many boiler tubes myself, so I just stand, sweating, in front of a boiler the size of a locomotive, and I give Carmine a long angry stare. He turns his back to me, looks out the window.

We could get done, I say, and just get out of here.

"They send us on these shit runs," Carmine says, "we take our time." He's still looking out the window. "I can't believe this neighborhood," he says. "Used to be all Italian and Polack." He's shaking his head. "Come here, look at it."

I go over to the window, which looks out ground level on a little asphalt schoolyard, spray-painted with so much silver and red and green graffiti that there isn't one understandable word. The yard's surrounded by the rusty skeleton of a chain link fence, and just past that are two stripped cars, rusted and smashed and windowless, sitting on just wheels, with hoods and trunks sprung. Loitering near the cars are four boys, black kids, none of them old enough to be out of school.

"Look at the little bastards," Carmine says, "criminals. Hanging around, looking to get into trouble."

A police cruiser goes by, smashed like somebody had beaten it all day with a crowbar. The kids don't move, or even take notice of the cop, who slows down to eye them, then drives away.

Carmine's sputtering. "When I grew up in this city," he says, "the cops would take you in for being out of school. And slap your face if you wised off to them. Now? They're afraid of these little nigger kids. That's what's ruining Newark today."

I just roll my eyeballs.

"You don't believe it?" Carmine says. "Look around. Look at that street."

He's talking about a string of rundown, boarded-up houses, with mud front yards, on a treeless street littered with broken glass, the only visible industry being a storefront with a hundred mismatched hubcaps, and the whole neighborhood crowned by an abandoned brick apartment building, black fire scars where there used to be windows.

"When I grew up," Carmine says, "the Polack ladies would be out there every morning, sweeping them sidewalks."

Silence from me.

"True?" Carmine says.

True, I say.

"Then if the niggers didn't cause this, who did?"

At one time, I say, I would have blamed the bozos.

"The who?"

Bozos, Carmine, I say. Never mind, I say. What difference does it make whose fault it is? Are you going to help me with the rest of those boiler tubes?

"You're the kind of guy," says Carmine, but I lose the rest of whatever he's saying. Because I'm watching the tallest kid out there, he's picked up a rock, now he's throwing it at the school, it sails off to the right and hits something metal, the JS&T truck, parked near the basement door. All the kids are laughing. Carmine doesn't notice anything, he's on a tirade, about white people not sticking together, and that being the reason Newark was lost to the blacks. "But I'm going to stay and fight," he says. "I ain't like you."

Fight for what? I say.

"My city," he says.

But this isn't my city, I say.

He gives me a disgusted look. I just walk away from him, start down the narrow, twisting, dirty concrete corridor, so many turns in it you can hardly get one twelve-foot boiler tube through at a time, and then only by scraping the walls. I'm halfway up the corridor when I hear a shout, Carmine back in the boiler room. Then furious pounding footsteps in back of me, I stand aside as Carmine goes rushing by. Up ahead, where thick metal doors are pushed open to a square of sunlight, Carmine stops and shouts, "Hey! Who's throwing rocks at that truck? Knock it off!" He's answered by the thunk of rock hitting the truck body, he runs out of the doorway and into the schoolyard.

By the time I get up to the doorway, Carmine's already across the street, he's chased the kids, three running one way and the big kid splitting off, down the street alone with long strides, almost tripping on the length of his mustard-colored vinyl coat, he turns around, Carmine's stopped chasing him, the kid puts out his middle finger, raises his arm high in the air.

Carmine coming back across the schoolyard and unzipping his blue JS&T jacket, sweating, he stops to look for damage to the cab, doesn't find any, then walks around the whole truck, looking for where the rocks hit, cursing the kids nonstop, and in the meantime I get busy humping boiler tubes. Two at a time now, I'm managing to get them down the corridor somehow, but not without a lot of cursing. Finally, on my fourth trip back to the truck, with Carmine still on his inspection tour, I say, come on, Carmine, help me will you? Big deal if there's a scratch on the goddamn truck, so what?

"You don't know this company," he says, "you don't know how fussy they are about these trucks." He's squatting now, running his hand over the right fender. I grab two boiler tubes, cold steel against the yellow oilcloth of my gloves. Pull the tubes out of the flatbed, lay them at an angle between the truck bed and the asphalt, grab them around the middle, lift. If you're worried about the truck, I tell Carmine, the sooner we get out of here the better. I grunt with the weight of the tubes, lift the two of them to one shoulder, balance, start down the corridor, to my surprise Carmine's behind me, a pair of tubes on his shoulder too. Sound of steel hitting concrete as we bang down the narrow dark corridor and into the boiler room. Bong, I drop my tubes in the pile, jump out of the way as Carmine lets his roll off his shoulder. Hostility. Watch my feet, will you? I say.

He ignores me, goes to the window, puts his hands up on the bars and looks out. He grunts something. I shift my head to look out the window, and there's ten, maybe twelve kids out there. The only one I recognize is the tall kid in the mustard-colored coat. He looks like he's got a rock in each hand.

"Throw it, just throw one," Carmine says almost to himself.

Carmine, I say, let's not start a war over some rock throwing, okay?

"Someday, Hollaran," he says, still looking out the window, "you're going to get another office job. Not me, I ain't going nowhere but Newark. No way I'm going to let them stone my truck."

More kids gathering. Fifteen, maybe twenty now. The tall kid's coming closer, leading a pack across the street and to the edge of the schoolyard. I see what he has in his hands, not stones but heavy sticks, tied together with what looks like clothesline. More kids, I don't know where they're coming from, must be thirty of them by now, mostly just little boys, hardly any of them could be even fourteen. But they have

rocks in their hands, some of them. And one kid looks like he
has a pipe. They're all coming through what used to be the
fence and into the schoolyard, now the big kid's swinging the
sticks in front of him. From somewhere in the crowd a rock
flies up, cracks against the hood of the truck.

Carmine cranking hard to open the window. "Hey!" he
shouts. "Put those rocks down. Get away from that truck."

A rock comes flying toward us, skips on the asphalt,
cracks the half-open window as we duck away. Carmine and
I down under the window, a rain of rocks hitting the concrete
and asphalt above us, I feel like I'm in Vietnam all over again.
You're not going out there now, I tell Carmine.

"No?" he says. "What are we going to do then, college
boy?"

Find a way upstairs, I say. Another rock cracks the window, glass shards fall to the floor between us. Call the cops, I
say. Maybe somebody up there's calling them already.

"You kidding?" Carmine says. "Newark cops? It takes
them four hours to scratch their ass. By the time they get
here . . ." He doesn't finish because there's a loud thud out
there, then a dull sound almost like hail, Carmine stands up, I
look just over the edge of the window, the truck's windshield
has been busted out. Kids all around the truck, one tiny boy
pissing on the tire, a couple of kids on the flatbed kicking at
the boiler tubes, the tall boy in the mustard coat is climbing
into the cab, puts his hand on the steering wheel and hauls
himself in, starts going through the glove compartment. All I
can think of is the basement doors, wide open.

Carmine taking off his belt. Holds it in his hand, buckle
end loose. "I'm going to take out that big one," he says. "The
rest of them will run."

Carmine, I say, let's call the cops. Let's try it, the truck's
already busted to hell.

"You go up," he says, "I'm going out. Go ahead, call the
cops." He's taking off his jacket.

You're crazy, I say. They're little kids but they're mean,
look at them, don't be stupid, Carmine.

But he's already halfway down the corridor, walking

hard, now he breaks into a run, starts shouting, a war cry, I look out the window, see him burst out the doors, jump on the flatbed, swinging his belt, kids jumping off the truck left and right. A rock flies far over his head, I should go out and help him, go, I can't seem to move, call the cops, I can't seem to move. Carmine jumps off the flatbed, rips open the driver's door, then his head pulls back, hands go to his face, he backs away from the truck. And jumping from the truck seat is the tall kid, swinging the sticks over his head, Carmine backing off, the kid charging a couple of steps at a time. Call the cops, Hollaran. From where?

Carmine surrounded by kids now, a circle of them, takes his hands away from his face, bleeding from the lips, he backs around, dukes up like a boxer, the tall kid still whirling the sticks, lets them fly at Carmine's head, Carmine ducks, a kid kicks him from behind, a fist goes out for his head, misses. Move, Hollaran. Go! Drag him back here. I grab his jacket, maybe a little protection against flying rocks, I try to wrap it around my head as I run down the corridor. Huffing already, I run right out the door, expecting a hail of rocks, nothing. All the kids running away, toward the street. Carmine on the run in front of them, ducks the fence rail without losing stride, makes a sharp turn down the sidewalk, a rock thumps him in the back.

Kids after him in a swarm now, rocks flying, kids shouting, a neighborhood mutt's even joined in the chase. I run to the fence rail, look, Carmine's got maybe twenty yards on them, no time for the cops or anybody else, I feel in his jacket for the keys, turn and run for the truck.

My hands shaking, tight around the key, stab, stab, trying to get it in, fire the truck up, sitting on broken glass, air for a windshield, jam the gearshift into first throttle to the floor, quick look and out of the schoolyard, sharp turn to the right, lose some boiler tubes clanging to the street, Carmine down two blocks, pack gaining on him, stick-swinging kid just out of reach.

More gas, jam through the gears, swing around a double-parked car, where's the fucking cops when you need them,

I'm standing on the gas pedal, my ass cut and bleeding, I
know it, bang the gears, catching up now, Carmine dashes
across the street in front of me, gang of kids follow. I pull
alongside the curb, blowing the horn, I'm even with Carmine
now, he won't look up, I pull ahead, bang, the outside mirror
shatters, no choice, I cut right up on the sidewalk, Carmine
sees me, rocks hitting the truck everywhere, Carmine grabs
the mirror frame, swings up on the running board, I turn
right, give it the gas, bounce off the curb, into the street, out
of control, turning the steering wheel hard, oh my God, sideswipe a derelict car, Carmine still hanging on, his face
bloody, I'm zooming down the street.

Eddie's lying stomach-down on top of a big scaffold he's
built over and around the helicopter, he's got a huge torque
wrench in his hand, tightening down the nut that holds on
the main rotor. His face a rock of concentration. Just inches
between him and the cellar ceiling. I'm staring up at him,
half blinded by work lights hung on the rafters.

My job all night has been to help put on the main rotor,
and then keep it in balance, holding cables attached to each
tip while Eddie works. But that part's over now, and I'm idle,
leaning against the Plexiglas, watching Eddie up there, his
face all sweat and grime. Hours ago I told him the story of
what happened in Newark, and all he said was something
about it being more dangerous at home than it was over
there. With Eddie it's always *over there,* he hardly ever says
the word *Vietnam.* Anyway, for the past half hour or so nobody's said anything in here, not with the final critical moment coming, when the helicopter will be all put together.
Eddie grunting as he turns the torque wrench, now he stops
to read it, a change comes over his face, a spreading grin, I
expect a whoop or a holler, but all he says is "There."

He climbs down from the scaffold, lays the torque
wrench gently on the floor, steps back and admires the helicopter, shiny black, yellow blades, clear bubble, all under the
glare of the work lights.

"A balancing job, that's all I need," Eddie says.

I thought you were done? I say.

"No, that rotor's got to be balanced," he says. "Just like you balance the wheel of a car, so it don't get wobbly. The rotor gets wobbly you could bend the mast, anything could happen. The ship could shake apart in midair." He takes out a Winston, sticks it in his mouth, lights it, but doesn't take his eyes off the helicopter. "That's not going to happen to this baby," he says. "Balancing's next, then we go up."

Then *you* go up, I say.

"You're coming along," Eddie says, "I know you will."

I shake my head.

"You ain't never had your hands on the controls," he says. "Have you? It's just sheer engine power that keeps these things up. They ain't natural fliers, you know. You never seen a helicopter glide, did you?"

Ed, I say, you don't even have a pilot's license, do you?

He ignores the question, limps past me, headed for the helicopter. Sits in the pilot seat, starts going through his ring of keys. "You don't understand helicopters, Hollaran," he says, "that's your problem." He finds the right key, unlocks the map compartment. "They're always trying to go in three directions at once. Up, down, and sideways. The same motions that makes them fly tears them apart. That's why a good pilot . . ." He trails off, hands me an ordinary road map, it says JERSEY CITY on the outside. "Here," he says, "look inside and you'll see what I'm up to."

I unfold the map and there in the middle of it is a shaky red *X* drawn on a corner of Kennedy Boulevard.

This means nothing to me, Ed, I say, and hand the map back to him.

"Morelli's Auto Parts," he says. "That don't ring a bell? Auggy Morelli, my old boss. The one that never gave me my last paycheck. The old thief, cheats everybody."

Okay, I say, I remember. What are you going to do, Ed, bomb the place?

"No, sandbag it," he says, and grins.

Ed, I say, you can't, you could kill somebody, you'll go to jail.

"I ain't going to drop them right on the bozos' heads," he says. "Don't worry," he says, "I got it all worked out, the targets and all, chimneys, house roofs, cars, skylights . . ."

Ed, I say, you just can't do it.

"Why not?" he says, "I done it over there."

That was a war, I say.

"This is a war," he says, "and it ain't over. Everybody thinks we lost it, don't they, Hollaran?"

We did lose it, Ed, I say.

"You're wrong," he says, loud, anger rising. "I thought you knew better, Hollaran. I thought you were going with me, you're supposed to be my friend."

Can't you see what's going to happen? I say. You're going to make one of those bomb runs, maybe two, then you'll be arrested. You'll rot for twenty years in Trenton, Eddie, and the feds will take your helicopter and auction it off.

"You're a liar," he says.

They'll sell it to some bozo, I say.

"I've had enough of you, Hollaran," he says, "shut up, I'm warning you."

You'll be in jail, I say, and some bozo will be flying this thing up to his ski lodge.

"All right," Eddie says, and swings out of the seat. Takes two steps at me, hands at his sides, curled into fists. "Put up your dukes," he says.

I step back.

"You're backing out on me, ain't you?" Eddie says, and takes another step at me. "Up with your dukes."

I don't want to fight, Ed, I say.

He's still coming at me, breathing hard through his nose, I back toward the tail of the helicopter. Duck under it, Eddie after me, I trip over a toolbox, bang into the scaffolding, hurt my arm, grab it, keep backing away. "You're worried some bozo might get hurt?" Eddie says. "Let me ask you something. Was they worried about us?"

No, I say.

"We could have died, we could have rotted over there, admit it, Hollaran."

True, I say.

"Then come with me," he says, fists still up, still coming at me as I back away. "This is your last chance, you never backed out on me in your life."

I'm not flying in any helicopter, I say. I'm not sandbagging anybody, count me out.

Roundhouse swing, I duck under it. Watch out, Sadowski, I say, and back up. He jabs, misses. You could get hurt, Sadowski, I say. He's got me backed against the helicopter, the only way out is up, I grab the rungs of the scaffold. Eddie coming at me, kick to keep him away, pull myself up. Climb to a wooden platform over the bubble. Hoist myself up on it, stay on my knees to keep from bumping the ceiling.

"Get down here you bastard," Eddie says.

I just shake my head.

"I'll fix you," Eddie says, and drops his fists, steps back, looks on the floor around him, kicks at some tools with his bad foot, bends down and grabs a wrench. Shakes it at me. Limps under the scaffold, right underneath me. I look over the edge of the platform, he's working the wrench, loosening the nuts and bolts that hold the scaffold bars together.

Ed, I say, stop, are you crazy?

A bolt clangs to the floor, the scaffold underneath me shifts and shakes.

Cut it out, Sadowski, I say, before you hurt somebody.

"You drank to it," Eddie says. Working the wrench like he's in a fever. "You swore you'd help me get back at the bozos."

Well, I've done some thinking since then, I say. Things have happened since then, Ed.

Another bolt clangs on the concrete, the scaffold sags, instinct, I grab the edge of the platform and hold.

Ed, stop, I say. Answer me one question, and I'll come down, okay? Stop will you? He's working the wrench like a madman.

Ed, I say, who is a bozo?

He stops turning the wrench. "That's a stupid question,"

he says, "everybody knows who's a bozo and who ain't." He's turning the wrench again.

Am I a bozo? I say.

"No," he says. "You're a liar and you can't keep a promise, but you ain't no bozo."

Says who? I say.

No answer, a nut drops to the floor with a small solid thunk. "You ain't going to talk your way out of this one, Hollaran."

Ed, I say, tell me something. Why did those kids throw rocks at me in Newark this morning?

"Because you were a white guy," he says.

But I never did anything to those kids, did I? They don't know me, or anything about me. They just decided I was a bozo, and started throwing rocks.

Eddie stops turning the wrench. "Bozo? They didn't throw rocks because you were a bozo."

Yes, I say, it's the same thing, can't you see it? They just picked me out as the enemy, but they were wrong, weren't they? Kids do that by instinct, Ed, they don't know any better, but we're not kids, Ed, stop turning that wrench, will you, and listen? Anybody can be a bozo, you, me, anybody at all, you can't just . . . Ed! Will you listen? Forget the bozos, take this chopper out to the airport, get yourself a pilot's license, you could have fun with it or make money even, and think of the girls, Eddie, you could have all you want if you'd take them for a ride in your helicopter.

Another bolt clangs to the floor, the platform shifts and sags, I'm ready to jump, platform's at an angle, I could almost slide off, I'm clinging to it, Eddie stops. He's listening to something and now I hear it too. Crunch of shoes on the gravel driveway outside. Must be midnight, sounds like two men, robbers? Thieves? Eddie puts down the wrench, bends, picks up a crowbar. Crunching stops in the driveway, a loud knock at the door. Eddie looks at me, I start climbing down. Eddie limps to the door, crowbar held at his side. "Yeah?" he says.

"Edward Sadowski?" a voice says.

Silence.

"Mister Sadowski," the voice says, "Elizabeth police."

"Yeah?" Eddie says.

"We'd like you to open the door," says the voice.

"What for?"

"Questioning, that's all."

"You got a warrant?"

"We'd just like to ask a few questions about Thomas Hollaran."

I'm creeping toward the stairs, holding my breath, Eddie looks back at me, frantic, he points upstairs.

"Are you acquainted with Mister Hollaran?" asks the voice.

"Yeah, I know him," Eddie says. "Unfortunately. What's he done this time?"

"Please open the door," says the voice. Eddie looks around, sees I'm on the stairs, slowly draws back the three bolts on the garage door, then opens it a crack. I'm at the top of the stairs, at the kitchen door, it's locked, damn that goddamn Sadowski.

"We have a warrant for his arrest," the voice says. "Do you know his whereabouts?"

"You mean where he is?" Eddie says. "I couldn't tell you. But if you find him, let me know. I'd like to get my hands on him myself. He's a liar and he can't keep his word, and he's a bozo too."

14

THE RECOVERY ROOM

Failure to complete a work assignment, I say, mumbling almost to myself. Unauthorized control of a company vehicle, I say, and take a throat-burning sip of Jack Daniel's from a shot glass. Violation of insurance carrier agreements, I say, and bang the shot glass on the bar. Leo, the world is lousy with bastards. Bastards like Carmine, they'll stab you in the back and walk away like nothing happened. You know what I mean, Leo?

"Do I ever," he says. And then smiles. Dressed in a gray sweatshirt, dark wet spots show how hard he's been working in the back room. But right now he's sitting on a stool inside the horseshoe-shaped bar, sipping club soda and lime out of a mixing glass. The clock behind him says nine-thirty, two hours ago I was employed, one hour ago I was sober, a half hour ago Leo stopped hammering in the back room, came out to see how much of this bottle I'd drunk, and stayed to listen.

Heartless, that's what it is, Leo, I say. It's a heartless world when you're fired not by a person but by a piece of paper left in an envelope on your workbench at seven in the goddamn morning and you're not even awake yet, the bastards. And you look for Carmine and he's called in sick, and you ask for Gripper and they tell you he's out in the yard somewhere, and so you run up panting like a dog to the main office and Jerri pats her beehive hairdo and puts away her mirror and says, Oh, Mister J's in a management huddle, no calls, no interruptions. And then you run back across the yard and trip on the goddamn railroad tracks and fall in a filthy puddle and your uniform's all wet and you look like a fool, soaked, racing through the warehouses, they're laughing at you in stainless, copper, and aluminum, and you're yelling out Gripper's name and finally you find him in the coffee room, sitting at the head of the break table, surrounded by all his guys, and they're kind of smirking when you ask why you're being fired and all Gripper does is spread his arms and say, Babes, I had nothing to do with it, that's the rules. And you stand struck dumb for anything to say and the Gripper's telling you how he feels for you, and how he fought for two weeks' severance pay for you and then he's got you thanking him and slinking out like a fool while all the guys are trying to hide the smirks behind cups of coffee and you walk out and close the door and you imagine the whole room breaking out in lousy laughter.

And you walk across the yard and ask yourself why you feel so bad. When it's a stupid job anyway and greasy and cold besides. And then you look up at the big green-tinted windows of the main office and you realize that once again you're a loser, you've taken a fall.

What I want to figure out, Leo, is that miserable bastard Carmine, and why he did it to me. Because after he jumped in the truck yesterday, blood still running down his face, he was all thanks and gratitude. I owe you one, Hollaran, he said, don't worry. I'll talk to Gripper, he said, I'll smooth things over, I'll take care of everything, that's what he said. But I should have known, Leo. Because when we got near the yard and he wasn't bleeding anymore and had spit on his handkerchief and got his face cleaned up a little, he was telling another story. About how he could have beat those kids off. How he was just waiting for them to catch up so he could whirl, surprise them, kick for their balls. By the time we drove through the company gate he was practically in a rage, saying how he'd remember every one of those kids, how he'd get them back one by one, how he'd spend the rest of his life stalking them on the streets of Newark if he had to.

I can just imagine him last night in Gripper's office. I can imagine the story he made up, with him as the loyal employee, trying to deliver the company's goods in the ghetto, fighting off a street gang to do it. With me as the wiseass college boy who panicked, took the truck and smashed it up. But it doesn't make any difference what lies Carmine told. Because facts are facts, Leo, and this morning he's working and I'm not. I'll have another shot of this Jack if you don't mind.

I guess what bothers me most, Leo, is that John Johnson has the last laugh. His plan worked and I'm gone, he's rid of me. It's enough to make a guy join Eddie on the *Bozo Bomber*, it really is. And you're sworn to secrecy, Leo, about that helicopter, remember. If Eddie finds out I told anybody, he'll kill me. But maybe he's got an idea there, Leo. Sandbag the bastards, that's what they deserve. Right now I'd like to drop one through Johnson's office roof. Could you see it? The look on his face? Him sitting in that big La-Z-Boy, reading *Iron Age*. And boom, this sandbag comes crashing through, and beans him. That would be justice finally, wouldn't it, Leo?

He just smiles. Gets off the stool and comes forward, makes himself another club soda. Squeezes a half lime over it. Drops the lime in, lifts the thick giant glass to his lips, his Adam's apple working through layers of fat. Takes half the glassful in a long gulp. "Justice?" he says. "I don't know much about justice. But ask yourself sometime. What have these people won?"

A paycheck, Leo, I say. Don't you understand? I'm going to be out of work.

"Not for long," he says.

I'm glad you're so sure, I say.

He laughs.

Don't laugh, Leo, I say. The worst part is yet to come. Because sometime today, I don't know when, I'm going to have to tell Annie. Another humiliation. And Leo, we were starting to get along, things were going real nice. I've been going over there a couple of nights a week, waiting for her to get off work, making her dinner. Of course, I told her I had been married to Sandra, and she doesn't care about that. You know where I made my mistake with Sandra, Leo? I thought it was enough that she was pretty and sexy and smart. And for a while it really was enough. There we were, trying to avoid the draft and pay our bills and get the nice things of life, but that's all we had in common. And at the first big crisis we fell apart. Because she was absolutely determined to control the future, hers and mine. I guess because we were headed in different directions all along, only neither one of us knew it.

And so with Annie, you know, I'm trying to make things different. Like last week, we had a big talk. It was a conspiracy, really, the two of us. Because she wants to go someplace too, and doesn't look forward to retiring from St. Elizabeth's forty years from now.

And I said, you know, if I got the credentials of a first-class chef, we could go anywhere in the world. I said Italy would be high on my list. She said she'd like that. And if we ever went to Europe, could we stop in England, because London was a city she just had to see. I said, hell, we could live there if we wanted to.

Then she showed me her road atlas, with her trips colored in with green pen. Just to Pennsylvania, Maine, Virginia Beach. A lot of territory left to explore, I said. All over, anywhere. She was real excited about it.

"Why don't you call her now," Leo says, "before you have any more to drink?"

I would, Leo, I say. I'd go down to the hospital right now, but I don't know what she'll say or what she'll think. She's got plenty of reasons already to think I'm a loser.

"Maybe you'll find out what she's really made of, then," Leo says. "If she sticks with you, you've got the right one. If not . . ." He shrugs.

I pour myself another shot. Hot glow in my face from the last one. But Leo, I say, if I lose this girl, I'll have nothing left. Absolute zero.

"That might not be a bad thing," he says.

I just look at him. A little anger welling up through the heat of the whiskey. Easy for you to talk, Leo, I say. When you've got everything, and all the luck in the world.

"I want to show you something," he says, and steps back from the bar. "Come on, off the stool and come this way." He comes around the end of the bar, I'm following, up a short set of carpeted stairs, he pushes through a double door and into a dark room. Hits a switch and lights go on dim, then come up bright. Chandeliers, four big ones hanging from the ceiling. Walls paneled in dark wood, except for the back, which is just studs and silvery insulation, wiring snaked down through the walls, a pile of dark wood paneling ready to be nailed up. And one half of the room filled with tables and chairs, antique slot machines, framed photographs, all pushed together and protected under sheets of clear plastic.

"I'm hoping to open next month," he says. "But I don't know. There's a lot of work to be done, and I haven't figured out the menu yet."

He pushed open a swinging door, holds it so I can look in the kitchen, a framed skeleton of a room, stoves and sinks already in place, a big stainless counter gleaming in the middle.

"There's two ways to go," he says, "do it yourself, or owe the bank money the rest of your life. I'm learning as I go along, carpentry, plumbing, even a little electric."

I back out of the way and Leo lets the kitchen door swing shut.

"Unfortunately for me," he says, "I once had a small inheritance." He smiles. "There was no way you little kids could have known it, but I was an angry, bitter veteran back then when I lived on your block. I was trying to make sense of what I did and what I saw in Korea. I shut myself in that basement apartment, and when I wasn't eating I was a TV zombie. And when the TV signed off, I read. History and philosophy mostly, I was trying to figure out what was wrong with the world. Seven years I lived down there, and gained nothing but weight. Then I got lucky. My inheritance ran out.

"I took a good look at myself. I had to. After a lot of thought, I realized that my anger, my bitterness, it was all directed at one person. Me. Who else was there? I lived in my own little world, fighting my own private war. And then I realized I was in a hell of a position to call a truce."

That's when you left Boyle Place? I say.

"I decided to trust to luck for a while," he says. "I went over to Port Authority, took the first bus I saw, it was going to Florida. I got there almost broke, and all I knew was I wanted to be around people again. So I applied for jobs tending bar. Dozens of them. Slept on the beach. Ate rolls and butter. Finally I walked into this run-down place, the Shamrock, Betty was behind the bar, the owner. In three weeks we were married. In a year we were making money." He reaches over, turns the chandeliers down, then off. Pushes the swinging door open, holds it for me, I walk down the stairs and into the bar. I'm thinking, standing at the bar, pouring another shot into the shot glass.

"You're welcome to stay and drink if you want," Leo calls from the door. "But I've got to get back to work."

One more drink and I'm out the side door of Lucky Leo's, and grinding the starter on my Volks. Two tries and it catches, my luck might be turning already. And so many things to think about, all running through my brain, diluted with whiskey. One thing I've got to do is get to Annie. And if she doesn't want me, what the hell, I'm taking the bus south, like Leo. And I'll have to do it quick, because tomorrow's my appointment with the lawyer, and after that I'll be broke for sure, not even bus fare left out of my last paycheck. It's now or never, Hollaran. Drive.

Down Westfield Avenue like a madman. Up Broad Street, zooming, zigging, zagging through morning traffic, past the broad steps of the courthouse, big white hospital up ahead, pass it, out to Bayway, cutting patterns between the trailer trucks. Down the ramp to JS&T. Along the outer fence and there's the boiler tube shed, door open, is that Carmine inside? Stop the car. Look hard. That's him at the saw, I can tell from here. I think about Leo's question. What has he won? And it occurs to me, Carmine's hate, his anger, his resentment, it's bound him here. Here and to the streets of Newark. He's not very smart about picking his fights, that's Carmine's problem. And maybe mine. I don't want to be bound to Gripper and Johnson and Carmine forever. By hatred or anything else. So I admit it, I've been a fool, I let you win, the three of you beat me. And now I give you all my blessing, a wave good-bye. I don't blame you anymore. I don't blame you for anything.

Drive, Hollaran, and don't look back. Up the ramp and out on Bayway and going like a bullet toward the hospital. In the parking lot and stop the Volks with a jerk and out running, a whoosh of air and I'm through the revolving doors and into the wide white corridor. Long strides across the hard shiny floor and just as I get to the elevators a door opens, I get in, out of breath, step around a stretcher bed, door closes behind me. And on the bed, a skinny wrinkled ugly dying old lady curled up in the fetal position. Big square bandage where her nose used to be, and tubes running out of everything but her eyes. Pushing the bed, a young girl in candy stripes, long shiny black-Irish hair, complexion right out of a soap commercial, slim legs in white stockings. A polite little smile at me, and she pushes the button for seven. Elevator rising and I ask in my soberest possible voice, where's the recovery room? A wider smile and she shows somebody's big investment in plastic-and-steel braces. "Wait," she says, "I think . . ." and I find myself staring at her shamelessly. And trying to ignore the foul pus smell coming up at my nose from the dying old lady who, I know it without looking down, is twitching and squirming right beneath me. "I think it's on six," the candy-stripe girl says, and I push the button but don't take my eyes off her, I've seen enough of the ugly for a while, and when the door opens on six I'm almost sorry and she even says a sweet good-bye to me, must look like a bum in this old army jacket and smell

like a brewery besides. And now that she's gone I'm on the
sixth floor and don't know which way to turn, green tile
hallway, double doors each way I look, signs on both doors,
NO ADMITTANCE, AUTHORIZED PERSONNEL ONLY.

Pick the doors on my left, looking through one of the
little square windows, into a bright corridor where everybody's dressed in pink, green paper masks tied over their
faces. I have to back away from the door, two women in pink
push through, walk past me without even looking, one's saying she brought a cheese sandwich and an apple for lunch. I
push through the door. Nobody yells, nobody seems to notice
me.

I take four steps to a cross corridor, my shoulders
hunched, waiting for somebody to yell at me, but pink-robed
people just keep passing. A small boy with a crew cut, looking
healthy and awake, is wheeled past me by two nurses, and I
look down, there's a wide yellow line on the floor. The line
runs up the wall too, and every foot or so it's stenciled with
the black word STERILE.

I look down the three corridors, straight ahead, left,
right, nothing to guide me, except it's got to be near the
operating rooms somewhere. Three doctors turn the corridor, their faces still in masks, I look directly away from them,
they're arguing about the Knicks, and when their voices fade
I take a quick look and run. Straight ahead. My work boots
sounding down the corridor. Somebody yells "Hey!" in back
of me but I keep running, don't turn to look. Past unmarked
doors, four, five, six of them, "Hey! Hey!" A man yelling
behind me. Past another yellow sterile stripe, double doors
on my left, I burst through. Past doors marked BLOOD GAS
ROOM, I'm running hard, LINEN ROOM, STORAGE ROOM, RE-
COVERY ROOM, hard right, I fling open the door, out of
breath.

A wide white room with beds shoved up against windowless tiled walls, people unconscious in the beds, hooked up to
quiet clean green machinery all around them.

No Annie. No nurses at all in sight.

"Well, finally." A voice in back of me, female. I turn, a

middle-aged woman with half glasses, dressed in white, she walks up to me, a sheaf of paperwork in one hand, and says, "I called down there two days ago, what's wrong with you people?"

I give a dumb shrug of my shoulders.

"Didn't Al tell you to bring up any tools?" she says. All I notice is her name tag, M. JOHNSON, RN, CHARGE NURSE.

"You are maintenance, aren't you?" she says.

I back off a step. I'm looking for somebody, I say.

"Young man," she says, "are you employed here or aren't you?"

I shake my head.

"You're to leave at once," she says.

I just want to know who's on duty now, I say. What nurses.

"The insolence!" she says. "What business is that of yours?" She backs away from me, to a white desk where she picks up the telephone. She dials, I go to the middle of the room, hoping to see Annie somewhere. "Security?" she says. "This is recovery on six. We have a male intruder. I believe he is intoxicated."

She just finishes saying that when the door opens and it's a fat security guard, an older guy, he reaches for his belt, unsnaps a pair of handcuffs. "You stay right there," he says, and points at me.

I run at him, he tries to block me but I bump him, duck, squirm, twist, snap, something on my wrist, I throw an elbow, the guard huffs, I break away, a handcuff locked around one wrist, dangling, but I'm free, running down the corridor, head low, full speed. Burst through a door and into a stairwell, jumping down stairs, floor five, floor four, at three I try the door, handle won't turn, down to one, door striped in red and white, stenciled with the words FIRE EXIT ONLY ALARM SOUNDS IF DOOR OPENED.

Noise above me, voices. Men. Stomping feet coming down the stairwell. I charge the door, bang it open, burst into sunlight, a Klaxon practically blows out my eardrum. I'm running across the courtyard, right handcuffed hand shoved inside my jacket, over the asphalt past leafless trees, up the stairs, knocking like a madman on Annie's door.

The door opens wide and it's Annie in a white bathrobe and she doesn't even get out my name before I push in, shut the door behind me.

"Slow down," she says, "you're breathing like . . . what's going on out there?"

I bring my arm out of my jacket, show her the handcuffs.

She looks at them, her only reaction is to help me off with my jacket. "My God," she says, "you're all flushed." Jacket off and she's examining my wrist where the handcuff's pinching the skin red.

I'm trying to explain things, can't catch much breath. Guards, I say, after me.

She leads me out of the kitchen and into her bedroom, picks up her telephone. "I'll call them," she says.

No, wait, I say. I go over and kneel at the window, raising the shade slow and careful until just an inch of daylight shows. Out in the courtyard, the fat security man, I could swear he's pointing at this building. With him is a doctor in pink and a tall guy in a business suit.

"Why did they call security on you?" Annie asks from behind me.

I crossed the sterile line, I say.

"They can't put you in jail for that," she says. "I'll just call and tell them you're a friend of mine, you were just lost, and everything's okay."

No, I say. I watch the security guard, the doctor, and the businessman start moving toward the spiked fence that surrounds the courtyard.

"They're probably just worried about molesters," she says. "They get a lot of that here." I hear her dialing the phone. "I know this guy Scotty," she says, "Laura used to date him, he's the assistant chief of security."

Outside, the security guard at the fence waving, red lights are flashing, a city cop car pulls up, I feel my stomach turn right over. Annie, hang up, I say.

"Why?" she says. "It's ringing."

No, I shout, and run to the telephone, plunge down the buttons. Annie looks at me like I'm just out of the mental ward.

You'd have to give them my name, I say. Wouldn't you?

"Probably," she says, "why not?"

More sirens sound outside. "Is there a fire or something?" Annie says.

I sit down on the bed. Pound the mattress in frustration. Okay, I yell, and then I see the fear on her face, try to calm myself. There's a warrant out for my arrest, I say.

"You haven't done anything wrong," she says.

Yes, I have, I say. I did something nasty to Sandra. I mean to her cabin, I wrecked it. And to her boyfriend, I just went out of my mind and slashed his clothes with a knife. All kinds of charges against me now.

Her lips turn down. A look of disappointment on her face, it's drained of something, love, sympathy, I don't know.

"I didn't think you could hurt anybody, Tom," she says.

Well, you're wrong, I say. I punched her boyfriend, too. A good one, right in the stomach. I'm glad, too, I'm not even sorry. And one more thing, this morning I got fired. And then I went right to Leo's and got plastered.

She sits down in the chair opposite me. "You're in a lot of trouble, aren't you?" she says.

And nobody can help me out of it, I say. Not even you, Annie. I get up, kiss her full on the lips, hug her hard. I love you, I tell her. I'll be back if you want me, but right now I've got to go. She's up out of the chair. No, really, I say, I've got to go.

And I'm running. Out the door blindly. Hop over the stair rail and into the dirt behind the hedges. Crawling.

I hear the slam of police car doors, the static from the cops' radios. I'm down, low as an ant. Voices of my old drill sergeants running through my brain, keep it down, stay covered, break up your profile, move in quick bursts. I'm on automatic now, elbows, knees, feet moving me in a silent low crawl behind the hedge. Then a bent-over sprint along the spike fence, hoist myself up, even with the fence, leap for it,

over, fall tumbling, into the gutter and I stand right up. Walk.
Make myself. Pace myself. Like a guy out for a winter stroll.
Past the big blank white side of the hospital, past the emergency room doors, across Broad Street, heart pounding,
stomach churning, bruised on the elbows and knees, handcuffed wrist shoved deep in my jacket pocket. *Make* yourself
walk, Hollaran. Like an innocent man.

My neighborhood now, I could hide anywhere, Doctor
Rhinehart's right here on the corner, the church and school
up the block, I could run to Satriano's in two minutes, or go
home to Boyle Place, I know where they hide the key. But I
turn away from the old neighborhood, cross Pearl Street,
head downtown, I think I'm starting to understand now,
where I've got to go. I start to hustle a little, almost run.
Down Broad Street and over the Elizabeth River, a filthy
brook. Past the Greek grocery and the place that redeems
Gold Bond stamps, hop the low wall of the public library,
cross Elizabeth Avenue against the light. Run up the big wide
marble stairs, the courthouse, police station, jail, all in one
building. Push through the revolving door, the first office,
right there, that's it. A skinny bald sergeant standing in front
of the booking desk, lighting a cigarette. "What's your problem?" he says.

I put out my arm and dangle the handcuffs. Thomas
Joseph Hollaran, I say.

15

You're on Your Own Where There Is No Phone

The cop clicks the door shut and I'm alone in this little room, looking at my hands, black smudges all over my fingertips. I hold my hands away from me and walk to the sink, once white porcelain but deep purple now with a thousand criminal washings. Hot water on, I jiggle some powdery soap out of a rusty dispenser and start scrubbing. Working the gritty soap over fingers and thumbs. Rinse, black still there. Another mound of powder in my hand, scrub harder. Practically taking the skin off.

Give up and dry my hands on a paper towel. Pace this room, five steps long, four steps across. Sink, towel dispenser, a metal wastebasket, two chairs, a table, green walls. And on the table a big photo machine, with the camera and flash dish at eye level, held up by a metal arm attached to what looks like a photocopier. Which right now is humming and glowing with a soft green light, processing pictures the cop just took of me. Also on the table, a stack of blank fingerprint cards, a can of ink, a pad, a roller, more paper towels.

That's it in here. I wish I had a way to tell time. Was it ten minutes or maybe an hour ago that I finally got to make a phone call? And dialed Annie but got Laura on the line. Who said, Annie? For the last couple of hours she's been driving around looking for you. Where are you? What's going on? And I said, Laura, I need a thousand bucks bail, in cash, please, I know it's a big big favor but could you drive over to

Eddie's and tell him to get down here with the money?
Because otherwise they're going to take me downstairs and
lock me up.

That must have been an hour ago. At least. But will
Eddie even be home? My luck, tonight he's stopped off at
Leo's or the White Castle or he's got himself barricaded in
the basement with that helicopter. Damn him anyhow, why
doesn't he get a phone? I can just see myself, locked up all
night with rats and cockroaches running around, God knows
what kind of maniac with me in the cell, and me holding on
to the bars and screaming for mercy. I could be black-and-
blue, bleeding, or even dead by morning.

Pacing the room faster and faster. Try the doorknob, of
course they've locked me in here. Hard to breathe. Hot in
here. Sweaty. A guy could suffocate. Never get out to breathe
the real air. Can't let that happen. Can't waste my life. Got to
get out of here, do You hear me, God? I'm making a direct
appeal, just in case I'm wrong, and You're loitering in some
corner of the universe.

All I'm asking for is a miracle. Like the ones in the Bible
stories. Where the walls of the prison open up, and the pris-
oner walks out, laughing and praising Your name.

Go ahead, do something, will You? Open up the walls
right now. Why wait? I'm not asking for a big catastrophe.
Just a little hole. I'm perfectly willing to crawl through.

Please, anything. Unlock the door, make me invisible,
anything. A lightning strike, a hole even, a beam of light.

You can do it. Or maybe You can't. Maybe You're not
even there, and I'm wasting my breath. Maybe You are
around but don't care. Or maybe You're a loser too.

A series of clicks from the photo machine, and coming
out between the rollers, thick black-edged paper with two
gray rectangles on it. The paper drops flat on the table, faint
outlines already forming in each rectangle. Photos of me the
criminal and I watch them develop.

Faint outline of a thick Irish skull, stuffed with thirteen
school years of Catholic ideas. The answer to everything,
printed right there in the catechism. Variations will not be

tolerated. In anything. Everybody takes two years of Latin. And wears the gray uniform. And marches over to mass as a group. And says the Pledge of Allegiance together, and the Apostles' Creed. You're just moving your lips, aren't you, Mister Hollaran? Yes, Sister.

Head and shoulders in outline now, shoulders drooping, defeat. That boy has a good head on his shoulders. But he needs to walk the straight and narrow. Because he's a deliberate underachiever. Uncooperative and socially awkward and resists authority. Could get excellent grades but won't buckle down. My constant report card.

The profile shot, coming in all nose. Pure Italian, that nose, that's what my uncle Anthony always said. All the good cooks have the nose, he used to say. And if size means anything, Tommy, you'll end up cooking at the Waldorf. And he'd laugh. But I always knew there was a compliment hidden in there, and the whole time I was growing up, it was just Anthony who ever let me go with my instincts.

The full-face shot developing, I guess you could call that a weak chin. Something weak about me, that's for sure. Because after high school, when I had a chance to do almost anything, I kept marching along, right in step. To Fort Dix, to Fort Ord to Vinh Long airfield, hardly missing a step. Well, not until those days in the middle of my tour. When I saw Charley fire back once at the helicopter. And when I came out of that tunnel with the baby girl.

At that time Hoover was coming through the barracks handing out mail, and saying, nothing for you, Hollaran. Day after day.

I kept writing to Sandra, though, and in one letter I told her the whole tunnel story, every detail. No answer. Seven, eight, nine days went by, no letters at all. My daily letters got shorter and shorter until they were just notes. Practically begging her to write.

I got so worried I signed up for a MARS call. I was two weeks on the list, waiting my turn. All that time, no letters. I was worrying, imagining all kinds of bad things. Most of those days we were making patrols, and I was getting really jumpy out there. Seeing things. Charley everywhere. Behind that paddy dike. Up that tree. Lucky for me it was a quiet time in the Delta war.

Finally the day for my call came and I walked up, an hour early, to the end of the flight line where they had this little shack. With a big bizarre-looking crisscross antenna planted on top of it. I waited in this long line of guys, and about every three minutes a helicopter came by, just a few feet off the ground, blowing up dust and small stinging stones.

As the line got shorter and I got into the shack, I could hear the guys talking. They were sitting at this little school-type desk with a regular black telephone on it, saying, Hi Mom, how are you? Over. I'm fine, don't you worry about a thing, honest. Over. How's Grandma? Over. Is Daddy there? Over. And three minutes exactly from the time they sat down, they'd be cut off. In the middle of saying tell so-and-so I said hi. And then they'd get up and walk past the line of guys, their faces turned away like they were trying to keep something private.

When I finally sat down, the seat was sweaty and so was the handset on the telephone. I put the handset to my ear and a voice, some sergeant somewhere, asked what number I wanted. In front of me, on the wall, a sweep hand started to move around the face of a black timer clock. I fumbled the number, stuttering. The voice asked me to say it slow. And then said this was a radio call, and the conversation could only go one way at a time, and I would have to say Over or the other person couldn't speak. Did I understand? Yes, I said. Then there was a lot of loud static and finally a phone began ringing.

It kept ringing and I closed my eyes and said like a prayer, Be home, and finally she did say hello.

Over, I said for her. Sandra? I said. It's Tom. Listen, this is a radio call, so whenever you're finished saying something, you've got to say Over. Okay? How are you? Over.

I could barely hear what she said through the static. She asked if anything was wrong.

No, I said. Are you okay? Over.

Just static. Could you speak up, Sandra, please, I said. Have you been getting my letters? Over.

Yes, she said, shouting.

When you're finished, say Over, I said. I haven't been getting any of yours. Have you sent a lot of them? Over.

Just crackle on the line.

Sandra? I said. Over.

I haven't been writing much, she said. Not lately, I'm sorry, Tom, but things have changed around here.

Over, I said. What do you mean, changed, I said? How have things changed? Over.

I can't explain it, Sandra said. Tom, I can barely hear you anyway. Are you sure you're all right? You haven't been hurt or anything? I'm going to sit down and write a letter tonight. And take it right to the post office, okay?

Over, I said. Listen, we haven't even got a minute left, I just wanted to tell you I love you and I miss you, that's all. Over.

You're breaking up, I can't hear you, Tom, she said. Look, I'll explain everything in the letter, it's too complicated. Don't do anything stupid, Tom, promise me. Take care of yourself, okay? Over.

I started to say something, something angry, but the line went dead. And the guy behind me tapped me on the shoulder. The first thing I saw when I got outside was a helicopter, it was landing, a narrow mean little Cobra with big teeth painted on it.

The letter came in three days. I got off tower guard one morning and there it was, lying on my bunk. No stamp, of course, free mail to a combat zone. Just Private First Class Thomas Hollaran and an APO number in Sandra's slanted writing. I tore it open and reached under my bunk for a warm can of beer.

She was confused, the letter said. That was her exact word. Confused but she didn't know why. And she was afraid, living alone. She had been having nightmares about someone breaking in. Always a man, always at night. She didn't know who this man was or what the nightmare meant. But things were driving her crazy. And she was on tranquilizers. And going to a shrink somewhere in Cranford.

The shrink had definite opinions about me, she said. The shrink had helped her see that her feelings were okay, too. And also to see that I was very immature.

She had shown part of my last letter to the shrink, she said. About the tunnel and the little girl. And the shrink said the story was meant to worry Sandra. And besides, he knew very well that I didn't give a damn about the Vietnamese people at all. So why was I over in Vietnam? he wanted to know. What had made me go there?

The shrink had made her see that she was right to feel abandoned and betrayed, the letter said. Because it was obvious I had made my choice, and had left her for the war. And war was an adventure that attracted immature, hostile men, the shrink said. Who, no matter what they said, deep down wanted to fight. To prove their manhood.

Then there was the end of the letter, a simple statement. I can't live like this, Tom, she wrote. And then her signature, no *love*, no *be careful*, no anything.

I put the letter in my locker and sat on my bunk, finished the beer. Took off my shirt and tried to sleep. Flopped around for a few minutes and then got up, grabbed my pistol belt out of the locker, strapped it on. Walked all the way out to the perimeter, no shirt on, no hat. Stood there all alone, right up against the barbed wire. For I don't know how long. And it kept going through my mind that maybe there were snipers out there, across the river.

Finally I picked my way through the barbed wire. Stepping on it, straddling it, the beer cans hanging from it rattled, the little razors cut me on the hands, the thigh, I got tangled, pulled free, ripped my pants. Stepped over a Claymore mine, disarmed for the daylight. Walked around a trip flare.

Then I was out on the bank of the river. Sat down, took off my boots and pistol belt. Took out the pistol, whatever I was thinking of doing with it, forget it. Took the pistol by the barrel, flung it out into the middle of the Mekong.

Then I followed. A barefoot step into the river and I sunk halfway to my knees in muck. All I could think about was to get to the other side, for some reason. So I started to swim, strong current, nasty-smelling water. And the river wider than it looked from the banks. Had to be as wide as the Hudson, really. And after a while I got too tired, started to fight the current, drifting out toward the ocean. It crossed my mind that maybe I really wanted to drown. For just a moment, I felt at peace. And then I started to go under, like I was getting sucked down. That's when I panicked and started to swim again. Breathing in gulps, heading for the near shore of the base, splashing the water like a maniac, the strongest strokes I had in me.

There's my mug shot, fully developed now. And what can you say about a face like that? Especially when it's got numbers underneath. And look, the collar of the JS&T uniform. It seems like I've been in one uniform or another all my life.

I think I see, now, how the trail of my life led here, to jail. Because when I wasn't drifting along, I was marching to somebody's orders. Always somebody else to blame.

The rattling of keys outside the door, I take a deep breath, surprised. Coming to take me downstairs, I guess. Key slides into the lock, knob turns slowly, door opens, the uniform sleeve of a cop, gold buttons. And then the door's pushed open all the way and the cop stands aside, and in back of him, the face of Eddie Sadowski, big Polack grin. "Hollaran," he says. "I see they finally caught up with you."

"Five cans of white spray paint," Eddie says.
Check, I say.
"One five-gallon can of hydraulic fluid," he says.
Check, I say.
"One Sears toolbox, locked."
Check, I say.
"One bundle of fifty sandbags."
Check.

"One AWOL bag with long johns, jacket liner, gloves, socks, spare flight suit."

Check, I say. We're doing this in the basement by flashlight, freezing in here, I'm squatting in the helicopter, the steel all around me radiating cold. Eddie's just outside the helicopter, a tiny penlight held between his chest and chin, sending a slim light beam down to the clipboard he's holding.

"One copy of the Holy Bible," Eddie says.

I play my flashlight around until the light beam falls on the *Procedures, Maintenance, United States Army Rotation Wing Aircraft.* Check, I say.

"One shitfish spear, and sheath," Eddie says.

I spot a Ranger survival knife and say, check.

"Two cases of Lurps," he says.

I play the beam around, catch the smoky cold of my own breath, finally see two tightly strapped cases of army dehydrated meals. Check.

"Five quarts of pilot fuel and a case of vitamins," he says, and I say check when I spot the vodka bottles in an open cardboard box, and filled in around the bottles, small cans of V-8.

"That's it," Eddie says, "the works. How's it look for balance in there?" He sticks his head in the door.

I move the light beam slowly, right to left inside the helicopter. Hardly any room, really, between the seats and the engine compartment, but it's stuffed with all the things we just checked off, plus a rolled-up sleeping bag, folded tent with stakes, kerosene stove, a case of emergency flares, box of powdered milk and giant jar of instant coffee, a toiletries bag, a pair of steel-toed boots, a huge torque wrench, an army mess kit folded into a round canvas case, a pair of binoculars, an orange lifejacket, two smoke grenades, a flak vest, a bed pillow, a deck of cards, maps in a tubular case, an eight-pack of Big Bargain toilet paper, a transistor radio, a Canon 35-millimeter camera in leather casing, four cartons of Winstons.

"Can you think of anything I left out?" Eddie asks.

No, I say. In fact, this is why we lost the war, Ed. Dragging all this crap around.

"Be serious," Eddie says. "Do you think the load's balanced? It's got to be evened out, just like on a boat."

The load looks balanced, I say, and then stare Eddie square in the eyes. I don't know about the pilot, though, I say.

A long look from Eddie, then he clicks off the penlight and drops it, along with the clipboard, into the pilot's seat. "Time to get going," he says.

He limps to the garage doors, throws back the bolts, takes a hesitant look outside. It's actually brighter out there, full-moon night, Eddie insisted that we work in the dark in here, using just flashlights. He's pushing the doors open now, their bottoms scraping on the asphalt driveway. The doors swung wide into the moonlight, Eddie heads for his jeep, and I'm left in the helicopter to think.

In the hours that have passed since Eddie bailed me out, I've tried to tell him that sandbagging the bozos won't work. Won't be justice and won't change a goddamn thing in the world. Except to cause trouble, most likely for him. But I don't think he's heard a word of it. And I'm starting to realize that Eddie, too, has to learn things the hard way. So I'm going to try to keep my mouth shut from now on. And just help the guy take off, if that's what he wants to do.

Red taillights of the jeep backing through the doorway, they go bright as Eddie taps the brakes. Engine running, he gets out, drags heavy chains across the concrete floor, hooks one end to the jeep, another end under the helicopter. Gives a tug on the chain. His face as tight as I've ever seen it. He's waving for me to come out of the helicopter, and I squeeze past the seat, step down from the bubble.

Garage filled with jeep exhaust, I'm choking, Eddie doesn't seem to notice. Walks all the way around the helicopter once, looking and touching. Gives a tremendous long sigh. "It'll fly, it'll fly," he says, almost to himself. "Tom, guide me out," he says, and goes past me at almost a running limp, opens the door of the jeep. "Watch the mast and the rotor blades real careful," he says, and shuts the door, revs the jeep engine.

I go out of the garage, stand facing the jeep, lift my arms and wave them for an okay. Yellow parking lights flicker, then I'm blinded in the glare of jeep headlights. I step aside and wave my arms, the jeep moves an inch. Eddie watching backward in the mirrors. Jeep moves another inch and the chain clanks and thumps, helicopter jerks forward on its wheels. I'm waving my arms, the jeep and the helicopter moving out of the garage as one, top of the mast just clearing the hole in the house wall, Eddie looking backward all the time, air smells of burnt clutch, black helicopter coming out of the garage like it's being born, coming out into the moonlight, yellow rotor blades catching the light and almost reflecting it, the main rotor tied down by wires, bouncing a little as the helicopter makes the final bump out of the garage and into the driveway. Eddie with his head poked out the window, face wide with a grin, he pops open the jeep door, stands in the moonlight and looks at his creation and says, "Wow, I never thought I could do this."

I swing the garage doors closed and head for the jeep, sit in the passenger seat and start calling for Eddie. I have a strong sense that what we're doing is somehow illegal, and now that the helicopter's out of the garage I want to get it moving. Away from me. I have no desire to spend time in jail because of a helicopter. Eddie, I call out, come on. He's standing there like he's hypnotized by the helicopter. Sadowski! I yell. Then I gather up all my lung power in one breath and scream, *Polack!*

That breaks the trance, he comes back to the jeep slowly, gets in, grabs the wheel with one hand, throws the other arm over the seat, he's driving forward and looking backward. Driving a big arcing circle over the frozen mud of his backyard, and won't take his eyes off the helicopter, except for a couple of frantic glances frontward to keep us on course. The circle complete and we're going down the driveway at maybe two miles an hour, the jeep engine straining and giving off a hot-metal smell, "Be my eyes up front, will you?" Eddie says when we get near the street.

Must be midnight, no traffic, no people, and across the road, an empty cinder-stone lot, a knee-high wall of railroad ties, then the Arthur Kill, water black even in full moonlight, and across the river, dull yellow lights of Staten Island warehouses, wharfs, tugboats. "Clear?" Eddie says. Roger, I say.

We roll across the street and into the lot, cinder crunching under the tires, stop just a few feet from the railroad-tie fence. Eddie turns the jeep engine off, it's clicking with its own heat. He breathes out, reaches for a Winston, puts it in his mouth. "I guess you ain't going to change your mind," he says, and lights the cigarette.

I guess I'm not, I say.

"You could learn to fly it," he says.

I hate helicopters, Ed, I say. You know that.

"I could really use a copilot," he says.

Sorry, Ed, I say.

He shrugs, breathes out smoke. Opens the door and says, "Here goes." I watch him walk back and take up the chain, then he opens the back hatch of the jeep, feeds the chain in, makes a neat, snakelike spiral. "Move the jeep away, will you?" he says. "About fifty feet."

I drive it forward, park it right at the edge of the river, turn to look. Eddie out there in the cold, doing one last walkaround inspection. I get out and walk toward him across the cinder stones, I can feel the beginning of an argument rumbling inside me. I should hold him down, hold him back, punch his lights out, he'll thank me someday. Or maybe I should let him go, I can't run his life for him, I can barely run my own. I owe the guy a lot of favors, but which would be a real favor? Hold him back or let him go? I thought I had the answer a few minutes ago, but now that he's ready to take off, I don't know. And now I'm standing right next to the helicopter, with no idea how to really do the right thing.

Eddie's pulling the wires off the main rotor, rolling them up tight, dropping them inside the bubble and behind the pilot's seat.

"You're going to show up, ain't you?" Eddie says. "For court? I got a thousand bucks invested in you."

I'll show up, I say.

"What's the date?" he says. "Maybe I should send you a telegram a couple of days before, just to remind you."

You don't have to, I say. And besides, I'll be getting a phone while you're gone.

"As long as it's in your name," he says.

You can call collect anytime you want, I say. In case you get into any trouble.

"Don't forget the electric bill," he says. "They'll charge you for reconnection if they cut you off. Forty bucks."

Don't worry, I say.

"There's oil in the tank, but if you need more, my company gives a discount."

Okay, I say.

"And don't tell them nothing, if they ask," he says. "You ain't seen me, you don't know nothing. I didn't tell them I quit or anything, the less they know the better."

I'm nodding.

"And that goes for Laura, too. And 'nnie. And everybody else, including my old man and old lady. I don't want to tell nobody nothing, because I might be back sooner than you think."

Okay, Ed, I say.

"And take care of the house," he says. "I might be back looking to sell it. I don't want to find it full of beer cans and dirty dishes."

Will you stop worrying? I say.

"I guess that's it," Eddie says. He reaches into the bubble, pulls out a flight suit. "And let me ask you," he says, "don't use the jeep unless you got to. Unless your car breaks down or something. And if you use it, premium gas. Always." He takes off his army jacket, puts it in the bubble, then unbuttons his blue work shirt, takes it off. Sits on the edge of the pilot's seat, brings his pants down over his boots, steps out of them, he's in white underwear now, doesn't seem to feel the cold. Rolls up the work shirt and pants, ties them together with the belt, throws them as far as he can, over the railroad-tie fence, they plop into the Arthur Kill.

"There," he says. And unrolls his flight suit, all one piece, thick and army-green. He steps into it, zips it up.

"I got to tell somebody," he says, "and you're the last guy I can trust, sort of." He reaches into the bubble for his flight helmet. "I'm aiming for Texas."

What the hell do you know about Texas? I say.

"Shhh," he says, "don't say that word again."

What word? I say.

"Begins with a *T* and has an *x* in it," he says. "Don't ever say it again, especially in front of anybody who knows me."

Ed, I say, what the hell are you going to do in T . . . that place you're going?

"You know that list of bozos," he says. "That's where the last one is, right? So afterwards, when I even the score, when I get a mission accomplished, I'll be in the perfect place to make myself a fortune." He brings the helmet over his head. Seats it. Flicks the visor up and down.

How are you going to make this fortune? I ask.

"Taking workers and freight and stuff out to the oil rigs," he says. "I got it all figured out."

But Ed, I say, this helicopter's too small for that. And besides, you don't even have a pilot's license.

"That's why it's perfect where I'm going," he says. "Where you don't need no piece of paper, just as long as you can fly."

Who told you that? I say.

"I know it," he says. "It's like that down there."

Ed, that's a myth, I say. Didn't you ever hear of the FAA?

"A technicality," he says. "I got it all worked out, going to make my connections with the oilmen, sell this chopper, come back, sell the house, buy me a big six-seater, you can make five hundred bucks a day just flying."

Ed, I say, I wish you could. I wish it was that kind of world, too, but it isn't. You need the goddamn piece of paper, Ed. Or they're going to haul you right out of the sky. And I'll be down there bailing you out. Please, Ed, listen to me, hook this thing back up to the jeep, bring it back to the garage, take those sandbags out, burn them, forget all about the bozos, think of all the fun you could have with this helicopter, no more traffic jams, you'll have bimbos lined up waiting for a ride, you can be down the shore or up the lake in fifteen minutes, Ed, please, think about it, that's all I'm asking you. Think about the fun you could have with this thing.

"No, I'd need a license up here," he says. "They'd have me swamped in paperwork, taking tests and all, I can't do it."

Okay, I say, then go to Texas. Sorry, I mean, go down there. But forget the bozos, forget the sandbags, everything, clear it out of your mind.

"Maybe you can do that, Hollaran," he says. "You ain't going to be gimping around the rest of your life."

I find myself looking at the ground, an argument I can't win. I look up at his face, surrounded by helmet, my mind's made up, I have to let him go. Okay, pal, I say, and stick out my hand. We shake. Take care of yourself, I say. I hope you understand why I can't wish you luck.

"Ain't going to need luck," he says. And grins. Salutes me and I salute him back. He gets into the pilot's seat and straps himself in. Flicks a switch and there's a soft green glow from the instrument panel. Gives me a thumbs-up and a wide grin. The red light on top of the chopper starts flashing, I back away. Feel the chill of Vietnam up and down my spine. Five steps back, ten, I bump backward into the low wall of oily railroad ties, steady, almost lost my balance. From the helicopter there's a series of low mechanical coughs and then the beginnings of a whine. The big blade turns weakly once, twice, then catches, a slight cold breeze as both rotors become blurs of speed. A rhythmic chopping sound in the air, from across the road the far cry of a junkyard dog, then the engine noise picks up, drowns out everything and the blades are whirling faster and faster, raising a dust storm of little stinging cinders and the red light's still flashing and the engine's screaming now and I almost have to turn away for all the cinders stinging my face and I hear the chopper lift, look up, it rises and goes right over my head, tilting sideways, I duck, a horrible crack as the helicopter hits the surface of the river, it's like I'm shocked by a million volts, wham, main rotor, hits the water, breaks like a toy. I'm up on the railroad ties, chopper sinking fast, landing lights on, red light still flashing, fifteen feet out there, I strip off my army jacket, ready to dive, see something bobbing in the black water, Sadowski, I'm screaming, he's screaming, I can see by the landing lights he's paddling, swimming, making his way, I get off the railroad ties, stretch across them on my belly, reach out as far as I can, screaming, Eddie's hand, I grab it, lose it, get him by the wrist and pull. Got him by two hands now, he's struggling for a foothold in the railroad ties, I yank as hard as I can and he's arms over the ties, legs still down in the freezing water and I'm ready to yank again when there's a big gulp out there, and the Plexiglas bubble disappears under the surface and the white landing lights dim to gray, then go out.

16

Moonlight Serenade

Smoke from the Pall Mall in Betty's mouth drifts up in a narrow stream, past her cat's-eye glasses, the deep lines of her forehead, the boyish cut of her gray hair. I'm concentrating on that smoke, nervous, trying not to look too hard at her or Leo. Who's sitting beside Betty, right across the bar from me. And slurping, a cup of soup to his lips.

"What did you call this?" says Leo. He puts the cup down and wipes his mouth with a bandanna.

Stracciatella, I tell him. A simple egg-drop soup. But good because it's made fresh every time. Swirl in the egg, grind in Parmesan and fresh nutmeg, throw in a pinch of chopped parsley, that's it.

Leo looks at Betty. "I like it very much, dear," he says. "Will you have some?"

"Later," Betty says, frowning. She hits the total button and her adding machine starts to whirl and click.

It takes only a few seconds to make, I tell Betty, and it's a nice alternative to the minestrone. Which would basically be our leftover soup, I say. She's looking down at the cost sheets and menu proposals I gave her about ten minutes ago.

I tried to make the whole menu like that, I say. Economical. It's not a big selection, but there's a minimum of ingredients, and hardly any waste. And the food will be fresh, first-rate stuff.

Betty doesn't react. She pulls the tape out of the adding

machine and stares the column of figures up and down. I shift in my chair and keep talking, concentrate on Leo. I haven't forgotten what Anthony taught me, I say. Make everything you serve your own, special. If people can't get it anywhere else, they'll have to come to you, you'll always have business. Leo's nodding, a half meatball on a fork, ready to go into his mouth. "Absolutely, I agree," he says, and eats the meatball, dips his fork down, twirls it in tomato sauce, brings it up to his mouth for a taste. "I like that sauce," he says.

It's my own, I say. Not Anthony's, not my grandfather's. It took a long time for me to get it just right.

"I think we can make you a deal here, Tom," Leo says. "If the numbers work out." He looks at Betty. She looks at me. "You're sure you can handle the kitchen yourself?"

As long as it's just lunch hour, I say.

She's got the adding machine going again, fingers moving almost faster than I can follow, then she lifts the tape, bends forward, stares at the numbers through thick gray glasses. "Looks okay from my end," she says. "How about you, husband?"

Leo's tasting a forkful of eggplant roulette stuffed with sausage. He raises one finger for a moment of patience, then swallows, smiles, holds his hand out to me.

We shake, but I don't have time to stay around and talk over the details. Not tonight. So with Betty and Leo eating the food I've brought in, I get ready to leave. Zip up my army jacket and take a copy of the sample menu, I want to show it to Annie. A wave and a see you later and I'm out the door. Twilight. Last glow of orange behind the gritty houses and bare trees. And dirty leftover snow pushed into the gutters of Westfield Avenue. Tired of winter and wondering whether it will ever end. But when I get in the Volks and coax a start out of it, I look back at Lucky Leo's and start to feel better. Cheers me up to know that next week I'll have work, the kind I enjoy. And I'm going to need all the cheer I can get, too. Because of an appointment I've got. In ten minutes and I'd better get moving.

Down the same old dirty streets of this city where I've

lived my whole life, except for one year. Could probably make this drive blindfolded, and it's a good thing. Because I can hardly pay attention to the traffic now. My mind busy trying to put together the exact words that will cut down Sandra. And put her in her place forever. The lousiest things in the world going through my mind right now.

It was a surprise yesterday, the first call on my new phone, from the lawyers. I was ready to make excuses for missing my appointment, but that wasn't why they called. They're representing Sandra and Wolpenheimer, and they wanted to make a deal. A peace bond, in the amount of bail. I thought it over and called them back and said okay, on two conditions. That it be on neutral territory and that Sandra come along. The lawyer just laughed, and said I was in no position to bargain. I hung up. Two hours later he called back and said we had a deal.

The corner before the courthouse and I pull over on busy Broad Street. Double park with the rush hour traffic honking, swerving around me. Drop a dime into the pay phone, Annie's number, no answer. Been doing this for three days now. And it's no answer or Laura saying Annie's not home. Phone still ringing. Cop car pulling up behind the Volks, I drop the phone, run. Wave at the cop, try to look friendly, get in the car and pull away nice and slow. Cop lets me go, good, turn the corner at the courthouse, behind it an office building. Waiting for me in front is a young guy, built like a football player, dressed in a white trench coat, I've seen him somewhere before.

I pull in a few spaces away, get out and slam the door of the Volks. I'm walking toward the guy in the trench coat and he says, "Are you Thomas Hollaran?"

I nod. I realize this is the guy, Sandra's friend, who was the draft counselor at St. Peter's.

He sticks out his hand for me to take, I hesitate, shake it, he's dry, I'm sweating. "Daniel Houlihan Junior," he says. And leads me through two doors. "Please," he says, "have a seat."

For a moment I expected Sandra to be in here, but I

realize now she must be up in another room. It makes me
nervous to know she's that close and I can't get to her. Houlihan sits behind a thick dark oak desk. "Drink?" he says, and
reaches behind him, puts two glasses on the desk, and says,
"Mine's Scotch." He shows me the bottle, it's the kind that
comes in a velvet bag. I'll have some of that, I say.

"With ice?" he asks. I nod. "Soda? Water? Twist?"

Just ice, I say. And while he makes the drinks I keep an
eye on the smoked glass of the other office, but I can't see
anything behind it, not even a shadow.

Did Sandra come? I ask when Houlihan hands me the
drink.

"First things first," he says, and smiles. Reaches into a
drawer and brings out a thin legal document, puts it on the
table. "This should be relatively painless," he says. Tight
smile. Hands me a pen. "I take it you're still determined to
proceed without an attorney."

I don't have one, I say. Besides, I can read.

He pushes the document to my end of the table, I start to
read. . . . *neither in person nor by any form of written or
verbal correspondence whatever . . . Sandra O. Hollaran or
Robert Wagner Wolpenheimer . . . nor cause himself to be
in unnecessary proximity thereto . . . forfeit and relinquish
all claims to the sum of one thousand dollars . . . dismissal
of criminal and civil complaints . . . against Thomas Joseph Hollaran . . .* And then a date and the place for my
signature. I take a big drink, heavy with whiskey, and almost
choke.

I read it over again and look at Houlihan. Neutral, drink
to his lips. I sign Thomas and half the Joseph and then I have
to stop, drink shaking in my other hand, the ice cubes rattling. In my side vision I could swear I see the wisp of a smirk
cross Houlihan's face. I put my arm around the document to
block his vision and finish signing, the pen shaking, signature
looks like it was written by a madman in a fit. But I'm re-
lieved it's over, and hand the pen to Houlihan.

"The other copy, too," he says. "Please. It's underneath."

Oh, I say. And take another sip of Scotch. And this time

I'm steady, a normal signature, and then Houlihan takes both copies, inspects them, hands one back to me. "That will do nicely," he says. "I hope you're pleased. I know my client will be."

I finish my drink in a long gulp, put the glass on the desk.

Can you bring Sandra out? I ask. So I can speak to her.

"Mister Hollaran," he says. "You've just signed a peace bond. You have a copy, read it. It prohibits all contact between you and her."

But we made a deal, I say.

"As a matter of fact," he says, "my client has declined to be present."

You mean she didn't come? I say.

"I'm afraid she declined," he says.

God damn it, we made a deal, I say.

"I only know what's in writing," he says. "You have the document there in your hands."

No, no, I say. This is a lawyer's trick. I know she's there in that room and I demand to speak to her.

Houlihan goes to the smoked-glass door and opens it. A completely empty office. No Sandra. Nobody at all.

Drive to the hospital, burning with anger, two blocks and a good thing nobody gets in my way. Park in a doctor's space, just let somebody challenge me. Slam the door. Kick the car, damn it, done in by Sandra again. Beaten and tricked. When will this kind of luck ever end? I walk up to the main entrance, asking myself that. And when I get to the doors I stop for some reason. And find myself staring down at the courthouse and jail. And I realize that for all I've lost, I've been spared something, too.

I pull open the door and head right for the telephone, it chimes with my two nickels and I'm dialing Annie's number. Busy, a good sign. An encouraging sign. I hang up and dial again, still busy. Give her time, Hollaran.

Dial Doctor Rhinehart's number. She answers and I invite her to the preview opening of Leo's dining room, a week from today.

"Perhaps I can make it," she says, her voice coming in very faint. "But first tell me, is today Tuesday or Wednesday?"

Doctor Rhinehart, I say, it's Monday.

"Of course," she says. "Well then, Monday of next week, yes, it seems so. I can be there."

Good, I say. Because I've fixed you up with a date already.

"Oh?" she says.

A fellow professional, I say. I've arranged for you two to share a corner table. He practices at the VA in Newark. I'll bet you two find you have a lot to talk about.

"Delightful," she says. "So tell me, are you anxious about this debut of yours?"

Nervous as hell, I say. But I'm going to do my very best. I have to. Just about everybody I know is going to be there. And Doctor Rhinehart, I'll call you next week to remind you. Because I know you're busy and you sometimes forget.

"I'm sure to remember," she says.

I'll call you anyway, I say. Thanks, Doctor, and good-bye.

Hang up the receiver and lift it again, dime in, dial Annie's number. Ringing, come on, answer. It's not even a hundred yards from here, but behind a fence and a locked gate, and damn it if I need more trouble with the cops. Still ringing, come on Annie, answer, please.

"Hello?"

Laura? I say.

"Tom, I don't know where she is."

Laura, I say, please. She can't be gone every single time I call.

"Tom, really, she is not home now."

Then where is she? I say.

A sigh on the phone. "She went to get something for her supper."

With who? I say.

"To the best of my knowledge she went alone, Tom. But I don't keep track of her."

Laura, I say, she's been avoiding me. I want to know why.

"Because," she says, and hesitates. "I'm not sure I should be saying this, Tom. But Annie is very confused at the moment. And I can hardly blame her. First you cause an uproar in the hospital, then you come running to her with the police in hot pursuit. Then you sneak away like a criminal. She spends half the evening searching for you, and the other half worrying. You go in and out of jail and you don't even bother to come by with an explanation."

That was because—I say, and Laura cuts me off.

"To make matters worse, Ed turns up in the emergency room, the victim of his own irrational schemes, which you were aware of all along."

Laura, I say, I tried.

"Frankly I can understand why she doesn't come to the phone when certain people call."

Okay, Laura, I say. Look, when she comes back, please tell her I called. And that I'm going up to see Eddie now. And I'll call again in maybe half an hour.

I hang up, ride the elevator to the fourth floor. Slink past the nurses' station and they're too busy with paperwork to notice me. Here it is, 409, Sadowski, a double room but no other name on the door.

Slip in and there's the food cart at the edge of the bed, everything eaten but a melting square of green Jell-O. And Sadowski sleeping, his head held stiff by a neck brace. Shiny metal, clamped under his jaw and around his shoulders. And they've taken most of the bandages from around his head. A Winston, burnt to the filter, is still smoking in an ashtray. And lying on the floor, a magazine, I bend to pick it up, *Kustom Kar*, and a picture of a shiny old-fashioned station wagon, the kind with wood on the sides. I put it on the night table, reach over and snuff out the cigarette.

He moans. Moves his head and grabs at the neck brace like it's a cage. Opens his eyes and says, "Hey! Hey!"

Sadowski, I say, it's all right.

"Huh?" he says. "I must have been dreaming." The words slurred by the fit of the brace.

How are you, soldier? I say, and salute him. How's the head feeling?

"Aches," he says.

How's the neck?

"Hurts like hell."

You'll be feeling better soon, I say.

"No, I won't," he says. "Not until I get out of here. Light me a cigarette."

I pick a Winston out of the pack on the nightstand, stick it just over the metal bar and into his lips, hold a lit match under it. "That's better," he says, and exhales, takes the cigarette out of his mouth. "I'm going crazy here," he says. "I can't wait to get out. I got this new idea."

Oh, no, I say.

"It don't have nothing to do with helicopters," he says. "I'm through with them. I'm thinking about woodies now. Remember them? The old wagons? Fixed-up ones are going for a fortune."

I'm listening to Eddie. I sit on a chair in front of full-length white curtains.

"Turn the light off, Hollaran."

For what? I say.

"Just turn it off."

I reach for the little bedside button, click, the room goes dark. "Open the curtains," he says. I do and the view is a full-moon night. Patterns of white, yellow, and red dots, trucks and cars moving on the Turnpike. Beyond that, straight rows of streetlights. The rectangles of warehouses and factories, and there, the biggest rectangle, all yellow lights, JS&T. Somewhere lost in the glow of lights and the gray moonlit shadows is Eddie's house, then the black water of the Arthur Kill.

"You see what I see?" Eddie says. "I been looking at it for three days now. Thinking. Of what I done right and what I done wrong. Going over every step of it because she didn't handle right. She lifted okay but then she started shaking, I thought the cyclic was going to come off in my hand and then she was shuddering, I mean shuddering, and then I tried to turn her back and land . . ." He stops talking. Staring out the window. "We lost her, didn't we, Tom."

Yes, we did, pal, I say.

"Nothing we can do about it, is there?"

Not a damn thing, I say.

"I had my chance at the controls, though," he says. "I was flying there. Just for a few seconds, but I was up there."

I'm a witness, I say.

"Put her there," he says.

We shake hands. The overhead light goes on. It's Annie at the door. "Oh, excuse me," she says. And just stands there like she's not sure whether to come in or go away. "I brought this for Eddie," she says, and holds up a white bag. Looks at me. "Hi," she says.

Hi, I say. And she's up at the foot of the bed. Puts the bag down on the swing table that holds Eddie's tray. "Ed," she says, "you finally ate some hospital food."

"Yeah," he says, "I couldn't hold out no longer."

"Well, I brought you a snack anyway," she says. And from out of the white bag she pulls a big foil-wrapped hamburger, a paper cone of french fries, I recognize the wrappings, Jersey Joe's. "But you're not hungry, are you?" she says. "You just ate."

"You kidding? I'm starved," Eddie says. "They give you kiddie meals here."

Annie's pushed the tray in toward him, and now Eddie tears open the hamburger wrapper like he hasn't eaten all day.

Annie's standing there, watching him eat, and I'm watching her. Long blond hair falling over the shoulders of her flannel shirt. What first attracted me to her, that hair. And a smile like she's smiling now at Eddie. Who's breaking open a little squeeze bag of ketchup and spreading it all over the french fries.

"How's your head?" Annie says, "does it still hurt?"

"Nope," Eddie says, and puts a raft of french fries in his mouth.

"How about your neck?" she says.

"Perfect, no problem," he says, and swallows.

"I took a look at your chart," she says. "You're doing really well, Ed. You should be out of here in a couple of days."

I hope so, I say. And look right at Annie. Because I had this thing planned, I say. For next Monday, at lunchtime. You're not working then, are you?

She shrugs her shoulders.

I'd really like you to make it, I say.

She won't look at me, eyes down. Ed, I say, could you excuse us for a minute?

"Take all night if you want," he says.

Maybe I will, I say. I touch Annie's elbow. Can we talk somewhere else? I ask her. She nods.

"Just do me one favor," Eddie says. "Hand me that magazine before you go."

I do that, and tell him I'll see him tomorrow, and that he'd better be out of the hospital in time for Monday's lunch. And then it's just me and Annie, on a slow walk down the hall. She's brought the white bag out with her.

Is that your supper in there? I say.

She nods.

A hamburger? I say.

"Cheeseburger," she says. We keep walking.

I'm sorry about last Friday, I say.

"You don't have to apologize," she says.

I just want you to understand, I say. After Eddie bailed me out Friday night, I *did* stop to call you.

"I was driving around," she says.

I'm sorry I missed you, I say. Didn't you go past Eddie's?

"It looked like nobody was home," she says.

He's got his windows painted black, I say. I was down there all night, I couldn't get away, I'm sorry. Eddie was practically in a fever, he wanted to get that thing off the ground, neither one of us thought it would take the whole night. And I want you to know something, I did try to talk him out of it, but there was no stopping him and I owe him so many favors.

We're walking, she won't even look at me.

I admit it, I say, my life's been a mess lately. But I'm trying to get it straight, Annie. I finally know what I want to do with myself. I'm going to be the cook at Leo's, but that's only a start. I've been thinking about chef school again, I've still got the GI bill and everything. I want to go places, far and wide, and then I want to come home and open a restaurant someday. A place all my own where people can eat and relax and have a good time. It's the best way I can think of to earn a living.

We're walking, Annie in silence, past the nurses' station. Can I ask you to have supper with me? I say. She stops, looks me in the eyes. "I don't know," she says.

Just supper, that's all I'm asking, I say. Come on, come with me. I reach out and take the white bag from her. Lay it on the counter at the nurses' station. We'll go to Leo's, I say. I'll make something special. Just for the two of us.

Down the hall, down the elevator, into the Volks, neither one of us saying a word. Driving in the early moonlight to Lucky Leo's. And somewhere on Broad Street when I get it into third gear, I touch her hand. Then we're holding hands, and I don't want to let go to shift. Turn a corner, the Volks bucking and coughing up Westfield Avenue. Practically a miracle, a parking spot right in front of Lucky Leo's.

Big crowd inside, the place blue with cigarette smoke, "Moonlight Serenade" coming out of the ceiling speakers, louder than the babble at the bar. I've got Annie by the hand so I won't lose her, trying to make my way through the crowd. And there's Leo and Betty in the middle of the bar, all around them, dollar bills held up like the torch of the Statue of Liberty. Up the steps with Annie, push through the doors and into the back room, into the kitchen, lights on. Take off my army jacket and tie on a white cook's apron. Get myself a heavy frying pan, Annie sits on a stool.

I can tell you're not in the mood to talk, I say.

She shakes her head.

I'll just kind of talk while I cook, then, I say. Don't mind me, it helps me relax and concentrate, I say. I light a fire under the pan.

I really like this song, I say. "Moonlight Serenade." Miller's best stuff is just music, no words. Listen. This kind of music is going to make a comeback, I know it. Leo thinks so too. Why I like it I really don't know, except maybe it's the music I heard as a boy. But it's not just nostalgia, listen to how tight that orchestra is. Everybody playing together, beautiful harmony. And you know, Annie, music and cooking have a lot in common. Harmony's important. So is timing, counterpoint, little surprises, keeping things fresh. And simple. Like this dinner I'm making us. I don't know how many recipes start the same simple way. Take this onion and slice it thin. Sauté it in a little butter and olive oil. After that you can make just about anything. Anything at all.

Return to the savage storm of VIETNAM in some of today's best novels.

VIETNAM